The Richmond Diary

Also by Peter Rawlinson

Non-fiction
A Price Too High – an autobiography
The Jesuit Factor – A Personal Investigation

Fiction
The Colombia Syndicate
Hatred and Contempt
His Brother's Keeper
Indictment for Murder
The Caverel Claim

THE
RICHMOND DIARY

Peter Rawlinson

Constable • London

First published in Great Britain 2001
by Constable, an imprint of Constable & Robinson Ltd
3 The Lanchesters, 162 Fulham Palace Road,
London, W6 9ER
Copyright © Peter Rawlinson 2001
The right of Peter Rawlinson to be identified as the author
of this work has been asserted by him in accordance with the
Copyright, Designs and Patents Act 1988

ISBN 1–84119–298–8

Printed and bound in Great Britain

A CIP catalogue record for this book is available from the
British Library

Once again, for Elaine

Part One

Chapter One

Bolton Gardens, London. Tuesday, 16 April
Tomorrow I lunch with Kitty McClaren. Or Peregrine, as now his friends must call him. It is many years since he answered to the name of Kitty and certainly not these days – when he is a Right Honourable with a government car, an office in Whitehall and a Diary Secretary to organise his engagements. The voice on the telephone said 'One o'clock, lunch at the Garrick Club, 17 April', indicating how fortunate I was to have been granted an audience. 'The Minister', the voice went on, 'must leave at two fifteen for the House. I trust that won't be inconvenient.'

He trusts right. An hour of Kitty will be quite long enough to get the gossip. When we meet I shall, of course, formally call him Perry. But it is as Kitty that I shall think of him, the undergraduate whom I used to visit at Cambridge thirty years ago. We'd take a punt on the river in the Backs behind King's, he and his friends, with their shining young faces. Then he had the profile of a young god, golden hair falling over his forehead, startling blue eyes. Now he has thickened and his hair is receding.

I myself have retained a full head of hair. I am told it makes me look much younger than my years, those years that, alas, advance so inexorably. Within weeks I reach the biblical three score years and ten. And lately I have not been feeling well. I am getting pains in the chest. I should see my quack, Peter Webster, but I am a coward and I keep putting it off.

Wednesday, 17 April

I was early at the Garrick. I am not a member, so I stood
waiting for my host in the hall at the top of the steps
within the swing doors.

I saw the terrible Mordecai Ledbury struggling with
his sticks up the steps. I thought of the friends that brute
of a QC has bullied and insulted in the Law Courts, one
a dear, close friend. He was halfway up the steps, so
I fled to the loo. By the time I emerged, happily he had
disappeared into the dining room.

Kitty, of course, kept me waiting. He was twenty
minutes late. The modern manners of our modern masters! Eventually I saw him emerge from a large black car.
He bounded up the steps and flung his arms round my
shoulders as though I were some constituent whose vote
he was soliciting.

At lunch he was as indiscreet as I hoped he might be.
(How distressed he'd be to know that I am recording all
he said. But he'll not know. I write my journal for my
own amusement and read it now and then as I lie in
bed, and chuckle. When I am tired of it I shall destroy it.
A bonfire of the memories!)

Kitty declared that he likes government, especially
now that he is in the Cabinet. He claimed that he gets on
famously with the PM. He said that he liked the old
man's style, so much more patrician and elegant than
any of his immediate predecessors, a welcome reversion
to times past, before the modern 'Cool Britannia' men
and women invaded Downing Street. Now this PM,
Kitty said, has restored the place and the office. Kitty
also enjoys listening to the old man's stories, and the PM
knows it and often takes him upstairs to the flat for a
whisky and soda after an evening meeting in No. 10,
and gossips about his colleagues. The Home Secretary,
she of the populist style, is quite out of favour – confused performances in the House, too loquacious in
Cabinet, while the Home Office resent her vulgar husband, who keeps dropping in.

The Foreign Secretary, sharp, supercilious, dozes

through Cabinet meetings and Tancred, Kitty suspected, was drinking rather heavily. However, Tancred has the ear of the PM who regards him as his political heir. I'm not sure exactly what is Tancred's post in the Ministry, something to do with the Services. I asked about Tancred's life, and Kitty shrugged and said he knew nothing. Tancred was a loner, solitary. A man of mystery. Kitty added that nowadays ministers have to be very careful, what with the media snooping and bribing, and the Cabinet Secretary and the MI5 boys watching. 'So continence,' he said, winking at me, 'rigorous continence, that's the order of the day. You wouldn't last long in government, my dear Fanny.'

This irritated me. 'Francis,' I replied tartly, 'Francis. Unless you wish me to call you Kitty.' He has become more common since he has become important. I suppose it's the company he keeps. But I shall stay in touch. The gossip amuses me.

I passed the Dell where Nanny used to take me nearly seventy years ago. I remember the rabbits and the squirrels while she gossiped about her employers with her friends in their smart uniforms of grey or navy-blue. There are no nannies now in the Dell. Nor rabbits. In my childhood we had servants – a butler, a chauffeur, a cook, two parlour maids – and, of course, Nanny. Today, in my house off the Little Boltons with the studio used by Millais, I have only Mrs Evans and a daily, although, thank heaven, I am not poor.

Wednesday, 24 April
Reception at the Italian Embassy for their visiting PM, a dapper little man who looked like the maître d' in an inferior restaurant. I suppose I'd been asked because I'd written an article about Etruscan figurines for *The Connoisseur* last January. It caused quite a stir among the cognoscenti and at Sylvia Benedict's a month ago the Cultural Attaché at the Italian Embassy complimented me.

Amid the scrum I ran into Emerald Cunliffe, her lips

as scarlet as a Rank starlet's in a Forties movie. She said she was just back from spending Easter with Franco and Serena Pallocinni in Umbria. Such dears, she said, sighing. As though I didn't know that she's been sleeping with Franco for years. Or rather, was. I'm told she's switched to the new Italian ambassador who arrived a month ago. But perhaps she's enjoying both at the same time? Her appetite is insatiable.

I have known her since she was a child when I was at Balliol with her much older half-brother, Bolton. She was then a scrubby little girl with braces on her teeth and from that moment for some reason she made me her confidant. I've seen her through affairs without number and through her marriage to the wretched Willie, whom she killed through sheer exhaustion. Now in her late forties, she is still remarkably handsome under the layer of paint – and still indomitable in her lusts. Or passions, as she would term them. But her skin is turning leathery – light tan colour under the powder – and her mouth much puckered, the result of her annual 'lift'. But I am fond of her. Gallant is how I think of her.

While we were talking, or rather she was talking, I saw the dark head and face of Tancred. He was talking to a tall, fleshy man with a sensuous mouth. At first I couldn't place him. Then I remembered. Oscar Sleaven, the billionaire head of a vast manufacturing and property empire, one of whose companies, incidentally, pulled down the houses next to me and developed the site as a block of luxury flats. During the rebuilding I wrote, complaining about the noise and the dust, and received a very cool reply from a firm of lawyers called Levitt and Sleaven. The Sleaven is, I assume, some relation of Oscar Sleaven. I wrote again but got no reply. Typical!

On my way out of the Embassy I ran into the young George Templeton, looking very bronzed and athletic. Why was this young man invited? For the Ambassadress?

Friday, 3 May

Kitty McClaren is in trouble! At least, his government is. If it falls he would be stripped of his official car and Diary Secretary – and I should lose a source of amusing gossip. Apparently the son of Kitty's friend, the PM who takes him up to the flat in No. 10 and feeds him whisky, has been involved in some trade machinations in Japan and the Opposition are alleging improper influence for personal gain. The newspapers, especially the *News* and the *Telegram*, are full of it. There is to be a motion of censure next week. I tried to get hold of Kitty – to gloat, I'm afraid – but he's gone to ground. Anyhow, I never got further than the superior young man in his Private Office. If the government falls and Kitty leaves office, and I lose what access to the few crumbs of insider gossip that Kitty condescended to fling me, I shan't be too sorry, for Kitty has been corrupted – by the little power that the modern politician enjoys. He has become conceited to compensate, I suppose, for his loss of hair and swelling waistline. When we lunched together I sensed that he had coarsened. It is odd that political power, so transient and meretricious, can turn the head of even so basically harmless a creature as Kitty. Of course, he was always weak. It is his charm that got him where he is.

Thursday, 16 May

Dinner at Sylvia Benedict's. Another female sexual athlete to whom I am also close, a great friend of Emerald Cunliffe. They hunt in pairs, searching out their prey.

But I had quite a shock when I entered the salon: Mordecai Ledbury, sitting in a chair, looking as ugly as sin, his two sticks obscenely poking up between his legs, talking to a woman I didn't know but who seemed oddly taken by him. I have heard it said that, despite his hideous appearance, some women actually like him! Why I cannot imagine. It is rare to see him in society, so how dare Sylvia invite him! She should know what her friends think of him. Fortunately it was a large party and I managed to avoid him.

Royalty was present – but I was not presented, which was rude of Sylvia. Food as inferior as ever. On my left, Sylvia's daughter-in-in-law, the wife of the young earl. She talked about children and the school run. To me, of all people! As though I could conceivably be interested. I endured her, just, through the fish and when the over-done tournedos arrived I turned thankfully to the woman on my right – handsome, with masculine features, a creamy white skin and a mole beside her mouth. She seemed to think I should know who she was but I didn't. After some fencing I discovered she was a journalist, Julia Priest, who has a column in Ogilvy Grant's *Telegram* and does political 'pieces' on TV. She seemed very taken by some woman minister in the government called, I think, Patsy Something who, the journalist said, wrote poetry. She waxed quite enthusiastic about this political poetess. Both Sapphics, I assume. She enquired if I knew any of the Ministry. I said only Peregrine McClaren – and Tancred slightly, once upon a time. I hadn't seen anything of him for some years. She asked what I thought of Tancred. He's said to be very able, I said. And honest? I suppose so, I replied flatly. But I did not say it convincingly. I kept thinking of seeing him talking with the vile, unspeakable Sleaven. Radical? she asked. No, said I, not radical. Promiscuous? I don't think so, I replied. Celibate, monk-like, I have been told.

After dinner I was cornered by Emerald until the odious Digby Price, the proprietor of the other news-paper group, News Universal, joined us. He ignored me and talked to her in his grating South African accent. He lives in Paris with, I believe, some Hungarian woman. But he changes his women as often as he changes his vulgar ties and I am told that the Hungarian is on her way out.

I moved on and talked a little with Sylvia and a military man with a military moustache whose name

I did not catch. I assumed they were lovers. Or had been lovers for, like Emerald, she changes her men so often that the body language may only have been a farewell salute – to a former love. What she could see in the stupid fellow I do not understand.

Later Kitty arrived from the House, jubilant. He said the motion of censure had been easily defeated, the government won the vote – and the debate. The Opposition had been crushed. Tancred had made a brilliant speech, without a note, defending the PM. 'He's a clever devil,' Kitty said proudly. But is he honest? I thought to myself, echoing the woman journalist as again I thought of his intimacy with Oscar Sleaven. However, I said nothing. Kitty looked so pleased with himself. He was almost affectionate. So my small window into the shabby world of politics remains ajar.

Saturday, 1 June to Sunday, 2 June
On the Saturday morning I drove to Wainscott for a weekend with Sylvia and arrived just before lunch. A large house party including a charming and handsome young actor called Job Streatley and, to my surprise, Tancred. Later, to my increased surprise, the awful Oscar Sleaven and his wife Ethel arrived. After luncheon I noted that the young actor was in the garden alone so I joined him. He said his ambition was to play Richard II at the National. I told him he'd make an excellent Richard. He took me by the arm. 'Do you really think so?' he said. I was quite affected.

After changing for dinner I came across Tancred with Oscar Sleaven, both as yet unchanged, in the library. Tancred had a sheet of paper in his hand. When they saw me Sleaven said, 'We must be late' and they hurried off to change. As they passed I couldn't resist saying to Sleaven, 'How's business?' He smiled, or rather leered, but said nothing. Tancred yet again with Oscar Sleaven! Why? What have they in common? What are they up to?

At dinner I was next to Henrietta Plaistow. She is the

kind of Englishwoman who doesn't bathe sufficiently and it is noticeable. Like Sylvia and Emerald, she is voracious sexually. How her lovers stand the body odour I cannot imagine.

Next morning, just before lunch, Tancred and Sleaven came in– from a stroll, they said.

Emerald brought over her house party from The Waves for lunch. The Italian Ambassador, of course, and his wife; the journalist Julia Priest and another woman of about forty with short hair and a clever, interesting face. I sat next to her. She said she had been a don at Cambridge but was now in the Lords and the Under-Secretary of State at the Home Office. Not many decades ago, I thought, she'd have had the Metropolitan Police enquiring into my then illegal activities. Not that there's any activity now!

I asked if she had much to do with Perry McClaren and she said she did. She found him very agreeable. Trust Kitty, I thought. What exactly is Tancred's post in the Ministry? I asked. He's Minister for Defence Procurement, she said briskly, and in charge of defence exports. Is that, I thought, Sleaven's interest? Is that why the pair are so intimate?

While we talked I saw Julia Priest looking at us across the table and smiling. So my luncheon neighbour must be the Patsy of whom the journalist had spoken so fondly at Sylvia's dinner party. An improbable poetess, I thought. But then, lovers rarely see the beloved as he or she really is.

In the afternoon I overheard Job tell Sylvia that he had to get back to London for an interview with a producer. I pretended I had a dinner engagement and gave him a lift.

2 July

Some weeks ago I accepted an invitation to dine at the Inner Temple with my brother-in-law, Henry Baines, at one of their Private Guest Nights, black tie.

Henry is a bore, a Chancery Judge, very much the

Learned Friend, but he was kind to my disagreeable sister Eileen who died two years ago after twenty years of marriage. How they tolerated each other I never understood but they seemed reasonably content and, to give Henry his due, he was bereft after her death. I do not willingly endure the company of lawyers but I feel obligated to dine with him from time to time.

Quite an interesting collection of guests. Tancred was one, the guest of the Lord Chief Justice who, I later noticed, is very fond of port. Henry introduced me to a youngish middle-aged man who, Henry said, wanted to meet me. He had apparently read my small book on fourteenth-century Chinese porcelain and shared my enthusiasm. He was very complimentary but, I thought, oleaginous. At dinner Henry told me he was the solicitor, Sebastian Sleaven, younger brother of Oscar. His must have been the firm that wrote such a disagreeable reply when I complained about the noise and dirt when they were building next to me. I imagine he's as sharp as his brother, although not so gross. He has not his brother's sensual mouth. He looked, indeed, the kind of lawyer you need if you are really in trouble.

Before this conversation I had an unpleasant shock. Ledbury again! I've now seen him three times in the past month. Of course, I should have anticipated that he would be there. After all, it is from the Temple that he makes his forays to bully people in the Law Courts. Yet somehow it had not occurred to me that he would be. I'd been too busy gloomily contemplating the company of my brother-in-law. Fortunately Ledbury was in a corner of the room; sitting as usual, making the most of his disability while everyone else was standing. I prayed I would not be near him at dinner. As it happened I was not but I could see him for he was further down the table on the opposite side. With his twisted face and humpback he looks what he is – a monster. He was drinking, I noticed, none of the excellent white burgundy or claret but champagne from a silver tankard and eating very little. Next to him was a severe-looking, rather prim woman in her early fifties. At first I saw her looking at him with distaste. I sympathised, but later I noticed she was smiling as though she were enjoying herself. Why? What could there be to smile about in the company of that brute? I asked Henry who she was. 'A new judge,' he replied. 'Mordecai only takes trouble with the women judges, never the men.'

I snorted.

We retired to another room for dessert. Candlelight and port, and puerile legal anecdotes. I saw Tancred talking with the smooth lawyer, the younger Sleaven. He is certainly very close to that family.

I managed to get away at half past ten, exhausted.

3 July

I had a bad night after the dinner in the Temple. Severe pains on my way home in the taxi. The food? I wondered. But I knew it was not. When I got home I didn't trouble Job. I looked into his room. He was asleep, on his back, his head on his arm, looking suspiciously innocent. He's not often in the house. He's usually in the studio annexe where he takes his friends.

At about midnight I began to feel seriously ill. The attack was bad, worse than ever before. I grew increasingly worried. I really must see Peter Webster. He's an excellent doctor but when I consult him he gives me the impression that he rather enjoys my ailments. He says they're always so interesting. But these attacks, I know now, are serious. However, I'm such a coward I don't think I shall see him – not yet. Not until I must. I don't want to know the worst, if the worst it is. It's surely better not to know, not to have formal sentence pronounced. If these attacks signal the approaching end, it is better to go suddenly rather than waste away, poisoned by drugs – which, I understand, make your hair fall out – a humiliation I could not bear. I'd prefer to go suddenly rather than drift off into senility.

Looking back over my life, as I do now more and more frequently, I am struck by how pointless and useless it has been. I've made no stir in the world, even in the world of the collectors of 'virtu'. Who will remember Francis Richmond for his two slight volumes, his minuscule success as a minor scholar and writer? Never.

4 July

I am feeling better today but I have resolved to take it more quietly for the rest of the summer. This last attack has given me a nasty turn. I ought to get away and fortuitously this afternoon I had a letter from Dolly Partiger in New York, inviting me to stay at Euston Farm at Oldhaven in New England in the first week in August. I think I shall go. I like Oldhaven, with its 'Robber Baron' palaces and their turn-of-the-century opulence – although the 'cottages', as they call the vast Edwardian mansions, have now mainly been turned into apartments. But not Euston Farm. That remains, an enclave outside the suburban quaintness of the town, an enchanting house, a little inland, set in proper grounds, unlike the meagre strips around the palaces nearer to the ocean. And I like Dolly. She's kind – vulgar, of course, but hospitable in the way that only Americans are – and I like her house, which is comfortable in the way only American houses are. I expect she'll have the usual stagy crowd down from New York, actors and songwriters and so on. They are always amusing and it might help Job to meet them. But I'm afraid he won't come. He's not very kind to me.

15 July

As I thought, Job won't come to Oldhaven. He says he'll be on tour. He has a small part in an Ayckbourn play. Silly boy!

Euston Farm. 6 August

I haven't written this journal for several weeks for I had little to write about in London in July. I thought I should abandon the Season on account of my health, except for special occasions with special friends. So there has been little to record. Except that one day about a fortnight ago I had a curious sighting. It was lunchtime and I took myself to the Tate, and in a distant corner of the room with the Impressionists I saw Tancred and that gross Oscar Sleaven, once again engaged in intense conversation. Then I watched them part, Sleaven looking about him furtively as they wandered around separately, pretending to look at the pictures before they separately disappeared. How odd, I thought, to see Tancred at a gallery. Tancred was never a man for art or culture. On the other hand, a gallery or a museum is a convenient place for a discreet meeting. In my day it certainly was for lovers. But this was no lovers' meeting. What can they be up to? The Minister and the industrialist talking so secretively?

Anyhow, here I am at Euston Farm, in my attractive room overlooking a meadow and I am enjoying my visit. I needed a change of scene, even if the scene here is a little too social for my present comfort. Clarissa Stoneley, by origin from Alabama and more recently the relict of Jimmy, the Duke of Midhurst's younger brother, is here with her lover, a Latin who looks and probably is a gigolo from Rio, much younger than the ancient Clarissa who is certainly making an exhibition of herself. But either she doesn't know it or doesn't care. Apparently they are living in a suite at the Westbury in New York. The gigolo, incidentally, is barely polite to me.

None of Dolly's usual Broadway/Los Angeles set in the party, so Job is missing nothing. Lester Chaffin arrived this morning. He's a senator from one of the mid-west states and Dolly says he's tipped to be the new Under-Secretary at Defence. She also told me, to my surprise, that she's expecting Tancred tomorrow evening on his way home from some ministerial meeting in Washington. He's only staying two days but Dolly is determined to take him to the ball at the Ivory House on Wednesday evening. I don't know the Ivory House, the former home of the Van Mortens. It is said to be one of the marvels of Oldhaven. I shall be interested to see it decked out for a ball. At the beach I sit in my panama hat at a table under the awning amid a group of the elderly, listening to their gossip about the young while my companions drink innumerable vodkas on the rocks and I eat a tasteless salad and sip iced tea. There are some very leggy young wives, who wander into the bar after playing extremely energetic tennis, sweating and rubbing their noses – while their precocious children run around whining and getting under our feet. Clarissa says that when the parents have lunch, the children, even those aged eight or nine, meet behind the club-house and smoke marijuana! One young woman, a friend of Dolly's who seemed to keep herself rather apart from the others, came and sat with us for a time. She's a good-mannered, good-looking young woman. She told me she's visiting an aunt who lives in Old-haven. She volunteered to get me another glass of iced tea, and went all the way to the bar and brought it to me. She tells me she has no husband. I like her.

8 August

I am completely done up from last evening. I had a bad attack, violent pain, and I was brought home soon after one o'clock by the young woman I had met at the beach in the afternoon. I was on the point, I thought, of death.

But the ball in that extraordinary, *fin de siècle* house had been a splendid spectacle. Enormous late-Victorian rooms, swathed in flowers specially flown from Colombia. Drink, of course, flowed but the young nowa-days don't seem to get as intoxicated as we did in my youth. Perhaps they are all on cocaine? Or heroin. The music, as always in the States, catchy and tuneful – until later in the evening when it became too noisy. I had a dance with Dolly, which was constantly interrupted by her irritating habit of greeting and embracing everyone on the dance floor. I was glad when she led me back to the table that our elderly group had commandeered. She then demanded that the band play 'Hello, Dolly' and danced it like a dervish with Clarissa's gigolo, much to Clarissa's annoyance. She made a complete exhibition of herself.

Tancred had arrived in the morning. He greeted me, as I would expect, rather coolly. At the ball he didn't dance. He was unchanged, which was remarked upon critically. Dolly had to explain he'd flown straight from Washington and meetings with the administration, and had no dinner jacket. He did not come to the beach but spent most of the day talking with Chaffin. I suppose this was the reason he'd come; not to see Dolly, as she thought. I remembered what Kitty had said about Tancred's drinking but I saw that he was drinking little. Kitty, I suppose, being catty – like all politicians.

At about half past midnight I had gone to the loo. There was a cord across the bottom of the great stairs in the hall to show that upstairs was out of bounds, but so taken was I by the magnificent vulgarity of this extraordinary house that I thought I'd like to see more of it. No one was about, so I unhooked the cord and went up the great staircase. I proceeded with great caution, in case any of the upstairs rooms was occupied and I opened each door very quietly, so that I could peer inside. One, leading off the landing at the top of the stairs, opened on to a sitting room or library, very dimly lit with an open french window on to a veranda. I could smell the scent and indeed see the plumes of smoke from expensive Havanas and made out the backs of the heads of three men sitting and talking on the veranda. One of the voices I recognised. It was Tancred's. I heard him saying that the Prime Minister, whom he had defended so stoutly in the House in May, was of course a complete fraud, very manipulative, playing off his ministers one against another. There followed some talk about him and then I heard an English voice, I thought it was, saying, 'He's had a mistress for years, someone in his constituency.' Another said that the President should be careful. He shouldn't treat the PM as too close a friend. He doesn't, said an American voice. Tancred then went on to say he didn't intend to stay long in politics. He needed money. He'd only gone into politics to get the chance of making some, either while he was a minister or after he'd left the Ministry through the connections he'd made while in government. The American voice then said quietly, 'We must see what we can do.'

As this was said I thought of Tancred and Oscar Sleaven, but I heard a chair being pushed back on the veranda so I slipped out, closing the door silently, not feeling guilty at having eavesdropped but fearful in case I was discovered. Perhaps it was this anxiety that led to what followed next.

As I came down the stairs, I suddenly had a violent attack, piercing stabs of pain in the chest. I had to clutch the banister to prevent myself from falling. It was very hot and I began to pour with sweat. Somehow I managed to get down and I found a chair in one of the rooms off the dance floor. I was feeling very dizzy and faint, and was leaning forward, my elbows on my knees and my head in my hands, when I heard a voice. I looked through my hands and saw kneeling in front of me the young woman I had met at the beach and who had brought me the iced tea. She asked if I was all right and I said yes but that I ought to go home. 'I'm not drunk,' I added.

'Of course not,' she replied and asked if she should fetch Mrs Partiger. I said no but I would be very grateful if she could help me call a taxi to take me back to Euston Farm.

'I'll take you,' she replied. She took my arm, led me to the hall, sat me down and told the parking attendants to bring round her car. I suppose the servants and some of the guests who were in the hall thought I had drunk too much. Her car, when it came, was a small open tourer and the drive, with the cool air round my head, made me feel better. I said I was sorry to have taken her from the party but she said no, she was glad to leave. She said that as a child she'd often visited at Oldhaven but she preferred the winters when the place was empty. She remembered Christmases, with the houses and gardens decorated by lights and snow on the rocks. She said Dolly Partiger had been very kind to her when she was growing up. She knew most of the people at the dance but they were all much richer than she, married to Wall Street brokers. She said she lived in the Village in New York. She'd like to come to Europe next year to paint in London or Paris but she doubted she had the money.

When we got to Euston Farm she asked if she should help me to my room but I said no as I was feeling a little better. She helped me up the steps and at the front door she suddenly leant up and kissed me on the cheek. I was quite touched. I got to bed but didn't sleep much. I thought of the young woman's kindness. I hope she's a good painter.

9 August
I am still not feeling at all well. I should never have gone to that dance. It was too much for me. Today I declined going with the others to the beach for lunch and stayed in my room. In the morning an elderly couple arrived, an ascetic, thin, silver-haired academic from Yale and his plump wife with legs the size of a piano. Professor and Mrs Something-or-other. He, I thought, rather sinister. Clarissa says he is Dolly's latest, very imaginative in bed. I think Clarissa was still smarting from Dolly's dance with her gigolo.

When the others were at the beach, the young woman called and came to my room. She asked how I was. Better, I replied and thanked her for her kindness. She said she'd like to paint me. 'I have wanted to ever since I first saw you. You have such a distinguished head.' I laughed. She stayed about an hour and kissed me again on the cheek when she left.

Tancred departed in the evening. I leave tomorrow, feeling more exhausted than when I came. The pains last evening were the worst I have experienced. I should not have left London. It's been too much for me. I do believe that young woman, the painter, saved my life.

I shall be glad to get home for then I shall catch a glimpse of Job. But he never stays for long, just a night when he needs a bed. And, of course, money. I have grown very fond of the boy but he doesn't care for me. Why should he?

Since the attack on the night of the ball I have had a premonition. I dread the journey home. When I am back in London – if I ever get back to London – I shall see my solicitor, Oliver Goodbody, about my will and put my affairs in order. I am very tired.

What an unimportant life I have led! No one will mourn me when I'm gone, no one will remember me. I shall have left not a mark on the life of a single soul. Nothing, nothing, nothing – to show that Francis Richmond ever existed.

Part Two

Chapter One

Godfrey Lacey paused at the entrance to the kitchen. He could see the back of his wife's tousled blonde head. She was seated in a chair, feeding the baby. Once upon a time he would kiss the top of her head before he left in the morning. Not now. He was glad he didn't have to now. She didn't wash her hair as often as she used to. He called out, 'I'm off.' She said nothing, didn't even look up, went on feeding the baby with a spoon and scraping the food from the sides of its mouth.

In the hall he pulled on his raincoat. This morning he had butterflies in his stomach – like the old days when he was practising at the Bar before going into court. Their first home had been a flat in Putney. Alice would come to the front door to see him off and wish him luck. That was during the early days, during the sex time. Now, in the terraced house in Battersea where they'd gone after the baby and he'd taken the job at the news-paper, she let him go without a word or a glance. Not that he minded. He wasn't sure why he stayed with her. It wasn't pity. She had only herself to blame. She'd chosen to do what she'd done with a fellow cost clerk where she worked. Not, of course, to have the baby. But that had been the result.

It was raining and putting up his umbrella he hurried down the few yards of garden path and walked rapidly to the bus stop.

He'd been up half the night marking and tagging the manuscript, preparing. Eight o'clock conference with the managing director at the office of the editor of the

Sunday. When he'd got to bed in the small hours in his separate room in the small house, he'd hardly slept. Once he did, he'd dreamt of the characters he'd been reading about day and night for the past forty-eight hours.

He reached his office on the eighteenth floor in the tower block in Docklands at seven thirty. He went again through his speaking note. He'd prepared it as he had his briefs, those few, poorly marked briefs the clerk in chambers used to hand out, Legal Aid cases that wouldn't be paid for months. Now, on the staff of the legal department at the newspaper, he didn't have to worry so much about money. The cheque came in monthly, far more than he'd have earned if he'd stayed at the Bar.

He hadn't really liked the Bar. He liked law, the solving of problems and the searching for precedent; but court had terrified him. So he'd taken the newspaper job, and settled for regular office work, drafting letters, dealing with complainants, negotiating personnel problems, scrutinising contracts, none of which aroused the dreadful flow of adrenalin and fear of appearing before a sarcastic judge or a magistrate with a long list and a short fuse.

Today, however, might be different. For today the conference was with the new editor of the Sunday, and the new editor, they said on the editorial floor, was abrasive, with the language of the barrack room. Normally he'd have nothing to do with the editors. Dealing with them was the job of Harold Baines, the Legal Manager who'd hired him. Then, two weeks ago, Baines had had a stroke and been carted away in an ambulance. He would not be returning. Management was looking for a replacement. Godfrey knew he'd not be considered. He was too new, only three months into the job, and they'd be looking for someone with more 'bottle'. Meanwhile the routine work in the legal department without a legal manager was heavy.

Three days ago Ralph Spenser, the Managing Director,

had come to his office and dropped on to his desk a bundle of typescript nearly a foot high. 'I want advice on whether this is safe to print,' he said. 'Urgent.' Twenty-four hours later Spenser sent a message. Lacey was to give his opinion the following day at 8 a.m. in the office of the editor of the Sunday. During the day in his office and the night at home in the room next to where the baby was crying, Godfrey had been reading, marking pages and making a note.

At eight o'clock sharp he entered the Sunday editor's office. Spenser was already there, in a chair in front of the editor's desk. In his dark suit, he looked the accountant he was, as neat and sleek as ever, his dark hair smoothed back, his spectacles gleaming in the artificial light. The editor, even at this early hour, was smoking a small cigar. On the large desk was a bundle of typescript identical to that which Godfrey now balanced on his knee. He took a chair beside Spenser.

'I've just seen the latest figures, Ralph,' the editor was saying to Spenser, pronouncing Ralph the American way with an 'l'. Spenser nodded. 'Fucking awful. We've not stopped the rot.' Spenser nodded again. 'I need something for features, something cheeky – to get people talking, to make a bit of a stir. And this' – the editor patted the bundle on the desk 'could be it. How did we get it?'

'A young man has offered it to us. I've checked him out with the solicitors to the estate. He's the literary executor and he's also negotiating the book rights with publishers. He's after serialisation.' Spenser paused. 'He wants a lot of money. He's hawking it around but he came to us first.'

'Everyone will go for it.' The editor looked at Godfrey frostily and back to Spenser. 'It's what I need, Ralph. A bit of gossip about sex, a bit of chat about politicians. We can do with something like this.'

'Not if it lands us in a million-pound libel suit,' Spenser muttered.

'Who'd sue? The upper-class tarts he writes about?

Never. The politicians? They wouldn't dare.' The editor stubbed out the small cigar. 'It'll make a buzz, Ralph.'

'Not on the Clapham omnibus.'

'It will in Islington and Westminster. Who's in it, who's not. The chatterers will read it. The *Telegram* would print it all right. They won't turn it down. They'll take the risk.'

They, the *Telegram*, *News*'s rivals, can afford to, thought Spenser.

The editor went on, 'We must see those bastards don't get their hands on it, not in the middle of this fucking war.'

That's what it was, and had been for six months: a circulation war. Ogilvy Grant, owner of the Telegram group, made no bones about it. He'd announced he was out to kill News Universal. 'I'll bury them,' he'd said. He'd slashed the *Telegram*'s cover price and doubled the investment in editorial, bribing away top journalists from other newspapers with absurdly swollen salaries. It was costing Grant millions but he didn't care. He had the money. He'd spend a fortune. So long as he destroyed News Universal.

In reply *News* had been forced to lower cover prices and pump thousands into editorial, and thousands more into a TV campaign. But *News* was bleeding, haemorrhaging readers week by week. If it went on, they'd bleed to death, so Spenser said nothing.

The editor turned to Godfrey and glared at him. 'Who are you?'

Godfrey cleared his throat. 'Lacey, legal department.'

'Bloody lawyers,' the editor growled, lighting another cheroot. 'Only make trouble.'

'We have to check the legal risks,' said Spenser. He turned to Godfrey. 'You've been through it?'

Godfrey nodded.

'Well?'

Godfrey cleared his throat again and glanced down at his speaking note. 'In almost every entry on every day there are references to social or political figures, usually critical, often referring specifically to their—'

The editor cut him short. 'Sex orientation, sex activities. That's the whole point. Richmond was an old queen, and old queens are as bitchy as hell and obsessed with sex. But so are the readers – and the potential readers. That's why I want it. But no one's going to sue, not about sex, not nowadays.'

'But if the innuendoes or even the explicit statements regarding sexual orientation are untrue—'

Again the editor interrupted. 'What if they are? Who cares nowadays whether someone's homo or hetro? What's defamatory in publishing a story about sexual identity or sexual preference, even if it's wrong? Where's the libel in that?' Before Godfrey could speak the editor continued, 'When I was a kid on the *Star*, I was taught the definition of libel – to hold someone up in the eyes of right-minded persons to hatred, ridicule or contempt. Isn't that the bloody formula?'

'Yes, but—' Godfrey began.

The editor interrupted him again. 'Are you trying to tell me that to call a person gay in the twenty-first century brings them into ridicule, hatred or contempt?' The editor gazed balefully at him across the desk.

Godfrey tried again. 'Someone could take great offence at being described as gay or having an innuendo published about them that they are gay if they are not.'

'Fucking homophobia.' The editor waved the cigar threateningly. 'Are you saying that so-called right-minded people nowadays have contempt for gays, hate gays, ridicule gays?'

Spencer intervened. 'I understand that you as the editor want to publish—'

'I fucking well do.'

'Well, the Chairman will have to be consulted. He'll have to decide. He'll have to balance the advantages against the risks.'

'There's no risk, no real risk, Ralphie boy.'

'You are only thinking of the women. There are also the politicians,' Spenser added.

The editor waved the cigar airily. 'They wouldn't dare. The politicians wouldn't dare to take us on. No, Ralph, this could give us a boost. And kudos.'

'I understand that but the Chairman'll have to decide.'

'Well, make sure he decides quick. I wanted it this Sunday. Twenty-four hours?'

'Perhaps forty-eight. I'll get the seller to give us forty-eight hours.'

'Well, for fuck's sake don't lose it, Spenser, just because the fucking lawyers haven't any balls.'

Spenser rose. 'I'll call Paris from my office.' He beckoned to Godfrey.

They took the lift to the management offices on the top floor. This new editor of the Sunday had been the Chairman's personal choice after he had sacked the previous one two months before. He was a Scot, canny, concerned about cost. His successor was not. The new editor was different, very different. This editor, Spenser reminded himself gloomily, thinking of the evil-smelling cigar, was female.

As they walked along from the lift to his office, Spenser said, 'She lives with a merchant banker.' He paused. 'A woman merchant banker,' he added.

It was just before nine o'clock UK time, ten in Paris, when Spenser put down the receiver after speaking to the Chairman. He buzzed for his secretary. 'Get Lacey on the ten twenty-three Euro to Paris with an open return, the tickets to be collected at the booking office. The Chairman's office will get him a hotel room. Have my car brought to the front door.' To Godfrey, he said, 'Where's your passport?'

'At home, in Battersea.'

'Collect it on the way to Waterloo. Have you any money?'

'Not much.'

Spenser called his secretary again. 'Bring four fifty

pound notes and any francs we have.' Then he said to Godfrey, 'Change the sterling at the station, either end. We'll take care of your ticket.' He scribbled on a pad. 'Here's the address. Get a taxi at the Gare du Nord. Run for it as soon as the train gets in. There's usually a queue. You've tagged certain pages in the typescript?'

'Yes.'

'Make sure the Chairman reads at least the parts you've tagged. If possible, get him to read the whole of it. Don't miss the train. See that he fully understands the risks. Remember, he's not as stupid as he looks.' He paused. Then he added to himself, 'Nor so clever as he thinks.'

Godfrey had a seat in first class by the window at the end of a carriage. The seat opposite him was empty. His large briefcase, with the manuscript, a clean shirt and washing bag, was on the rack above his head. As he looked out of the window he saw a bareheaded young woman in jeans and a tan jacket pushing a loaded trolley hurriedly towards the carriage door. With difficulty she lifted a heavy suitcase and a wooden box on to the platform. The conductor normally stationed at the entrance to the carriage had gone. Any second the train would pull out. She struggled with the suitcase, trying to lift it up the high step of the carriage. Godfrey rose. 'Let me give you a hand,' he said. He hauled the luggage into the carriage and into the baggage racks opposite the door.

The young woman followed and sank into the vacant seat opposite his. 'Thanks,' she said. The train began to move. 'That was close. I shouldn't have so much kit,' she added in an American accent. 'I don't know what I'll do the other end.'

'Another trolley,' Godfrey said.

'If I can lift the kit on to it,' she replied.

'I'll help.'

'Thanks,' she repeated. She lay back in her seat and closed her eyes.

Godfrey studied her slyly over the top of his newspaper. Clear bronzed skin, oval face with a generous mouth; dark hair cut quite short. Shiny and well-kept, very different from the hair he'd left in Battersea. She knew he was staring at her and opened her eyes. 'Have you made this trip before?'

'Not by train.'

The stewardess came up with a tray of drinks. The young woman took some orange juice, Godfrey a glass of champagne. She lay back again and closed her eyes. As Godfrey sipped his champagne, he thought about the meeting with the Chairman of News Universal and the butterflies returned to his stomach.

The Chairman, Digby Price, a South African, lived in Paris, now and then coming to London to make sorties to Docklands to bully the staff, sack editors and threaten management. It was hands-on, personal government, the more harassing for its remote control. Godfrey was glad he had his note, hardly used in the meeting with the female editor. Would the Chairman, he wondered, read the whole manuscript? That would take time. He could be away for a couple of days. He'd like that. Perhaps he should recommend they get a member of the practising libel bar to read the manuscript and advise? But that would take more time. The editor would not like it. Above all, he must stay calm and not get fussed and make sure the Chairman understood the risks. That was what Spenser wanted.

He stared out of the window at the Kent countryside. He'd heard the train only really picked up speed on the far side of the Channel.

'You on business?' the young American woman asked suddenly.

He nodded.

'What sort of business?'

'Legal,' he said shortly. 'And you?' he asked.

'A commission to paint a portrait. That's the reason for all the kit.'

'So you'll be staying in Paris for some time?'

She nodded. 'Do you know Paris?'

'Not very well.'

'My first trip,' she said. When the steward brought the menu she looked at it and waved it aside. 'Airplane food.'

Godfrey nodded but ordered. As he unscrewed the small bottle of Bordeaux they had brought with his plastic tray, she watched him.

Then she called the steward. 'I'll have one of those,' she said, pointing at Godfrey's drink.

'Is it an interesting commission?' he asked.

'Portrait of a corporate wife. A friend of mine in New York fixed it up. I've booked into a hotel, the Lucerne on the Left Bank. Do you know it?' He shook his head. 'I'll have to do sketches and take photographs,' she went on, almost to herself. 'I'll have to find a studio.'

'Where are you from?' he asked her.

'New York, but I've just got the use of a studio in London. I hadn't settled in when this came up. I shouldn't have brought so much kit.'

She shut her eyes once more and lay back, and again he studied her. This time she slept, her glass of wine almost untouched.

As they approached Paris he asked, 'Have you any francs?'

'I was told I could change pounds or dollars at the station.'

'You'll need 10 francs for the trolley.'

'Hell.'

'I'll loan it,' he said. 'And put your watch on an hour,' he added.

At the Gare du Nord he jumped out of the carriage, found her a trolley and lifted on to it her suitcase and easel. 'I have to run. I've an appointment.'

She leant forward and kissed his cheek. 'Thanks for the help.'

He felt himself blushing as he turned and hurried away, following the signs to the taxis. When he looked back he saw she was pushing the trolley slowly towards the end of the platform.

It was three o'clock Paris time when the taxi drew up at the apartment block in the rue Casimir Perrier. A man in a dark coat and striped pants opened the door.

'*Godfrey Lacey, de Londres,*' Godfrey said hesitantly.

The manservant nodded and led him to a lift. '*Deux-ième étage.*'

Another man in a dark suit with silver hair but a young, unlined face was standing opposite the doors on the second floor. 'I'm Wilson. This way.' He led Godfrey down a corridor into a library cum office. 'I'm the Chairman's PA. You have the typescript?' He had a South African accent with a very English tone super-imposed.

Godfrey took the manuscript from his briefcase.

'Wait here.' Wilson disappeared through an inner door. Godfrey sat, the fear within him taking a hold.

Half an hour later Wilson reappeared. 'The Chairman will see you now.'

Digby Price, a short, stocky, balding man, with a lined, gnarled face, was sitting behind a large, important-looking desk. He didn't rise or put out his hand. 'I've spoken to Spenser – and the editor,' he began in his South African accent, uglier, more pronounced than that of Wilson. 'You've tagged the most contro-versial items?' Godfrey laid the bundle on the desk. 'I'll read it tonight. Come back seven thirty tomorrow morn-ing. Wilson will find you a room.' He waved his hand. Godfrey was dismissed.

In the library, Wilson asked. 'Where do you want to stay?'

Godfrey remembered what the painter had said on the train. 'The Lucerne,' he replied.

Wilson looked at him quizzically. 'You could do better.'

'The Lucerne will do,' Godfrey said.

'Then take a cab. I'll telephone ahead.' He stretched for the phone but rose abruptly from his chair. Godfrey turned, smelling the scent.

A woman had come into the room from the corridor. She was hatless, with bobbed blonde hair, in a long dark coat and tight black trousers, her lips very red. 'Is he in?' she asked in heavily accented English.

'He's in conference,' Wilson said. 'He will not be able to see you.'

'Then tell him to call me. If he doesn't, there'll be trouble.' She swung on her heel and left.

Wilson shrugged and picked up the telephone. 'Be here at seven tomorrow,' he told Godfrey.

When Godfrey had checked in at the Lucerne and handed over his passport, he asked, 'Has a young lady, an American, arrived this afternoon?'

The clerk shrugged. 'We have many guests.' He wasn't going to say more.

Godfrey took his briefcase to his room. It was like any room in any hotel in any city in the world: small, functional, with a bathroom. After he had washed he went downstairs and sat in a chair facing the entrance.

It was six o'clock before she appeared. 'Hi,' she said when she saw him. It was as if she had expected him. 'Have you come for your ten francs?'

He smiled. 'No, the office got me a room. I remembered you said you'd be staying here and I wondered if you were free for dinner?'

She looked at herself in the glass above the chair where he'd been sitting. 'God,' she said, 'I look a fright. I've been chasing halfway round the whole city, talking American French.' She looked back at Godfrey. 'Dinner? A stiff drink is what I need. See you here in an hour.'

Chapter Two

While he waited he asked the concierge to recommend a restaurant. After an hour she appeared, in an orange shirt and black trousers.

'It's a fish restaurant,' he said in the taxi. 'Is that all right?'

'OK,' she replied.

'I'm Godfrey Lacey,' he added.

'I'm Anna James, from New York.'

At the table in the restaurant he ordered a bottle of Chablis while he examined the menu. She pushed back a lock of hair, which kept falling over her forehead, and drank greedily, half her glass in a single swallow.

'A salad,' she ordered, 'followed by sole meunière.' She hadn't even looked at the card.

She knows what she wants; different from me. He thought of the bleak house in Battersea, almost a slum. Why was he still there? Why hadn't he left, as he'd said he would? He should have months ago. But he hadn't. So he was still there, with a woman, and a child who wasn't his. He ordered oysters and poached turbot. While they waited for the food, he said. 'You looked very worried when you came into the hotel.'

She pushed back the lock of hair. 'I spent the afternoon chasing after the woman I thought I'd come to paint. Eventually I located her husband's secretary, their social secretary, a very superior lady who seemed to think I was crazy.'

'Why?'

'Because I was here. She said they expected me to

send photographs of my work like the others. The husband – an American banker in Paris – hasn't made up his mind whom he wants to paint his wife, although the secretary said in her superior way that he'd probably prefer someone from Paris.'

'What did you say?'

'I had to say I'd send photographs of my work. She'll show them to the banker – or so she said. I left, with my tail between my legs.' She banged her hand on the table. 'I felt so *stupid*, turning up on their doorstep like a school kid.' Anna passed a hand over her forehead. He filled her glass and she drank again. 'June, she's the friend in New York, said it was all fixed. I could murder her.' He was swallowing the last of his half-dozen oysters. She watched him and pulled a face. 'How can you eat those awful things?'

'I like them,' he said. Especially, he thought, when it was his employer who was paying for them.

She went on, 'June made it sound like it was all pretty definite. I thought if I came over that would clinch it. Well, it hasn't.' She drank again. He watched her cut the sole with her knife, then put it aside as she ate the American way with her fork. He poured her more wine. 'You'll make me tight,' she said as she drank. 'What kind of lawyer are you?'

'I work for a corporation, in their legal department. I'm here seeing my boss who lives in Paris.'

'Was that why you ran off so fast from the station, to see the boss?'

'Yes. Have you painted many portraits?'

'I've sold one or two. Are you married?'

He paused. At last he said, 'I am, in a way.'

'What does that mean?'

'I have a wife.'

'At home?'

He nodded.

'Children?' she asked.

'There's a baby at home.'

The pictures flooded into his mind. Alice screaming,

telling him she was pregnant, he trying to calm her, to hide how horrified he felt, saying how pleased he was. You idiot, you bloody idiot, she'd shouted, sitting on the bed. It's not yours. Don't you understand? It's not bloody well yours. He wasn't altogether surprised. He knew she'd been up to something. When she said this he felt pleased, relieved. Now he was free, free of the mistake they'd both known they'd made only a few weeks after they married. Whose is it? he'd asked. It doesn't matter, it doesn't matter, she'd cried. Just help me get rid of it, you've got to help me get rid of it. But when he had she'd refused even to see the doctor. I can't, I can't kill it, I won't – and she'd called him a murderer. He should have left then but he hadn't. He'd go after the baby was born, he'd told her. She'd just nodded. But he hadn't. He was still there. Pathetic, Alice called him.

'The baby's not mine,' he said.

'Whose is it?'

'Someone at the office.'

Anna was watching his face. 'Why do you stay with her? Do you love her that much?'

'God, no. I meant to go. I shall soon.'

'I don't think I want to hear any more.' She lifted her glass slowly. 'I'm in a Paris with a married man – and I'm getting tight.'

With the coffee she ordered Crème de Menthe, iced. 'What my father called a tart's drink.' She looked around the restaurant, savouring the blue plumes that rose from the Gitane cigarettes. 'That bloody, condescending secretary,' she said as she drank the liqueur. 'I don't want to go back to the hotel yet.'

As they collected their coats Godfrey asked the coat-check girl where they could go for a drink, a bar, with music. The girl looked at them sourly and wrote on a piece of paper. In the taxi he showed it to the driver.

They were led down some narrow steps, he holding her arm, to a dimly lit circular room with tables against the walls, mostly unoccupied. In the centre there was a dance floor. A small band played on a dais and a middle-aged woman sang huskily into a microphone, trying to sound likes Edith Piaff. Godfrey pointed to a table at the back in the corner and ordered white wine. 'All right?' he asked. Anna nodded. By the time the wine had come the singer had sat down to desultory applause.

'Not so different from the Village,' Anna said. 'Perhaps not so noisy.'

A few couples took to the floor. Two women in dark suits began to dance together.

'Your friend at the restaurant had a sense of humour,' Anna said watching them.

'Do you mind?' Godfrey asked.

'Not unless they ask me to dance.'

'Shall we?'

'What would your wife say?'

'She wouldn't care.'

'Don't let them cut in.'

They danced for a few minutes, then sat and drank more wine. One of the two women dancing together smiled at Anna over the shoulder of her partner.

Anna looked away. 'One of the dykes made a pass at me,' she said. Suddenly she put her hand to her head. 'Oh, God, I feel dizzy. The bloody tart's drink. Take me home. I must get home. Take me home.'

In the taxi she leant against the side of the car away from him, moaning, 'The damn woman, the bloody secretary. June swore I had the commission.' She began to weep.

At the hotel he helped her across the foyer. He collected both their keys and guided her to the lift.

'Telephone, M'sieur,' the hall porter called after them. 'Second time, asking for you. They say it's important.'

The lift doors opened. 'What's my floor?' Anna asked, leaning back against the wall of the lift.

He looked at her key. 'Second.'

She snatched it from him. 'Go,' she said. 'Leave me alone. I'm all right, I'm all right.' Then she changed her mind. 'No, wait. Press my floor number.' He leant in and pressed the button. The lift doors closed.

He ran back to the desk, took the telephone and heard the angry English tones superimposed on the South African voice. 'Lacey? Is that you? Where have you been? You have been out all night. The Chairman wants you – at once. The car will be at the hotel in five minutes.' The line went dead.

Wilson greeted him silently at the lift door and led him to the Chairman's room. Digby Price was in his shirt-sleeves in an armchair. On a small table beside the typescript were a decanter and a tall glass.

Godfrey was left standing, Wilson beside him, facing the Chairman.

'The seller has given us twenty-four hours,' the Chairman began. 'After that he takes it to the *Telegram*. And I want it. As you're here, I suppose you'd better have your say.'

'There are several references and innuendoes which may or may not be accurate and—'

The Chairman interrupted him. 'If you mean the parts about sex, the editor says they're not defamatory but if they are, then they're true.'

'A jury might disagree that they are not defamatory, sir. Where the defence is truth, or justification, the burden of proof is on the defence.'

'I know that. But none of those women would dare. They'd look ridiculous. We'll put a team on to them to check them out. Unearthing sex affairs, young man, is a question of money. It never fails – if you offer enough.' He poured himself some whisky from the decanter. 'What do you say about the politicians?'

'The innuendo in respect of one or two is that they're homosexuals and—'

'McClaren and the woman Minister? Stuff that. What else?'

'The innuendo about the Minister of Defence Procurement, suggesting he was up to disreputable business dealings with an industrialist—'

'Ministers usually are, and this Minister more likely than most. Leave him to me. I'll deal with him.'

'If he sues and the defence fails, the damages and costs could be very large.'

'He's a crook,' Price said shortly.

'It could be difficult to prove that he—'

'I don't altogether care if we can't. It's a damn good story, him and Sleavens running a racket. But Tancred won't dare. We'll get the proof we need because, as I said, he's a villain and a crook. If he tries it on,' Price continued, 'we'll take him on.' He turned to Wilson. 'Corruption in the Cabinet! News Universal exposing bribery of a minister. The *News* performs a public service. How's that for circulation, eh, Wilson?'

'Indeed, sir, indeed.'

'If the defence fails, sir—' Godfrey said.

'The public'll think there was something to it, that the story was true but we couldn't prove it – legally. That we failed on a technicality. But the mud will stick and I intend to fling it. Especially at that bastard Tancred.'

'May I suggest we get an opinion from a barrister practising at the libel bar?'

'No, I've told the editor to print this weekend, in three days' time.' He looked at the clock above the fireplace. 'Now in two days' time. It'll be in copy on Thursday.'

'There is a considerable risk and—'

'Risk! What's newspaper publishing about, young man, if it isn't about risk, taking chances, giving the public what they want? The downside is what – a few thousands in damages? But it won't come to that. This is a true bill. That bastard is corrupt. I know it and soon the public will know it. I've waited a long time to get him and now I shall. I'm going to expose him and, even if I fail, there'll be kudos, sympathy because we couldn't technically prove what the public knows is true. That right, Wilson?'

'Quite right, sir.'

'So what does it add up to? If the women or their lovers sue, ridicule. If it's Tancred, we're a public-spirited newspaper playing our proper role in a democracy – exposing sleaze in public life. Win or lose, it'll be the end of Tancred. Even if we lose the verdict, we won't lose readers.' He looked at Wilson. 'Do you agree, Wilson?'

'I do,' Wilson replied.

'And as an extra bonus, we stop the *Telegram* from getting it.'

'There are the other ministers, apart from Tancred,' said Godfrey.

'I'll take care of that.' The Chairman looked at Wilson. 'I don't want those minnows coming in and muddying the waters when I'm after the big fish. Perhaps it calls for a visit to a nice country house in the Buckinghamshire countryside?' He grinned at Wilson. Then he went on, 'It's Tancred I'm after and I'm going to get him. We're in the middle of a circulation war, sonny. Now go back to London on the first train.'

'The six thirty-seven,' said Wilson, looking at the clock over the chimneypiece. 'Four hours' time,' he added with satisfaction. 'Waterloo eight forty-six. He'll be in the office by nine.'

The Chairman rose and waved a hand in dismissal. Wilson closed the door behind Godfrey.

'Is the decision to print the whole manuscript quite unexpurgated, exactly as it is?' Wilson asked the Chairman.

'Except what he writes about me. We can't have that, can we?' Price grinned.

'No, sir, certainly not.'

'And, as you guessed, I've cut the reference to the PM.' Digby Price rose to his feet. 'That little extract about the PM is the reason for my trip to Buckinghamshire, to Chequers – to have a little talk. I want to persuade him to make sure that none of his other ministers sue. I don't want any of those clowns bringing actions. I want a clean run at Tancred. Just him.' He paused, looking into the fire. 'Tancred. I want Tancred.'

When Wilson had gone, Price stayed in his chair drinking whisky, still staring into the fire. He was thinking of the iron bars, the door clanging behind him and the brick walls of the cell. The heat and the filth and stink and the dark faces, and the hands clutching at him, flinging him to the ground, tearing off his clothes. And what they had done to him.

That had been Tancred's doing. Tancred had been responsible for that.

Back at the hotel, Godfrey went to Anna's door and knocked. There was no answer and he knocked again. When there was still no reply he went to his own room and spoke on the telephone to the night porter, asking to be put through to the room of Mlle James. 'She's given instructions she's taking no calls,' the man said. 'She's taken the telephone off the hook.'

He scribbled a note. 'I have to leave Paris on the first train. I do hope to see you again.' He wrote the address and the number of his office, and pushed the note under Anna's door.

When Godfrey got to the office, Spenser was in Manchester, due back later in the day. Godfrey wrote a short memo on the meeting in Paris. Later he was summoned to Spenser's office. 'I spoke myself to the Chairman last night,' Spenser said. 'He'd already made up his mind. He's cut the reference to the PM. Did you say your piece?'

'I tried to.'

'Well, it's his newspaper.' Spenser looked out of the window. 'And his money.' But not all of it. Some of it, he thought, is mine. I, too, have an investment in News Universal.

Far below he could see men still working on the

Jubilee Line station. The journalists were happier now that the line was operational. The *Telegram* was in Battersea, much easier to reach. But morale was still poor at News Universal. Yesterday there had been two more defections to the *Telegram*, both from editorial, both experienced sub-editors; one from Sports, the other from the City page. They'd been offered nearly double their salary at *News*. It was part of Ogilvy Grant's campaign to seduce away *News*'s best people. The war was getting nastier.

He turned back to Godfrey. 'He told me on the telephone he'd read the manuscript. Do you think he had?'

'He didn't let me say much. He kept repeating that he wanted to get Tancred.'

Spenser looked at Godfrey. 'He and Tancred,' he said. 'That goes back. It's been like that ever since I've known him.' He began to walk around the room.

'The Chairman even seemed to want Tancred to sue,' said Godfrey.

That's now, thought Spenser. When it's then, he could think differently. Lose badly and there'd not only be the damages to pay Tancred; there'd be the damage to the group's prestige. Massive damages on top of massive costs added to the blow to News Universal's reputation could even put in jeopardy the existence of the whole group. That morning, before the copy was set and before even the copy editor had read it, Spenser had been on to his broker. His instructions: to sell, discreetly, a block of his holding in News Universal. The stock was in the name of a nominee. No one would know who was selling. Just a precaution, Spenser thought, in case the war was lost.

'Our job now is damage limitation,' he said as he continued to prowl around the office, stopping now and then to look down from the window. 'What's your opinion of Mordecai Ledbury?'

'They say he's the top man in libel cases. I've never heard him in court.'

'I have. Effective but sometimes too bellicose, alienating juries, quarrelling with the judges. The media generally don't like him. He's gone for too many proprietors and bullied too many editors but in this instance I think he's the man for us.' Spenser paused, looked again at the miniature figures thousands of feet below. 'I shall retain him. If I can get him.'

'There are several not very polite references to him in the diary,' Godfrey interjected.

'That's because of a case some years ago when Ledbury cross-examined some young friend of Richmond's. I've authorised cuts of the references to Ledbury.'

Price himself, the PM, now Ledbury, Godfrey thought. Only these three to be cut from the manuscript.

'Ledbury's another of the Chairman's pet hates but I shan't let that stop me from retaining him.' Spenser sat at his desk. 'Prepare me an analysis of the extracts of the diary with a list of all those who might have grounds for suing.'

In the afternoon Oliver Goodbody, patrician, very tall and white-haired, greeted Ralph Spenser at the door of the imposing room of the senior partner in the firm of Goodbody & Co., solicitors. It was a book-lined room looking on to the gardens in Lincoln's Inn Fields. As soon as he had sat in the chair opposite Goodbody, Spenser began, 'News Universal has bought the serialisation rights in the diaries of your late client, Francis Richmond, from a young actor, Job Streatley.'

'I expect you had to pay a stiff price. He's a greedy young man.'

'We accepted the manuscript after you confirmed that Streatley owned the rights.'

Goodbody nodded. 'He has the rights. He's Richmond's heir and gets the whole estate. As I told your secretary on Monday, the rights to all Richmond's writings were bequeathed to Streatley. So that includes the diary that the young man stumbled on, although I doubt if Richmond ever intended it should be published. There was only one other bequest, which concerns part of the property where Richmond lived, a studio annexe. A five-year occupancy was left to a young woman, an artist from New York. The young man did not like that. He wants to dispose of the property immediately. I expect that was one of the reasons he was keen to raise cash from the diaries.'

'The Chairman has decided that the first extract will be published on Sunday. We're taking a risk since it included references to individuals who may not like what is published about them. If any sue, we shall defend every action vigorously and I want to put in place the legal team to defend the newspaper in the event of any writs.'

'Very sensible.'

Spenser met Goodbody's eye over the desk. 'I wish to retain, as leading counsel, Mordecai Ledbury. I believe you know him well.'

Oliver Goodbody joined his fingers together under his chin and smiled slightly. He began to understand the purpose of Spenser's visit. Mordecai Ledbury had many enemies and few friends, at least few men friends; Oliver Goodbody was one of the few. 'He's a difficult man, a very difficult man,' he said, his eyes fixed on Spenser's gleaming tortoiseshell glasses.

'There have been several cases in the past, libel actions when Ledbury has been pretty severe about News Universal and my Chairman, Mr Digby Price.'

Goodbody nodded.

'Nevertheless I am anxious to retain him,' Spenser went on. 'I consider he's the right man in this instance for News Universal.'

Goodbody shifted his glance and looked out of the window. 'Ledbury', he said at last, 'is very particular about whom he represents. The rule of the Bar the cab-rank rule that obliges counsel to accept any brief offered, he often avoids by demanding exorbitant fees – or even by pleading ill health. He's a cripple, you know.' Spenser nodded. There was a pause, then Goodbody continued, 'He has pronounced likes and dislikes, of institutions as well as individuals. So you may have difficulty.'

'There is one further matter,' Spenser went on. 'I have decided that in this matter we shall not use our regular firm of solicitors. I would like to retain your firm as the solicitors acting for the Corporation in respect of all or any actions brought against News Universal arising from the publication of the Richmond diaries.'

Oliver Goodbody, his fingers underneath his chin joined almost as if in prayer, switched his glance back to Spenser.

'The retainer', Spenser said, 'will be payable even if no actions arise and none come to trial. I had in mind a level of fee commensurate with the standing and distinction of your firm and that of the Corporation.'

For a time neither spoke. Goodbody again looked out of the window at the gardens. That morning he had been in discussion with the firm's accountants. Despite the handsome rooms overlooking Lincoln's Inn Fields and every outward appearance, the situation of the firm of Goodbody & Co. was not healthy. Indeed, the accountant had used the word desperate. So Spenser's offer was more than welcome. It could be just what was needed. It could be a lifesaver. 'Ledbury,' he said reflectively.

'Ledbury,' Spenser repeated.

Goodbody rose. 'Ledbury and I have the habit of dining once each month at Penns Club where we are both members. It so happens that tonight is one of those evenings. Let me see what I can do, Mr Spenser.'

Chapter Three

On the last Wednesday night of every month many members of Penns, the dining club in Hanover Square, avoided the place for it was on those Wednesday nights that Mordecai Ledbury dined there. It was the custom that, when at dinner, members sat at a round table in the dining room in the order in which they had given their orders for food. No one chose his own seat, which was decided by chance, and older members had too often undergone the experience of finding themselves seated next to Mordecai Ledbury and suffering from his irascible conversation. The only sensible course was to eat silently and swiftly, and retire to the ante-room as soon as possible. Newer members who found themselves Mordecai Ledbury's dinner neighbours and who attempted to make conversation rarely repeated the error.

There was a further inconvenience on these Wednesday evenings, for when members arrived they often found their way down the narrow stairs blocked by Ledbury as he slowly descended from the entrance hall to the ante-room, awkwardly manipulating his two sticks with one hand, the other on the banister. Should any of the newer members try to assist, they were waved aside with a snarl, for all were forced to follow as Mordecai Ledbury made his difficult progress. When at last he reached the ante-room, he moved with his crab-like gait to a table by the fire, where the steward brought him his pint of champagne in a silver tankard. He drank neither spirits nor table wine, only vintage champagne.

There he would sit, awaiting the only member of the club who would join him – Oliver Goodbody, who alone seemed prepared to tolerate his company. If Goodbody did not appear, Mordecai sat in solitary silence until he went into the dining room, where his entry was greeted with an immediate exodus. He never had a guest. His only company in the club was Oliver Goodbody.

On this Wednesday evening Goodbody had arrived first and took his place at the small table in the corner of the room. He ordered a whisky and soda, and waited. Outwardly he presented his usual appearance of dis-tinguished imperturbability, but inwardly he was feeling anxious. Much depended on this evening.

The club, because it was 'Ledbury day' as some called it, was comparatively empty. Soon he heard the clatter of Mordecai's progress down the stairs and the buzz of talk from the small group of members who were queuing patiently behind him. He watched as, reaching the ante-room floor, Ledbury advanced slowly across the room to join him, while the members who had been forced to queue on the stairs hastily ordered their dinner from the steward and disappeared into the dining-room.

They made an odd couple: Oliver with his distin-guished, aquiline features and silver hair; Mordecai misshapen, saturnine complexion, his head bald except for a few strands of jet-black hair plastered across the crown. The steward, unbidden, having brought Mordecai his usual tankard of champagne and, having allowed time for Mordecai to take a gulp, as was his manner in drinking the wine, Oliver Goodbody began, 'I had an interesting visitor to my office this after-noon.'

Mordecai grunted over the rim of his tankard.

'Ralph Spenser, the Managing Director of News Universal,' Goodbody added.

'Rum company you keep,' said Mordecai.

'He came with a proposition.'

Mordecai grunted again. 'They're bad people. What did he want?'

'He wants you.'

Mordecai lowered his tankard on to the table. 'Me? What does he want with me?'

'Your services as counsel.'

Mordecai banged the tankard on the table, making an elderly but new member sitting across the room look up, startled, from behind his newspaper. 'My services as counsel! After the attacks I've made on their rag and that Afrikaner villain?' He drank. 'Have they taken leave of their senses?'

'No. They assume what you have said about them in court was in the course of your professional duty to your then client.'

Mordecai snorted.

'They want to retain you as a barrister. Not as a moralist, but as a QC who they believe holds himself out for hire like others in his profession.'

Mordecai snorted again.

Goodbody continued, 'This Sunday their newspaper, the *Sunday News*, is publishing what they believe could lead to writs for libel. Extracts from the diaries of Francis Richmond.'

'Richmond? He kept a diary?'

'He did.'

'And *News* intend to publish it?'

'Yes.'

'Why? Who on earth would be interested? It'll be nothing but yarns about him and his like.'

'I haven't read it myself but Richmond was a cultivated man who wrote several books and mixed much in society.'

'I am sure he did. I once had to cross-examine a youth, a friend of his. Richmond was in court. Afterwards he made a scene and insulted me in the corridor. He didn't like me.'

'No more than does Digby Price.'

'Well, then, how am I concerned?'

'They have decided to publish extracts from the diary

and they anticipate the possibility, even the probability, of writs from some of the people referred to.'

'Very likely, if it's as bitchy as he was.'

'They want to retain you on behalf of the newspaper.'

Mordecai shouted over his shoulder, 'George, bring me another drink.' He turned to Goodbody. 'Are they mad? Don't they know what I think of them?'

Goodbody ignored the outburst. 'They think you'd be the best man to represent them, despite what their proprietor may think of you. But that wasn't all. The Managing Director, Spenser, also had another proposition.' Goodbody waited as George brought a fresh tankard and returned to the bar. 'He wants my firm to act as solicitors for the Corporation.'

Mordecai Ledbury stared at Goodbody and drank slowly, his black eyes fixed on his companion over the rim of his tankard. 'So,' he said at last, 'they have got you to approach me.'

'Yes.'

'And the bait to land me is that you and your firm will have the lucrative task of acting as their solicitors.'

'Exactly.' Goodbody leant back in his chair. 'I am going to tell you what I would not tell another living soul. I'm in a bad way. I've had some hard financial knocks recently. The Caverel case and my support for that family cost me a great deal.'

'You got too involved. I warned you,' Mordecai growled.

'I've had to sell my country house at Whitchurch. The firm has not been doing well. Frankly, we are in grave trouble. We, that is myself as well as the firm, face the possibility of going under.'

Mordecai looked at him. 'Is it that bad?'

'It is. As you know, I have no partners. It's my money that has kept the firm going. But I can't go on. I have a large overdraft, which the bank is pressing me to reduce. The modern trend in the solicitor world is for clients to abandon small family firms like mine in Lincoln's Inn Fields and take their business to the legal factories with

a hundred partners in the City or the West End. Up to
now we have managed to retain a few of the old clients,
like Richmond whose estate I handled, but they are
dying, as he did.' He paused. 'The truth is that my
situation, both personally and professionally, is desperate.'

Mordecai looked down at the tankard he was holding
between his hands. 'I am sorry to hear it.'

He meant it, because Mordecai Ledbury had few
friends. There were some women who now and then
petted him and asked him to their dinner parties. One or
two had once loved him, for despite his appearance he
knew how to talk to women and these few had discovered the generosity and kindness beneath the
distorted exterior. Oliver Goodbody was the only man
he recognised as a friend. In his professional life,
Mordecai used his chambers in King's Bench Walk
solely for conferences, working mainly from home in
Albany where he kept his books. He wouldn't even have
been able to recognise any of the men and women who
were members of his chambers. The only person he
dealt with there was Adams, his clerk. Very rarely did he
go to the Inner Temple for a dinner, possibly once or
twice in a year. Oliver Goodbody was the sole friend he
met regularly.

The Wednesday dinners were important to Mordecai.

'This offer by News Universal could be the saving of
the firm – and of me. The retainer, which extends to
whether or not there are any actual writs, would be very
lucrative.'

'I don't doubt it.'

'And they want you, Mordecai,' Goodbody repeated.
'I know you are not doing as much business as you used
to,' he added.

Mordecai stared at the wine in his tankard. 'I do
enough,' he muttered. 'Enough to pay the bills. I don't
need much.'

'Enough for your vintage champagne, your apartment

in Albany, and your holidays at the Danieli in Venice? None of that comes cheap.'

'I told you, I have enough, more than enough.'

'My managing clerk is a good friend of Adams, your clerk. A retainer such as News Universal is now offering, he says, is what you need at this time in your professional life.'

'It's what Adams needs, you mean. He takes his ten per cent. He's a greedy old woman.'

'You're not getting any younger, Mordecai.'

'Leave me out of it,' Mordecai said roughly. 'I told you I'm all right and I am. I don't need News Universal. I dislike everything about them. They respect nothing and nobody. They corrupt every civilised standard this country once stood for. They pander to the lowest instincts of the modern yob. Left to myself, I wouldn't touch them with a barge pole.' He paused, studying the grave, handsome face opposite him. 'Left to myself, I said.' He paused again, then added, 'So it's a package they want. You – provided they get me.' Oliver nodded. 'Not one without the other?' Oliver shook his head. Mordecai leant back in his chair. 'So if I refuse, I ruin a friend; if I accept I have to sup with the devil.'

'You exaggerate, Mordecai, as you always do. This is a perfectly straightforward retainer.'

Mordecai emptied his tankard. The steward approached with his notebook.

'You have ordered?' Mordecai asked. Goodbody nodded. Mordecai did so and when the steward had gone they sat in silence.

'Spenser', said Goodbody after a time, 'is a respectable and competent man of business.'

'Price isn't respectable. I don't like Price.'

'Neither does he you. Spenser and I will keep Digby Price away from you as much as we can. This is business, Mordecai. That is all it is, good, professional business.'

'It is certainly good for you.'

Goodbody leant forward. 'Mordecai, listen to me.

57

Quite apart from me, you hold yourself out for hire in accordance with the rules of your profession, especially the rule which you barristers call the cab-rank rule and which requires you to accept the brief from whomsoever it is offered, irrespective of your personal prejudices and private opinion of the offerer or the subject in dispute, provided' – Goodbody paused – 'always provided, you are offered an adequate fee. And the fee in this matter will, I am sure, be more than adequate.'

'I'm sure that it will.'

Goodbody said quietly, 'And it could save me, literally save me. I don't like to do this but I am appealing to you as a friend.' Again there was a moment of silence, longer than the previous one.

'Is what you've told me about your troubles the truth?' Mordecai asked at last.

'It is.'

'And this retainer is that important for you?'

Goodbody nodded.

'You are asking a lot.'

'I know. I'm sorry to do it and I wouldn't if I didn't have to and you were not a friend.'

There was silence while Mordecai stared into his tankard and swirled his champagne. At last, he said, 'I am your friend.' Then he began to smile. It was a smile that lit his whole twisted face. It was not often seen but it was this expression that turned the ugly, saturnine face into something almost radiant, this smile that had captivated the women whose interest and affection for him so surprised those who could only see a crippled, humpbacked figure with fierce, darting black eyes and a snarl upon the thin lips. The sudden, surprising smile and the voice – the tone of the voice – those were the weapons which made Mordecai Ledbury so effective an advocate . . . and, for a very few, despite his appearance, so seductive a lover.

'You are quite the tempter,' he said finally, 'to remind me of my professional duty, but what has decided me is not that. I don't care a damn for the rules. But I do care about you, my friend. Very well. You can tell them I consent. I shall not enjoy doing what I have to do but I'll do my best to disguise it.'

'Which means you'll do very little. But Spenser is a realist. He won't mind. So long as they have you on their side.'

Mordecai picked up his sticks and stumbled to his feet.

Goodbody said, 'I'm very grateful, Mordecai. I hope you know how grateful.'

'And I hope you know what you're letting us in for,' Mordecai grunted.

Goodbody took his arm and they went slowly towards the dining room. As they got to the entrance two members came out, talking together and laughing, nearly knocking into Mordecai and Goodbody. The two stood aside and one, a tall, dark young man in his early forties said, 'I'm sorry, Ledbury, we didn't see you.'

'I'm hardly invisible, Foxley,' Mordecai said, limping into the dining room. 'This isn't a dance hall.'

Patrick Foxley looked at his companion and smiled. 'That's Mordecai Ledbury. As disagreeable as ever. He comes here some Wednesdays with that oily solicitor, Oliver Goodbody.'

They settled down to a glass of port in the ante-room. 'We're safe for a time – while Ledbury is eating,' Patrick said.

'How is Claire?' the other asked. He needn't have, for he knew very well how Claire was. Tearful and resentful.

Patrick shifted uncomfortably in his chair. 'I haven't seen her recently.'

'You've broken up?'

Patrick nodded. 'It's all very civilised,' he added.

Not according to Claire. Not according to her stories about how rude he was to her friends; about how his career in the law came before everything; about how little time he kept for her.

'She has her own life in TV,' Patrick went on. 'I believe she's hoping to become one of the presenters on some news programme. It's an odd world, her world, the media world. I never fitted in.'

His companion sipped his glass of port. No, he thought, you didn't. The elegant and clever Patrick Foxley, Eton and New College, Oxford, and the Bar. And Claire's friends, irreverent, sceptical, tieless, designer-stubbled, propping up another kind of bar, the bar at Television Centre. One glance at Patrick Foxley, one word from him and they assumed he was condescending to them. When, in fact, he was just being exactly what he was: as he was to everyone, including, it was said, the judges. It was a wonder he and Claire had lasted so long. Or had got together in the first place.

'She resented that I never got on with her friends but I found them very chippy. I suppose they thought the same about me.'

More than chippy. He represented everything they wanted to destroy. And Claire had never understood that.

'Then there's work. I have to work most nights, sometimes into the small hours preparing for next day in court. So it wasn't easy for either of us. It's best that it's over.'

'You've a lot on at the moment?'

'Yes. I've just broken into the libel work. There's not much of that but what there is of it is always fascinating.'

'And now you're a bachelor on the town?'

Patrick laughed. 'Not much on the town. Too busy. I've got my eye on the position of that old fellow in there.' He gestured with his head towards the dining room. 'Ledbury is the king of the libel bar. I aim to knock him off his perch.'

At the table in the dining room, Mordecai shook out

his napkin. 'That obstreperous young man who nearly knocked me over is Foxley.'

'The young QC? I've heard about him,' said Goodbody.

'Yes. He took silk two or three years ago and fancies himself inordinately. They say he's after my crown. He'll have to fight to get it.' He peered down at his potted shrimps. 'The pepper,' he growled at his neighbour on the other side. 'Have you reserved the pepper pot for yourself alone? Or are you prepared to share it?'

Part Three

Chapter One

On Sunday morning, at 8.30 precisely, Sylvia Benedict woke in her four-poster bed in the vast bedroom of her country house, Wainscott, and rang the bell for breakfast. She always breakfasted in bed, both here and at Eaton Square in London. At Wainscott at weekends the men guests breakfasted at 9 in the dining room; the women in their rooms. This weekend she had seven guests, three couples and an extra man, a young novelist with whom she was much intrigued.

Within five minutes of her ring her tray appeared. Coffee and orange juice, one slice of toast and honey, and the Sunday papers. She poured the coffee and spread the first of the newspapers on the bed beside her tray. It was a tabloid and she leafed through it as she sipped the juice and the coffee; then threw it aside. The next was the *Sunday News*. At the top, on its flaghead, her attention was caught by the flyer for the Review section. 'The diaries of Francis Richmond.'

She lowered the coffee cup poised at her lips. Francis Richmond's diary? Francis kept a diary? Francis Richmond's diary in the papers? She threw the rest of the newspaper aside and turned swiftly to the Review section to learn what her old friend had to say about the world in which he had lived and the friends who inhabited it.

Sylvia had known Francis Richmond for thirty years. He'd been a frequent weekend guest after Maurice, her husband, had died fifteen years ago. Maurice had not liked Francis. A pansy, Maurice had called him and so, while Maurice was alive, Francis had rarely come to dine and never to stay. But after Maurice's death he had, often, for Sylvia liked his company. He made her laugh with his tales and the gossip of which he was such an unfailing source. She thought him deliciously clever, so amusing, so well-read. She enjoyed, or rather she leafed through, his book on porcelain and at her dinner parties or at weekends she had him hold court at her table, talking about literature, the theatre, art – and, of course, people. Always people. But Francis Richmond was for Sylvia Benedict more than just a social entertainer. She relied on him to advise her what books to read or at least what books to talk about; what exhibitions to visit and even what clothes to wear – at least what colour clothes. She confided in him about her family and her son, the present earl who lived in Perth with his boring wife and children. She would discuss with him her own life, tell him about her followers, for even in her late forties there were many followers – although she claimed they were really 'walkers' who were only after a free dinner or an invitation to Wainscott. She had liked and trusted Francis and she had mourned him sincerely when he died.

It was, therefore, with agreeable anticipation that on this Sunday morning Sylvia Benedict opened the Review section of the *Sunday News* to read the serialisation of the diary of her old friend.

Fifteen miles to the south on the coast, at Emerald Cunliffe's country house, The Waves, a similar scene was being enacted. The breakfast tray was balanced on Emerald's knees as she sat up in bed to enjoy those agreeable hours on Sunday morning when in the peace and quiet of her bedroom she browsed through the Sunday papers. It would be noon before she would emerge, by then well acquainted with the political news and the reviews of the new books and plays, and descend, in what she described as her warpaint, to join her weekend guests for cocktails before Sunday luncheon. At the weekend parties at The Waves there were invariably some old friends, at least one ambassador, probably a junior minister or Opposition spokesman and one of her 'discoveries' or protégés, perhaps a painter enjoying a first exhibition or a young poet searching for a publisher for his inexplicable verse. The house party usually consisted of eight or nine people. They were expected to arrive before luncheon on Saturday and leave on the Sunday afternoon.

When Emerald, too, saw on the front page of the *Sunday News* that the Review section carried an extract from the diary of Francis Richmond she, like Sylvia, was surprised to learn that he had kept a diary and turned to it with perhaps even greater anticipation than had Sylvia at Wainscott.

For Francis had been one of her earliest friends. She had known him since she was a schoolgirl when he had been brought to stay by her older brother, Bolton, when he was up at King's, Cambridge and had met Francis Richmond at a party at his tutor's. Ever since that first visit, Francis had become almost a member of the family; and for Emerald a confidant, a second, although much older brother. Very soon – for her mother claimed Emerald had been born an adult – she realised the kind of man he was; that he was in love with Bolton. After her first Season, she began to appreciate what an advantage it was to have a man friend like Francis, so much older and so worldly wise. Such men, she realised were much more companionable: they posed no threat, no menace; there was none of the tension, as with her other men friends. When her love life went off the rails, as it so frequently did, Francis provided her with a shoulder to cry upon. When it was going well, as it sometimes did, she and he would giggle together. She confided in him all her secrets, confident that they were safe with him.

The reaction of the two friends who were simultaneously reading the extracts of the diary in the *Sunday News* was strikingly similar. The breakfast tray, which lay across the lap of each, was flung aside, the coffee and juice flowing over it, and anyone passing in the corridor outside their rooms in their respective houses must have heard their squeals of rage and betrayal. After the first surge of fury their immediate thought was to speak to the other and both reached for the telephone.

Emerald got through first. 'You've read it?' she began.

'I certainly have. How could he have written about us like that! I thought of him as my oldest friend. I trusted him. I told him everything and all the time he was writing down what I said and—'

'And sneering and laughing at us.'

'And now it's all over the newspaper! How could it have got into the newspaper?'

'Someone must have sold it to them.'

'Then it would have been that nasty little actor who made such a fool of him at the end of his life. And to think I introduced them! They were here for a weekend. It started then. I was told Francis had left the creature absolutely everything.'

'I have a full house, including the Italians. It would be the Italians! They'll be reading it now.'

'Surely it's libellous? Can't we have it stopped?'

'What good is that? Everyone's already reading it.'

'We must force them to retract and publish an apology.' Sylvia paused. Then she said excitedly, 'There's one person who might be able to help. Mordecai Ledbury. He'll know what to do.'

She put down the receiver and dialled London.

When the telephone rang in his apartment in Albany, Mordecai was in his dressing gown, a great oriental confection of red and gold, with a dragon down the back.

'It's Sylvia,' said the voice. 'Have you read the *Sunday News*?'

Mordecai had been expecting someone would call. 'I have,' he answered.

'Then you've read Francis's diary. How could he have done such a wicked thing, betraying his closest friends, writing down all we said to him? I've just spoken to Emerald. She's shattered. I thought you'd be able to help us. What can we do? What do you advise us to do?'

'I won't advise you,' he said.

'What do you mean, you won't? Why can't you advise us?'

'I can but I won't. All I can suggest is that you consult your solicitor.'

'You mean Oliver Goodbody?'

'No, not him. Some other solicitor. Oliver Goodbody won't be able to help you either.'

'I don't understand. Why can't you? Why can't Oliver?'

'Because News Universal has retained Oliver and myself. You must get advice from someone else. There's nothing either of us can do to help you.'

For a time she was silent. Then she hissed into the telephone, 'You bastard! You're on their side!' She raised her voice. 'I suppose they're paying you a fortune.' And she banged down the receiver.

Neither Sylvia nor Emerald appeared for luncheon on that Sunday. The guests were informed they had headaches and were staying in bed. At The Waves the Italian Ambassador said very little over the sombre and silent meal, and he and his wife departed soon afterwards.

Chapter Two

At Chequers that same Sunday morning the Prime Minister was breakfasting alone in the dining room. A novel, *The Card* by Arnold Bennett, was propped against the marmalade jar when Alan Prentice, his Principal Private Secretary, came to him and said that Mr Digby Price, the Chairman of News Universal, was anxious to speak to him in person. The Prime Minister was acquainted with Mr Digby Price. As far as he could bring himself to, he went out of his way to be polite to the man whenever they met. He'd even once asked Price to Downing Street to attend some function concerning a charity that News Universal was promoting. The only reason why the Prime Minister felt obliged to tolerate Mr Digby Price was that editorially the papers published by News Universal, as opposed to the *Telegram*, were staunch supporters of his administration. With the exception of one minister: News Universal were regularly critical of the Minister for Defence Procurement. Alone of all the present ministers they criticised him regularly – but only him.

The Prime Minister was not particularly distressed by this for in the rest of the media Richard Tancred was often, and as far as the Prime Minister was concerned, tiresomely, referred to as his obvious successor. Richard Tancred, these political commentators pointed out, came from a younger generation and, when the Prime Minister at last stood aside, as surely he soon must, Richard Tancred would infuse welcome new blood into a declining government, and would supply the energy and initi-

ative that the present ageing Prime Minister now so
singularly lacked. But while the Prime Minister did not
object to this one minister being so often singled out for
denigration in News Universal publications, which were
in general so politically supportive of his administration, even this could not make him like their proprietor.
'What does the fellow want?' he asked with distaste.

'He has something he wishes to say to you in person.
He said it was a private matter.'

'It must wait until I return to London.'

'He said it was so urgent that he was prepared to
come to Chequers today. I am to call him back when I've
spoken with you.'

'It must be important to make that scoundrel come all
the way here on a Sunday.'

'He said it would be no trouble; he'd come by helicopter.' Alan handed the Prime Minister the *Sunday
News*. Normally the Prime Minister made a show of
never reading the newspapers, relying on the summary
that was daily prepared for him. 'I've had a look
through the *Sunday News*,' Alan went on. 'I can only
think that Mr Price might want to speak to you about
the extracts they have published from the diary of
Francis Richmond in their Review section.'

'Who is Francis Richmond?'

'A minor scholar, a collector of objets d'art, an expert
in porcelain and china, apparently well-off and well-
connected. He mixed much in society in London, as well
as across the Atlantic. That is, he mixed in what you,
Prime Minister, might consider the more *louche* circles of
society.'

'Louche' was a favourite adjective of the Prime Minister who applied it, as far as Alan could judge, to anyone
who ever dined or lunched in a restaurant rather than in
a club.

'He published a small book on porcelain and wrote
articles on Etruscan antiquities. He died last year.' Alan
pointed to the Review section, which the Prime Minister
was holding away from him as though he feared that

too close contact might contaminate him. 'I think, sir, you should read the extracts from the diary. There are references to some of your colleagues. This may be what Mr Price wants to talk to you about. I can think of nothing else.'

With a sigh, the Prime Minister shut his well-thumbed copy of *The Card*, which he was rereading for the second time that year. 'Do you mean that I have to read the diary of some . . . some dilettante, published in the scurrilous columns of the wretched newspaper owned by the villain who threatens to disturb my Sunday?'

'Who also supports the policies of your administration, sir,' said Alan. 'So I think you should, yes.'

With Alan at his elbow, the Prime Minister began to read. After a few minutes he threw the newspaper aside. 'What a lot of tosh! How could anyone be interested in such rubbish?'

'The references to Mr McClaren and Baroness—'

The Prime Minister interrupted. 'Oh, the references to Peregrine McClaren. Of course I'd heard that McClaren in his youth was rumoured to be a homosexual. With his looks that could scarcely be avoided and for all I know he was, and still is, a homosexual – or? What is the modern word for it?'

'Gay, sir,' Alan prompted.

'Of course, gay.' The Prime Minister looked sadly at the marmalade pot. 'A misappropriation of such a useful word. However, I appointed McClaren knowing his reputation because he is a man of ability and was recommended by the Chief Whip – who is certainly not a man anyone could accuse of unusual or eccentric habits.'

He ran a delicate white hand over his fine head of silver hair. 'In my youth, when gay meant laughter and happiness and jollity, and indeed even up to only a few years ago, such an appointment would have been unthinkable. But not now. Times, Alan, have changed Some might say they have changed for the worse. What in my youth was called a pansy and more lately a queer is no bar to public office. Indeed, I have found McClaren a most agreeable fellow, clubbable and good company, and as far as I know a loyal colleague. Above all, he's an excellent minister. So I don't see what the fuss is about.'

'All I can say, sir, is that Mr Price wants to talk to you urgently and there is nothing else in his newspaper that would appear to concern the Administration except the references to the ministers. There are references to other ministers.'

The Prime Minister rose. 'Very well. I'll see him at three o'clock.'

The luncheon party that Sunday at Chequers consisted of the family, that is the Prime Minister and his wife, Joan, a redoubtable figure dressed like an Edwardian housekeeper in a long tweed skirt and flat, thick-soled shoes; their son, Gerard, a young man in his mid thirties whose business affairs in the East and, indeed, whose whole life caused his father personal as well as political embarrassment; and Joan's brother, the Bishop of Petersfield, a jovial and outwardly not very spiritual cleric, accompanied by his faded wife. The other guests were the Solicitor-General – red-headed, bouncy, in his early forties, said to be a high flyer – and his exceedingly pretty blonde wife; the Permanent Secretary at the Home Office, tall and grave, approaching the magic age of sixty when under the rules of the Civil Service he would be obliged to retire, and his already retiring wife. The party, seated at a round table, was completed by Alan Prentice. All were formally dressed, the women in dresses, the men in jackets and ties – all, that is, except for Gerard who wore an open shirt, a medallion round his neck in the fashion of thirty years ago and bright-yellow trousers. Before lunch he had insisted on making margarita cocktails, which he had forced on his uncle the bishop and the young Solicitor-General. The Permanent Secretary and his wife had prudently accepted sherry.

At the meal the Prime Minister was in his usual benign mood, delighted to have beside him the pretty wife of the Solicitor-General. He began to tell her his experiences in World War Two, when as a child he had been evacuated with his mother from Singapore before it fell to the Japanese. The wife of the Solicitor-General listened dutifully.

Across the table the Prime Minister's wife was complaining to her brother the bishop that Gerard had developed an 'estuarial' accent.

'Certainly,' Gerard said. 'It's not acceptable to talk posh any more.' He turned to the Permanent Secretary's wife. 'Don't you agree?' She didn't, but decided this was not the place and she not the one to start an argument, and kept silent.

The word 'posh' set off the Prime Minister. 'Posh', he announced, 'came from the jargon of the Raj. Sailing east, the sahibs booked their cabins on the port side to mitigate the heat of the sun; and on the starboard side on the way home for a similar reason: port outward, starboard home. Posh.'

Joan began a serious discussion with the Permanent Secretary about the drug problem in prisons but the table was silenced when Gerard leaned across the table and said loudly, 'I've been meaning to ask you for a long time, Uncle Harry, do you really believe in God?'

The Bishop, who he later confessed to his wife that he was feeling 'slightly *bouleversé*' from the effect of the margaritas his nephew had forced upon him and had not so far taken much part in the conversation, did not immediately respond.

'I mean, a personal god,' Gerard added. 'Do you believe in that kind of god?'

His mother answered for her brother, 'Don't be absurd, Gerard. Of course he does. He wouldn't be a bishop if he didn't.'

'The Bishop of Autun didn't,' said Gerald.

'A Roman, of course, a Roman,' muttered the Bishop.

The Prime Minister said, 'When Charles Maurice de Périgord, former Bishop of Autun, came here as Ambassador in the eighteen twenties, he brought with him his niece as his hostess. She was also his mistress. Think what the media would have made of that today,'

By now the question posed by Gerard was, to the Bishop's relief, forgotten, and Gerard turned to the pretty wife of the Solicitor-General and winked. When she smiled he lightly placed his hand on her thigh where she let it rest, apparently quite unconcerned.

Alan Prentice said, 'Prime Minister, you mustn't forget that you're seeing Mr Digby Price this afternoon.'

The Prime Minister put down his napkin and sighed. 'I had forgotten. The fellow arrives at three o'clock.' He looked at the clock over the chimneypiece. 'In half an hour.' He rose from the table. 'I fear that his arrival will disturb your afternoon's rest for he is coming in his personal flying machine – the badge of our plutocratic masters.'

Once the helicopter had landed in the park over the hedge that bordered it from the garden, Alan Prentice conducted Digby Price, who was accompanied by Wilson, to the house. In the hall, Alan invited Wilson to wait while he showed Price into the small white sitting room and then withdrew.

The Prime Minister greeted his guest affably, waving him to a chair, declaring that he thought that this agreeable room would be more comfortable than the long gallery in which to talk, attributing its grace to the renovations carried out by his predecessor Edward Heath many years earlier who, he said, had more taste and discrimination than any of his successors. He went on to speak of the generosity of Lord Lee who had given the house to the state for the use of the Prime Minister, using this preamble to take the opportunity of studying beneath his hooded eyes the figure and visage of his guest, both of which he found singularly distasteful.

'I have been here often before,' growled Price, 'in the time of your predecessor.'

'You know the house? Then I mustn't ramble on. We are both busy men and my private secretary told me you wanted to speak to me about something important and confidential. It must be important to bring you here in your machine on a Sunday afternoon.' He gazed benevolently at the squat, tough-looking figure now lounging in an armchair opposite him, trying to disguise his dislike of what he saw.

'It *is* important and it *is* confidential,' Price began and his host raised a delicate hand to his face to hide the wince at the harsh South African intonation. 'Have you had a chance to read what we published today in the Review section of my newspaper?'

'The Review section? Let me see. Ah, yes, my private secretary showed it to me. The extracts from the diaries of a literary fellow? Yes, I have glanced at them and noted certain references to some of my ministers. I must tell you, Mr Price, that I consider the publication of a public person's private sexuality unnecessary – unless his lifestyle affects the performance of that person's public duties. But I suppose this is the stuff modern readers enjoy.'

'The view my newspapers take is that the public has a right to know what kind of men are running the country.'

'In the days when a man was liable to blackmail if exposed as a homosexual I suppose that might have been understandable, but that is not the case today. Nowadays, Mr Price, we live in a very different kind of society. You refer, I suppose, to the paragraphs about Peregrine McClaren?'

'And to another minister, a woman.'

'Dear me, I didn't read as far as that.'

'There are also references to a third minister, the Minister for Defence Procurement,' said Price. 'The references to him are different. They suggest that he was associating in an improper manner with one of the manufacturers with whom his ministry does business.'

'An improper manner?'

'The inference is that there was some financial link between them. These references I have deliberately allowed to be published. If that minister chooses to sue, so be it. I would welcome it. But, Prime Minister, I must tell you that there were parts of the diary that we did not publish.' He leant forward and added conspiratorially, 'I had them removed from the text.'

'And why was that?'

'Because they referred to you, Prime Minister.'

'To me?'

'Yes, in the original manuscript the diarist wrote about overhearing a conversation in which Richard Tancred spoke about you. I had that excised.'

The Prime Minister's delicate white hand was once again before his mouth. 'But why was that?'

Price looked down at his own hands, at the gnarled, stubby fingers. 'When I decided to publish the diary, I realised that there were certain references to certain persons who might take exception to what was published about them and might even sue for libel, mostly men and women in society and their past or present sexual relationships. I don't care a jot if any of them sues. They'd be made to look very foolish. My people are looking into all that. I have no doubt that if it should come to an action at law we would be able to prove the truth of what was published. I have no worry about them. And, frankly, I'd welcome a writ from Richard Tancred if he were so foolish as to sue. But—' He paused, then he went on. 'But I wouldn't like your other two ministers to sue. If they do, of course I'll take 'em on but three ministers suing would seem like a confrontation between the News Group and your government, which I do not want. As I said, generally we support the government. I exclude the Minister for Defence Procurement of whom we've never approved, and whatever he chooses to do, I don't care a jot. So I hope you'll see that the other two ministers keep out of it.'

Both remained silent for a moment. Then the Prime Minister said 'You were, I believe, going to tell me what it was that Richard Tancred is reported to have said about me, which you decided to excise.'

'Yes. It's in the original manuscript.' There was another pause.

'Well,' the Prime Minister said wearily, 'you've come all this way to tell me so you'd better say what you want to say.'

'The diarist reports Tancred as saying, to use his words, that for many years you had been engaging in a long-standing love affair with someone in your constituency.'

There was another silence, a longer one this time. Then the Prime Minister smiled. 'I am flattered that anyone should attribute to me, at my time of life, such prowess.' He shook his head. 'You were wise, Mr Price, to have excised such a silly falsehood from the diary of this absurd author.'

'That is why I had it removed,' Price stated. He sat back in his chair. 'However, I have to warn you that what was in the diary was seen by some of my confidential staff. I have, of course, sworn them to secrecy.'

After a while the Prime Minister mused, almost to himself, 'Calumny, Charles de Gaulle said to Georges Pompidou, is the fate of statesmen. But in the words of his compatriot, Beaumarchais, playwright and pursuer of Queen Marie Antoinette, "Calumny, calumny, something will always stick".'

'I shall see that my people keep silent,' said Price. He paused and eyed the figure slumped in the armchair opposite him. 'I hope', he said at last, 'you will see that Mr McClaren and the Baroness Oxborrow do nothing silly in the courts.'

The Prime Minister's eyes were fixed on Price. 'I am obliged to you, Mr Price, for telling me all this, including that absurd report about me personally in which there is not a scintilla of truth and which you so properly decided not to print. You showed great judgement.'

'Thank you,' Price replied.

'And I agree with you that it is never best for people in public life to resort to the courts, however wounding the criticism levelled against them. That will be – that always has been – my advice. I am sure that Mr McClaren and the other minister would feel as I do. As to Richard Tancred—'

Price interrupted him, 'I do not mind what he does. As I said, I would welcome a writ from him.'

The Prime Minister nodded. 'So I heard you say.' He rose from his chair. 'But now,' he went on, 'as you have troubled to come all this way, the least I can do is to offer you a cup of tea.' He rang the bell.

Digby Price also rose to his feet. 'I am not a tea drinker, Prime Minister.'

'A whisky and soda then?'

'No, I have to get back to London.'

'In your machine?'

'In my machine.'

Alan Prentice entered the room.

'Mr Price', the Prime Minister said, 'has to return urgently to London. He cannot stay even for tea. Escort him, Alan, to his machine.'

Digby Price and Wilson remained silent in the noisy cabin as the helicopter brought them back to London. It was only when they were in the car driving them from the Battersea heliport that Wilson leant forward and closed the glass partition separating them from the chauffeur, 'Well, sir,' he asked, 'how did it go?'

'He got the message,' Price said grimly.

The following morning, Monday, was to be devoted by the Prime Minister to visits in his constituency before he returned to Downing Street. Accordingly only his detective accompanied him when he left Chequers and was driven to the county town which he had represented in Parliament since he had first arrived as a shining and enthusiastic young candidate over thirty years before. He'd cut a fine figure then, handsome, athletic with all the energy and idealism of youth, and from the start he had literally cut a swathe through all the feminine hearts which made up the bulk of the constituency workers and officials. There was much disappointment some five years later when he married the frumpish but well-connected and rich daughter of an earl. Nevertheless he retained through all the following years the devotion of the ladies who formed the backbone of the local party.

On this morning his first visit was, however, a municipal duty: to open the new town library where, as his car drew up, he was met by the mayor in his chain of office looking, as he felt, supremely self-important. His wife, the mayoress, was looking acid. She was not a supporter of the Prime Minister or his political party but she was obliged to be present and she stood beside her husband outside the doors of the library surrounded by aldermen and councillors and town officials. Before them had gathered a small crowd and the usual battery of cameramen. After a felicitous speech into a microphone, in which the Prime Minister welcomed the opportunity to join in such an agreeable task in such agreeable company, he declared the new library open and with the municipal group in close attendance he toured it, chatting to the staff, posing politely at all the demands of the photographers and making sure that the library staff were included in the pictures. This pleased them and infuriated the mayoress. After a glass of sweet sherry the Prime Minister made his excuses and departed for the local headquarters of his constituency party where there were gathered a group of constituency workers, mostly women, those devoted admirers who had so happily supported him for thirty years.

At the head of the group to greet their Member of

Parliament, now to their pride also their Prime Minister, was his political agent, Aidan Wills, a solemn, rather lugubrious, grey-haired man in his mid fifties. With him was his wife, Penny, a large, bosomy and friendly woman with handsome features, dark hair and a bright complexion.

The Prime Minister greeted Aidan with a hearty handshake and his wife with a kiss on the cheek, before similarly embracing the woman Chairman of the Party Association and several others. A modest buffet luncheon had been prepared; the Prime Minister made a speech, expressing his regret that his duties now prevented him from visiting the constituency as often as he had in the past and thanking them for the work they had done to ensure that he and the party now formed the government of the country. After toying with a sausage roll and accepting a glass of Spanish red wine, which he soon abandoned, he passed into the inner office where he remained with Aidan signing various constituency letters. They were joined by Penny. The Prime Minister asked Aidan if he would mind stepping out and making sure that his driver and personal detective were offered a sandwich. Aidan left the room and the Prime Minister was alone with Penny.

He was seated in a chair at the desk. She came behind him and put her hands on his shoulders. He raised his and covered hers, and patted them. She lowered her head and kissed his cheek. 'I have heard that there might be people, unfriendly people, coming round asking questions,' he said.

'What of it?' she asked, her head still resting against his cheek.

'They could be seeking information, gossip and letters. Have you any letters?'

'No. I promised you I would destroy them and I have. You needn't worry.'

'They'll offer money.'

She straightened. 'If I'd wanted money, I'd have got it

81

before now. If I were going to betray you, I could have done it years ago.'

'They'll have a lot of money. They believe they can get anything with money.'

'Not me,' she said. 'They'll never get me.'

'What about Aidan?'

'Aidan,' she scoffed. 'He has kept his head turned away for over twenty years. He'll not change.' She laid her head against his cheek once again. 'Darby and Joan.' She giggled.

Aidan came back into the room. 'Your driver says you ought to be leaving.'

The Prime Minister rose. 'Then I must say goodbye to my dear friends.' He took Aidan's hand and gave Penny a chaste kiss on the cheek. 'Goodbye.'

Perry McClaren had spent the weekend at his cottage near Petworth. For once he'd been alone, studying his departmental papers and preparing for a Cabinet Committee at No. 10, to be chaired by the Prime Minister on the following Monday. The Sunday newspapers were not delivered and he did not trouble to fetch them. He returned to London early on Sunday afternoon. In the car he listened to music on tape and did not hear any of the news bulletins. As a result he did not see the *Sunday News*, nor learn about the publication of the diaries of Francis Richmond until he was back in his flat in Islington. It was only then that he read what Francis Richmond had written about him. It wasn't long thereafter that the doorbell rang. From the upper window he looked down to the street below. He could see the reporters' cars and the small group outside the front door. He drew the curtains. He would face them, and his colleagues, in the morning.

On Monday afternoon, after his return to London from his visit to his constituency, the Prime Minister chaired the Cabinet Committee, which included Perry McClaren among the ministers attending. That morning Perry had been collected from his flat by his official car and walked, stony-faced and silent, through the group of reporters, one of whom yelled out, 'Is it true you're gay, Minister?' He had not replied and was driven away rapidly. At the Ministry he remained in his office, attended by his private secretary and later by the Permanent Secretary, preparing for the afternoon's Cabinet Committee. No one said a word about the weekend press. At No. 10, when the ministers assembled outside the Cabinet Room, no one actually spoke to him. Was that, he wondered, because of what they had read about him? Or was it because they didn't care? Or, which was equally possible, was it because none had reason to speak to him before they went in to the meeting?

Within a few minutes the ministers were ushered into the Cabinet Room and sat round the oval table facing the Prime Minister who was in his usual seat, his back to the fireplace, facing the windows overlooking the garden and the Horseguards beyond. When Perry's turn came to speak he did so quietly but with authority. The Home Secretary, who was seated next to him, disagreed with what Perry recommended. Perry maintained his stance and repeated his opinion. After others had expressed their views, some siding with Perry and some with the Home Secretary, the Prime Minister summed up. He said that having regard to the opposition of the Home Secretary, he would invite the Minister to take another look at the issue and report back later in the week. The business then concluded. As the ministers gathered together their papers and prepared to leave the Prime Minister called out, 'Perry, would you mind staying for a moment?'

Some of the ministers exchanged glances as they filed from the room.

'Come and sit here, next to me,' the Prime Minister said and Perry took a chair beside him at the centre of the table.

'I have, of course, read the extracts from the diary that silly fellow wrote and that awful newspaper saw fit to publish. I hope you will not let what was in the paper disturb you.'

Perry looked down at the Ministry file he was still holding in his hand. 'It was not very pleasant to read in print.'

'Perhaps not,' the Prime Minister went on, 'but today times are very different from the past when, as you may remember, poor old Willie Beauchamp, persecuted by that brute of a brother-in-law, Bendor, was forced to flee the country. Thankfully, that's the past. There's none of that nowadays. I wanted you to know, my dear fellow, that you have my complete confidence. You are doing excellent work, you are a valued member of my cabinet and I don't want you to do anything silly.'

Perry looked up. 'Anything silly, Prime Minister?'

'Yes, make an issue of it. I value your work and your comradeship, and I wanted to assure you that what has been published makes not a jot of difference to the regard in which I hold you.'

'My colleagues and the public, Prime Minister, may not think as you do.'

'To the devil with them. But I don't think any would. There's no cause for' here the Prime Minister paused for a moment – 'for the issue of writs or the courts or any of that nonsense. However, I'm sure you're not thinking about anything like that. If I, as an older man, may be permitted to advise, the dignified course is to say and do absolutely nothing. Treat it with contempt.'

'I had considered demanding an apology—'

'But why, my dear fellow? That is precisely what the wretches want. No, no. Legal action by a politician is rarely sensible. You have made an excellent impression as a minister and it would be a tragedy if you were provoked into doing anything of that kind.'

'Your advice is to do nothing?' Perry enquired.

'Exactly. Ignore it. Treat it as the ramblings of a malicious, minor literary gossip, which no one should take seriously. You are a good minister, and that is what public service is about and what the country needs.'

'But I never said what Richmond said that I did.'

'Of course not. No one will believe that you did. You must not waste time worrying over such a farrago of nonsense.'

There was a silence for a time. Then Perry said, 'Very well, Prime Minister, I shall do as you say.'

'Excellent. It is very cruel but the last thing we want is writs and actions in the law courts.' The Prime Minister rose, as did Perry. The Prime Minister took him by the arm. 'Courage and dignity, that's what is needed. Now, before you leave, let me offer you a whisky and soda.'

When Perry McClaren left Downing Street an hour later the reporters had vanished, believing that he must have departed through the Cabinet offices into Whitehall.

The Prime Minister sent for Alan Prentice. 'The undersecretary who was also written about in the newspaper? Baroness What's-her-name?'

'Oxborrow. The Chief Whip has spoken with her. She will take no action.'

The Prime Minister nodded.

'The Minister for Defence Procurement', Alan said, 'is in the Far East. He will be back the day after tomorrow.'

'Speak to his Private Office, will you. I'd be obliged if he would call upon me the moment he returns.'

How, he asked himself when he was alone, did Richard Tancred come to know about him? It had begun so long ago. The passion was long spent. He could trust Penny with his life. Indeed, he would have to, at least with his political life. She would not betray him. But how, he wondered, had this come to haunt him after all these years?

Chapter Three

At about noon the consular car drove him from Chek Lap Kok airport to the centre of the city. He had arrived in Hong Kong half an hour earlier off the Cathay flight from Beijing. An official from the consulate, grey-haired and solemn, had been at the airport to meet him. They had not spoken as the car carved its way through the traffic towards Central district and the official covertly examined the minister he had been deputed to greet. When the official had shown his pass at the barrier, he had seen approaching him a lean, tall man in a light-coloured suit, with dark hair liberally flecked with grey. Now that they were close together in the car he noticed the regular, rather hawklike features and the pock-marked skin on both sides of the face. And the dark circles beneath the brown eyes. I don't wonder, he thought, if he knows what is being said about him.

From the window of the car Tancred watched the teeming crowds on the pavements, before the car slipped expertly into the heavy traffic crossing the suspension bridge.

'Have you been here before, Minister?' the official suddenly asked.

'When I was a student. A long time ago.'

He thought of the day he'd arrived from Sydney. It was a very different city then. He had come again later when he'd been at the Bangkok embassy; his cover in Siam had been trade attaché. But those visits were secret, anonymous visits, known to few. He would not mention them. 'Last week I was here for one night on my way to Beijing. But it was dark and I could see nothing, except for the lights.'

'I was on leave when you came through.'

Once more they elapsed into silence, each staring out of the car window at the mass of humanity on the sidewalks.

'The Hong Kong Chinese are of very short stature,' the official began again, 'which is why the women have such small breasts.'

At the airport, when Tancred had complimented the official on his excellent Cantonese, the man had replied, 'I speak both, Mandarin and Cantonese.' Now he added, 'I have a Chinese wife.' Which is why, Tancred supposed, he knew about the physiognomy. Still, it was an odd remark.

'What brought you here on that first occasion, Minister?'

'Travel, curiosity. I was at the university.' He paused. 'I hardly recognise the city.'

In fact, he knew the city well enough from his later visits. But those secret entrances and exits to and from Bangkok would not have been recorded. They had not officially taken place.

'Indeed, it has changed greatly,' the official replied. 'The high-rise development began, I think, in the Sixties.'

Again they drove in silence until the official said diffidently, 'I have the English papers if you'd care to see them, Minister?'

So he too had read the *Sunday News*, thought Tancred. Who had not by now? 'No,' he replied. 'I have seen them. They came in the bag to Beijing. What time is my meeting with Mr Cheung?'

He'd instructed the consulate to arrange the meeting at the Mandarin Hotel, making it clear that this was a social not a ministerial occasion, a private meeting with a personal friend.

'Mr Cheung will be in the foyer at twelve fifteen. But we're going to be late.' The official reached for the car telephone. Tancred heard him speak to the hall porter in his excellent Cantonese.

It had been an exhausting trip and before him, in the early evening, there was the flight to London. But he was good at sleeping in aeroplanes. He'd had enough experience and his routine was neither to eat nor drink but read his ministerial papers and take a sleeping pill before settling down to sleep. Tonight he'd be alone, for Weston, who'd accompanied him from the ministry, was remaining in Beijing for two more days.

The ministerial visit had not accomplished anything serious: much talk, countless toasts, little real business. But they had not expected any. It had been goodwill, a promotional trip. His last official duty, he reflected, for in two days he would be a free man. But first he had to talk to Harry.

'I shall be back to collect you at three, Minister', the official said. 'We must allow ample time.'

It was nearly one o'clock when Tancred and Harry greeted each other in the foyer of the Mandarin Hotel. Harry was short, even for a Chinese, very well dressed in a dark suit, very soft-spoken. They went together up the stairs to the dining room arm in arm.

'Paris,' Tancred asked. 'How did it go?'

'Well.'

'You succeeded?'

'It has been accomplished.'

Tancred ate little. Harry helped himself freely from the many Chinese dishes; both drank soda water. With the coffee they sat smoking, Harry cigarette after cigarette, Tancred a cigar. Your only vice, Harry had said. My only indulgence, Tancred had replied.

'Digby Price is coming here,' Harry said. Tancred nodded. 'His people have set up a meeting with the regional government here. He has an appointment with C. T. Tung.'

'Is he travelling alone?'

'With his PA.' The two men looked at each other. 'His

new friend will not be with him. We thought that wiser.'

The lugubrious official was waiting for them when they descended to the foyer. 'We'll meet at La Ferme Blanche,' Tancred said, out of earshot of the official as Harry took his hand. 'When will you be there?'

'Next week.'

'Don't leave it any later.'

'I won't,' Harry assured him.

It was an even slower drive back to the airport than it had been from there at noon but they were in the VIP lounge an hour before it was time to board. 'Don't wait,' Tancred said as he took a seat in a corner of the lounge. He was anxious to be on his own.

But the official hovered above him. 'There's a message from your Private Office,' he began. 'The Prime Minister would like to see you immediately you arrive in London. Your office didn't seem to know what it was about,' he added. But he had a shrewd suspicion that they did. They would have read what had been published about their minister.

'What time is it in London?' Tancred asked.

'The early hours of the morning.'

'I won't trouble to call.'

The official leant down and opened his briefcase at his feet. 'I have this.. He handed Tancred a copy of the *Sunday News*. 'In case you haven't a copy.'

Tancred took it.

The official closed the briefcase. 'I hope you have a comfortable flight, Minister. Bon voyage.' Poor bastard, he thought as he sloped away. He'll not have a very jolly homecoming.

With the newspaper in his hand Tancred watched the stooping figure disappear through the swing doors. Then, for the tenth time, he read the extracts from the diary of Francis Richmond.

As the plane flew westwards through the night, Tancred sat awake in the darkened first-class cabin. Thankfully the seat next to him, Weston's seat, was empty. He waved aside the meal and the drinks, except for a bottle of mineral water. This time he took no sleeping pill; there were no ministerial papers on the table before him; there was no necessity. Someone else would have to read them now. The *Sunday News* was folded away in his briefcase; the reading light was off. For hour after hour he sat, reclining, his feet up on the footrest, his eyes open, thinking, left undisturbed by the stewards. Eventually he closed his eyes and slept.

An hour out from Heathrow he accepted a cup of black coffee and went to wash and shave.

Colin Senter, his personal assistant, was at the exit door of the plane – to avoid the press, Tancred supposed. 'The Prime Minister has asked you to breakfast with him in the flat at Downing Street,' Senter informed him when Tancred's luggage had been collected. 'I've told the driver to go straight there.'

'No,' said Tancred, 'tell Downing Street I'm going home to have a bath and to change. Find out what time would suit the PM for me to see him later in the day.'

Senter was put out. 'He's expecting you for breakfast, Minister.'

'Call them on the car telephone and tell them I won't be there. I'll come later in the morning.'

'It's Prime Minister's Questions today and he'll be preparing in the late morning so—'

'Then suggest the afternoon, after Questions, either in his room in the House or at Downing Street, whichever suits. Now take me to Chelsea.'

Downing Street was not best pleased by the rejection of the invitation to breakfast but fixed five thirty in the afternoon at No. 10.

There were no pressmen at the flat. But it was early and few knew where he lived. He had always kept that very private. Senter knew and the Permanent Secretary, no one else.

When Tancred entered the Cabinet Room, the Prime

Minister was in his usual seat, his irritation at the rejection of his breakfast invitation apparently forgotten. He swivelled in his chair and waved genially. 'Come in, come in, my dear fellow. I hope the journey was not too exhausting and the trip satisfactory. Those people in Beijing are devils to deal with.' He chuckled. 'I remember when I was Foreign Secretary—'

'I've dictated my report on the trip, Prime Minister. The Foreign Secretary and your office should have it by now but I wanted to give you this personally.' Tancred handed an envelope to the Prime Minister and remained standing.

'A letter?' The Prime Minister took the envelope and looked up at Tancred. He suspected he knew what it was about. 'Am I to open it now?' he asked.

'As you wish. It is a formal letter tending my resignation.'

The Prime Minister pushed back his chair, the legs squealing on the polished floor. 'Your resignation, Richard!' – making a good show of surprise – 'You are resigning from the Ministry! But why, my dear fellow, why in heaven's name should you wish to resign? Which of our policies has—'

'My resignation is not over policy. It has nothing to do with policy. I have made that clear in the letter. I shall continue to support your administration but not from Parliament for I intend to give up my seat in the House.'

'You are leaving the House? You are abandoning politics? Not, I hope, because of the wretched tittle-tattle in the newspaper? You mustn't throw up everything because of that nonsense. You must know that I have always considered you the most likely of all the colleagues to succeed me when I retire, as shortly I shall.'

'I am resigning from the government and giving up public life, Prime Minister, for personal reasons, which I'm sure are obvious to you.'

There was a moment of silence. The Prime Minister

looked at him warily, the envelope still unopened in his hand. 'You're not in trouble?' he asked.

'No, not in what I think you mean by trouble. No, I wish to be free to sue the *Sunday News* for libel. There is no truth in the innuendo that arises from what they published.'

'I'm sure there is not.' The Prime Minister half rose. 'Sit down, my dear fellow, sit down. We must talk more about this.'

Tancred shook his head and remained standing. 'My mind is quite made up. I have decided to take News Universal to court.'

'Suing News Universal! Suing a newspaper! Think for a moment. My dear fellow, that man, the proprietor, Digby Price is malevolent and malicious. He has immense resources. If you sue he'd leave no stone unturned to ruin you. Think of the risk!'

'I have considered that, but I am quite determined.'

'You are the rising star of this administration. I do not want to lose your services. Why not talk with the Attorney-General? He's a sensible fellow. I am sure he would advise you.'

'I have already retained my own advisers and I have spoken to them this morning.' Tancred looked at his watch. 'Thank you for the kind words you have said about me. In my letter I have myself expressed how honoured I was to have served in your administration. I have authorised my letter of resignation to be made public at seven o'clock. Good day, Prime Minister.'

'One moment,' said the Prime Minister. 'If you are determined, we must observe the niceties. There must be an exchange of letters. Do not, I pray, release your letter until after the ten o'clock news bulletin.'

'Very well, if that is your wish.'

The Prime Minister was fiddling with the still un-opened envelope. 'Before we finally part, you can help me about one other matter, a personal matter. It has been hinted to me that privately you may once have said something about me.' He paused. 'Something about my

private life. Something that the diarist, Francis Richmond, is said to have reported, although it has not been
included in what the newspaper published.'

Tancred looked at him steadily. 'I have never', he said
at last, 'spoken about your private life. I know nothing
of your private life and even if I did, I would not have
spoken of it. I may have said that in my opinion you are
not perhaps all that the public may think you are. But
who in public life is? The diarist may have reported
that.' He turned on his heel abruptly and went out of the
Cabinet Room, through the ante-room and into the
hall.

'Goodnight, Minister,' the hall porter said as he shut
the front door behind him.

That is the last time I shall hear that, Tancred said to
himself, or receive another salute – for the policeman
outside saluted. He had dismissed his official car and
walked rapidly along Downing Street, through the gates
and into Whitehall. Out of public life, he thought –
although not out of the limelight. For a time, yes. But
not when the libel action came to court. There would be
plenty then.

Once again there were no pressmen awaiting him, as
he had feared there might be, and he slipped anonymously into the crowd making their way to Westminster
underground station. He took a train to the Temple and
walked solemnly to the chambers of Patrick Foxley QC,
the counsel he had that morning retained.

The Prime Minister stayed on in the Cabinet Room,
pondering on what Digby Price had told him at Chequers and on Richard Tancred's denial that he had ever
spoken about the Prime Minister's private life. But, he
reflected, there must have been something recorded in
the diarist's manuscript for Price to have said what he
had. And if there had, then some of Price's staff would
have seen it. Eventually the story would come out.
Sooner or later the rumour would get around, especially

if Richmond's diary came before the courts, as Tancred intended that it should. He had managed to placate Price by preventing two of his ministers from suing but there was nothing he could do to stop Tancred.

He passed a hand wearily over his forehead. The time had surely come for him to carry out what he had hinted to his colleagues so often and so tantalisingly. To go, to retire, to hand on the burden, to surrender the role he had once found so delightful. But he wanted to leave the stage honoured for his place in history and for his political skills, remembered as a master of the House of Commons. For seven years he had played out what he had liked to call 'the charade of leadership' at the very top of the greasy pole. The colleagues he had surrounded himself with were, he considered, an ordinary, unimaginative lot whom he had cheerfully despised. It had amused him to weave webs about them, spinning around their dull heads the literary conceits that had so well disguised his purposes and so bewildered them.

Except for Tancred. Not he. Tancred had been the one minister whom he had never been able to fathom and whom he had watched beneath his hooded eyes with respectful wariness. Now Tancred, with his lawsuit, threatened to bring it all to an end. In ridicule. As he sat alone at the Cabinet table he knew that it would take all the good fortune that had so providentially followed him for so many years, the luck that had given him office and the comfort of Penny Wills, to enable him to go in peace, without the jibes engendered from beyond the grave by the gossip of the homosexual diarist.

Chapter Four

After leaving the conference with Patrick Foxley, Tancred took a number 11 bus to his flat off the King's Road in Chelsea. He rang his Private Office at the Ministry. It would remain 'his office' for a few more hours – until his letter of resignation was published after ten thirty that evening. Before he had left the Ministry for Downing Street he had warned the Permanent Secretary of the department of his intention to resign. The Permanent Secretary had in turn warned Colin Senter, the Private Secretary, so when Tancred telephoned from his flat, Senter knew what to expect. Tancred told Senter to inform the Permanent Secretary that Downing Street would release the news of his resignation to the media just after ten thirty that evening. He himself would not be returning to the Ministry.

Senter enquired where he should send the personal possessions in Tancred's room.

'There are none,' Tancred replied shortly.

'And any correspondence, Minister?'

'Send it to my bank,' replied Tancred. 'Coutts, Lower Sloane Street.' And rang off.

There had been no goodbye, no good wishes and no expression of gratitude for Senter's services. In Whitehall, relations between minister and private secretary were usually close, but during the two years that Senter had served Tancred the relationship between them had never been more than formal. Tancred had been invariably polite and courteous, never criticising or losing his temper. Equally, he had never congratulated for work well done. He had been admired for his administrative skill, his swiftness in reaching decisions and the civil servants had been impressed by his performances in the House of Commons. When Senter had to call at Tancred's flat on the ground floor of the tall Chelsea house to bring a red box, he had never once been invited inside. He'd stand on the doorstep and see only the long, gloomy corridor leading from the hall. He knew nothing of his Minister's life outside the office, except that the Minister had been punctilious in his official duties such as attending receptions at foreign embassies or trade fairs in connection with the business of the Ministry. As far as he knew, Richard Tancred had no club and dined only occasionally in private houses. For official engagements in London he had used his official car, whose driver said his boss rarely spoke except to give instructions. On the few occasions Tancred had spent weekends away from London, he'd travelled by train. Of Tancred's family and who were his friends no one at the Ministry knew anything. In the Private Office they had speculated about whether he had a girlfriend, but there was no evidence of one. No private letters came for him at the Ministry and no private telephone calls. Senter and the others in the Private Office felt they knew the man as little now as they had when Tancred had been first appointed.

When, once, the Permanent Secretary had been lunching at the Oxford and Cambridge Club with Harrington of the Treasury and they were talking about his Minister, he had said he thought Richard Tancred was 'a-sexual'. Gay? Harrington had asked. No, just not interested, the Permanent Secretary had replied.

'He has one particular friend or acquaintance whom I have seen him with,' went on Harrington. 'Oscar Sleaven. That's not very wise, is it?'

It certainly wasn't, the Permanent Secretary had thought. The Sleaven group were one of the conglomerates who tendered for the Ministry defence contracts so when he read the extracts of Francis Richmond's diary

published in the *Sunday News* he had been shocked. But
it had come not altogether as a surprise. He had always
admired his Minister but there was something about the
man that he, with all his experience of men and matters,
could not fathom. With his analytical mind, the Permanent Secretary had found this disturbing. He liked to
understand the ministers he served. But from the start,
Tancred had been an enigma.

Oscar Sleaven, the Permanent Secretary had repeated
to himself when he had read the extracts in the *Sunday
News*. The Minister meeting Oscar Sleaven at private
houses, in an art gallery! So that Tancred would be
forewarned of what had been published about him
before he returned to the UK, the Permanent Secretary
had seen to it that the newspaper had been sent to
Beijing in the Foreign Office bag. 'He'd better know
what he has to face,' he had said. When Tancred had
appeared in the Ministry on the morning of his return,
it had not been mentioned. Then he had announced,
confidentially, that in the evening he would resign. The
Permanent Secretary had nodded but said nothing.

'What a strange, cold fish he is,' Colin Senter said to
himself after Tancred had rung off. Then he joined the
others in the Private Office where they speculated on
who might be Tancred's successor. Senter wanted Peregrine McClaren – which was met by a giggle from two
of the women.

In the bedroom of his flat Tancred packed a large suitcase, placed two fifty-pound notes on the kitchen table
with a note to his cleaner who came three mornings a
week, saying he was going away and did not know
when he'd be back. 'My solicitor, Mr Burrows, will send
you your wages when the present £100 runs out. Please
keep coming in for an hour a week.'

Locking the front door behind him and carrying his
suitcase, he took a bus over Battersea Bridge. On the far
side of Clapham Common he walked down a small side

street until he came to a mews. At a garage halfway down the mews he unlocked the roll-down door, loaded the suitcase into the back of a Jaguar and, after locking the door of the garage, drove away. On the ring road round the south of London he made slow progress amid the heavy traffic until he reached the M20, when he drove fast in the direction of the coast. He stopped once for petrol and coffee, and made a lengthy telephone call from a call box. It was eight o'clock when he passed through the barriers to the Tunnel at Folkestone, paid for the ticket with cash and drove on to the train to begin the short journey under the Channel. He had waved his maroon European Community passport from the car window. It had not been examined.

From Calais he headed south, skirting Paris and driving in silence for many hours down the often empty motorways of northern and central France. He stopped once more for coffee and to make another telephone call, but otherwise he kept going until it was nearly dawn. It was in the half-light that he eventually left the motorway at Valence and drove on to the narrower side roads. After another hour he swung into a lane, passing through a village and at a fork turned left up an even narrower lane. Seven kilometres from the village he came to the courtyard of a farmhouse surrounded by farm buildings. By now the sun was fully up.

As the car drew up, the door of the house opened and a tall woman with short grey hair stood in the doorway. Tancred lowered the driver's window. 'You've made good time,' she said.

For answer he pointed to the barn beside the house, and the woman went back in and returned with a bunch of keys. She unlocked the door of the barn and disappeared inside. A moment later she backed a small Chevrolet into the courtyard and eased it into a lean-to shed, while Tancred drove the Jaguar into the barn. When he appeared with his suitcase the woman locked the barn door behind him. He put his arm round her shoulders as they walked side by side to the house.

'Was there anyone about when you came through the village?' she asked.

'Not that I saw.'

'They may have seen you, from behind their curtains.'

She led him down a stone-flagged hall into a large kitchen. From the stove she brought a tall brown pot of steaming coffee to the table on which were a long, thin baguette, butter and a pot of cherry jam. Tancred sat and watched as from the dresser she produced two mugs and from a cupboard a bottle of cognac. She poured the coffee and added brandy. 'You look exhausted,' she said.

He nodded and sipped the coffee. 'It's a long drive.'

'How long will you be staying?'

'For some time,' he said.

'You must get to bed. Tonight we can talk.'

When they had finished the coffee and he had eaten some of the bread and jam, they went upstairs to one of the bedrooms. Tancred put his bag on the bed. 'Hot water?' she asked, drawing the curtains against the morning light.

'No,' he answered. 'Later. Now I must sleep.'

She came to the room after an hour and looked at the sleeping figure. She closed the door and went silently downstairs.

Forty-eight hours after Tancred's arrival, during which he had never left the house, another car, an Alfa-Romeo bearing Monaco registration plates, drew up in the courtyard. The woman, who had obviously been expecting it, came from the house and pointed to the lean-to beside the barn. The driver of the Alfa-Romeo duly drove into the shed, parking beside the Chevrolet. The woman threw an old horse blanket over the back of the Alfa-Romeo, hiding the rear registration plate.

When the driver got out she kissed him on both cheeks. 'Welcome,' she said.

Harry Cheung took an overnight bag and a briefcase from the car.

'How long will you be staying?' she asked.

'One night. I have to be at Nice airport tomorrow evening. But I'll be back. How is he?'

'Very well, very relaxed.'

'Where is he?'

'Inside. He hasn't left the house since he came. He's expecting you. He says you have much to discuss.'

Harry nodded and followed her into the house.

In the weeks that followed, Tancred never left the farmhouse except in the hours of darkness when sometimes he took a stroll in the meadows. Four weeks after his first visit, Harry Cheung returned. This time he stayed three days.

On the night before the publication of the diary in the *Sunday News,* some three nights before Tancred left London, two other persons had taken the route under the Channel.

Oscar Sleaven and his wife Ethel had been driven to Folkestone, crossed by the Tunnel and arrived very late at an apartment in the boulevard Suchet in Paris. Next morning, when the *Sunday News* was on sale in the streets of London and was being delivered to the breakfast tables of its readers who then read the extracts from the Richmond diaries, Oscar and Ethel Sleaven left Paris on the early morning Concorde flight to New York.

On that same morning the City pages of the *Sunday Telegram* carried a report that due to ill health Mr Oscar Sleaven had resigned as Chairman of Sleaven Industries and was having to seek urgent medical treatment abroad.

At eleven o'clock, also on that morning, from his flat in Portland Place, which was conveniently situated on the floor above the head office of Sleaven Industries, Sebastian Sleaven, Oscar's younger brother and solicitor, issued a statement that was sent to all the news agencies. It read:

Mr Oscar Sleaven, who has resigned as Chairman of Sleaven Industries owing to ill health, has been obliged to go abroad to obtain medical treatment. He has, however, been informed of the publication of extracts of a diary said to have been written by the late Mr Francis Richmond and printed in today's edition of the *Sunday News*. He has not himself read what has been printed but insofar as any suggestion might arise from what was printed that he has been involved in any improper conduct, he will take whatever steps are necessary to refute such a falsehood, so far as his state of health will permit.

When reporters came to Portland Place, Sebastian Sleaven declined to answer any questions as to the present whereabouts of his brother or when he might be expected to return to the United Kingdom, but confirmed that he was under medical care.

Later that same day, Oscar and Ethel Sleaven flew from JFK in New York to Rio in Brazil in a private jet.

As soon as Sebastian Sleaven's statement had been issued, News Universal's investigators mounted a furious effort to discover the whereabouts of Oscar Sleaven, but they lost track of him in New York.

When, three days later, it was announced that Tancred was going to sue the *Sunday News*, Sebastian Sleaven issued another statement in which the legal action that the former Minister was taking against News Universal was noted and it was repeated emphatically that Mr Oscar Sleaven had never been involved in any form of improper conduct in relation to his dealings with the Minister or the Ministry. It ended by repeating that Mr Oscar Sleaven was presently receiving urgent medical care and was in no condition to comment. Again, Sebastian Sleaven declined to meet reporters or elaborate on the statement. Despite massive efforts by the investigators, lashed on by Digby Price, no trace could be found of Oscar Sleaven's whereabouts. He had apparently vanished.

Chapter Five

In the robing room of the Royal Courts of Justice in the Strand, Mordecai Ledbury tore off his court coat and flung his wig, originally grey but blackened with age, to his clerk, Adams. As usual after a day in court, his linen wing collar and bands were crumpled by sweat. He wrenched them off and Adams held out to him a clean white shirt. As well as being hot, Mordecai was angry. He had not had a good day. He had lost when he thought he should have won. On the other side in the case had been an elderly, rather prim counsel called Hayden Welsh who had a habit, which Mordecai found immensely irritating, of pursing his lips producing a whistling sound whenever he made what he considered a telling point in his argument. Welsh had pursed his lips even tighter and whistled even louder when the judge had given judgement in his favour. As Mordecai flung off his court clothes in the robing room he complained loudly enough for all the other barristers disrobing to hear that his defeat was an infamous miscarriage of justice entirely due to the bias and dislike of him of 'the judicial buffoon' who had tried the case, Mr Justice Traynor.

As everyone at the Bar knew, it was not unusual among the judiciary to dislike Mordecai Ledbury, for he was not known for his deference to the Bench. In court he quarrelled with judges as well as opponents, and the older he became the fiercer were the quarrels. But the dislike of most of the judges was tinged with a healthy measure of respect, for Mordecai Ledbury was a legend.

He had been at the business of trials far longer than any living member of the Bench, some before they had even been born – or certainly out of short pants. Mr Justice Traynor, who had so roused Mordecai's ire, was a blunt north countryman, who had spent his entire career in the north and had only fairly recently come to London on his appointment to the High Court Bench. He still retained all the prejudices of the Yorkshireman about southerners, whom he considered pretentious, condescending and devious. When he had first had the experience of Mordecai Ledbury as counsel in his court earlier in the year, Ledbury's attitude and aggressive manner had so offended him that he had privately complained about him to a friend, an older and senior judge, John Williams, a Lord Justice in the Court of Appeal.

Williams, aware of Jack Traynor's short experience of London counsel, had reminded him of Ledbury's decades of experience. 'He has a reputation for quarrelling with the Bench. You should handle him warily, avoid provoking him. It's not worth the trouble,' Williams said. 'Just sit quiet, keep your temper – and remember that you have the last word. It's you who decides the case.'

It so happened that in that same week Mr Justice Traynor's prickly northern sensibilities had also been affronted by another counsel who had been in his court two days earlier. This had been a young silk, Patrick Foxley, of Eton and Oxford, elegant, polished, with a forensic style very different from that of Mordecai Ledbury. Nevertheless he too, with what Jack Traynor considered his 'airs and graces', was not the kind of counsel to whom a judge from the north-east of England readily warmed. Again Jack Traynor grumbled to his friend John Williams, complaining that Foxley had been condescending to him.

Lord Justice John Williams had taken his friend by the arm. 'You're being silly, Jack. You've an outsize chip on your shoulder and you must get rid of it. Foxley's manner in court is the same whatever judge he's addressing, be it you or three of us Lords Justice in the Court of Appeal or even, I'm told, five Lords of Appeal in Ordinary sitting beneath the great tapestry in the Committee Room in the House of Lords. It's just his manner.' Foxley was clever, Williams went on. Maybe he knew it rather too well.

But in Mr Justice Traynor's opinion, young Mr Foxley was too clever by half. However, his feelings about that young man were nothing compared with his dislike for Ledbury. Nonetheless he had accepted the advice of John Williams and when, on this occasion, Ledbury appeared before him, he had kept control of his tongue and his temper, although inwardly fuming at the disdain with which Mordecai treated him. For Mordecai made no secret of what he thought of the provinces whence Jack Traynor came and which to Mordecai Ledbury were as uncouth as those distant lands overseas that Mordecai still described as 'the colonies'.

Jack Traynor was indeed a provincial, a fully-fledged 'Geordie', born and bred in the suburbs of Newcastle-upon-Tyne in the north-east of England. He had gone to school in that city and attended Newcastle University. When called to the Bar, he had joined the north-east circuit and acquired a large practice across the north of England, especially in criminal trials. At first he was popular with his fellow practitioners, for at convivial circuit dinners he made comical Yorkshire after-dinner speeches and played music-hall songs on the trombone. Like all his fellows, he never disguised his low opinion of anyone who lived south of the Wash, especially Londoners.

Then, in his late thirties, he had fallen in love. Lois was no more than nineteen years old, which made her twenty-five years younger than he. And she was from London, raised in Feltham near Heathrow with an Indian father. She worked in a couturier's in Mayfair and had ambitions to be a model. Jack had fallen head-over-heels in love and proceeded to lavish on her a slavish devotion – and his hard-earned Yorkshire money. Soon she was leading him around like a jolly bear on a chain. Somehow he managed to persuade her to wed him and they were eventually married at the Wandsworth Register Office in London. The only witnesses were a man and a woman from the couturier, both of whom kissed Jack enthusiastically when they parted after the ceremony. The honeymoon was to be spent, at Lois's insistence, in an hotel in Ischia off the coast of Italy near Naples, which had a *terme* with seaweed and mud baths and special beauty treatments. Jack Traynor was looking forward to a very jolly ten days with his very pretty bride.

When they arrived at the hotel, Lois's suitcase was missing. She made a scene in front of the concierge and the manager, and refused to go down to dinner but went straight to bed. Jack excused this as due to overexcitement and exhaustion on top of her irritation at the loss of her luggage, and he went alone to the dining room where he dined well and drank several glasses of cognac. When he came up to their room it was in darkness. He stood by her bed. She was asleep. He called her name but there was no response. He undressed in the dark and slipped into the other bed.

When he woke she was sitting on the balcony overlooking the bay, sipping orange juice. He came to her and put his arms round her and laid his cheek against hers.

She tilted her head. 'I've got the curse,' she said. 'I have a headache.' She complained she'd been kept awake by his snoring.

The suitcase turned up during the morning and she went to the *terme*, while Jack swam and watched the topless women by the pool. Her head was no better in the evening, although she consented to stroll with him around the small town. They dined together but she ate and spoke little. It's a migraine, she said and soon she went to bed. Jack stayed, drinking brandy. In the morning when he woke she was again sitting on the balcony and again complained that she had not slept, kept awake by his snoring. He persuaded her to come in a taxi to La Mortella, the garden created by William Walton whose music Jack admired, a magic forest of flowering shrubs and fountains, pierced by ribbons of paths cut from the side of a hill that had been a quarry. Lois said the walking tired her and sat on a bench drinking lemonade while he explored the garden. Her head, she said, was still troubling her. They did, however, dine together again but she left him as soon as he ordered coffee. Once again he drank brandy and undressed in the dark room. The next morning she told him she was going to spend all day having aerobic therapy and mud baths in the hope that this would help her migraine. She suggested he should explore the main town on the island. She set off down the corridor in her robe, and he caught a bus and wandered around looking at the sights. It was early evening when he got back to the hotel. She wasn't in their room; nor were her clothes. When he descended to the hall to enquire for her, the concierge said that she had departed in a taxi soon after he'd caught the bus. The man suggested he call the terminal where the ferries left from the harbour. Why? Jack asked. The concierge shrugged his shoulders and said the lady had had a suitcase with her. A little later he told him that a lady answering to her description had sailed on the noon ferry to Naples.

Jack eventually discovered that she'd taken the late-afternoon flight to London, so he rang the flat she shared in Wandsworth. There was no reply. Next morning he called the shop in Mayfair but no one could or would tell him anything. Later that day he too travelled to London. He went to the flat at Wandsworth. She was not there. Nor was she at the shop in Mayfair. They told her she had left. Disconsolate, he went back to Yorkshire.

At home near Leeds, he saw no one and waited for the lawyer's letter asking for money. But none came. She'd just gone. Some time afterwards he discovered she'd gone to Germany where she'd got work as a model. Still later he discreetly sought an annulment, which eventually terminated the marriage that never was.

Over a month after his trip to Ischia he returned to practise but it was a different Jack Traynor from the one his fellow barristers remembered. The trombone stayed in its black leather case as if in mourning and was never heard again at the Grand Night dinners of the circuit. He had become morose and misanthropic, but he threw himself into his work. He became known on the circuit as a savage cross-examiner but he didn't confine his tetchiness to witnesses in court. He lost what friends he had but prospered professionally, affecting a blunt joviality with juries – a joviality not retained in the robing room or in the Bar mess when the case was over. After a few years in silk he was appointed to the High Court Bench and developed into a rather sour, 'stand-no-nonsense' judge. As he now had few friends in the north and was often called to sit in the Divisional Court and the Criminal Appeal Court, he moved to London – despite his feelings about the south and southerners that had been so exacerbated by his experience with Lois. His spinster sister, Agnes, with whom he lived, found a villa in Hampstead where she joined the local Methodist Church and set about reforming it. From their bleak house he set out daily by bus to try cases at the Law Courts in London. So with his least favourite counsel appearing before him within the space of three days, Patrick Foxley on Monday and then Mordecai Ledbury, Mr Justice Traynor had not had the most agreeable of weeks in his short career on the Bench.

The case in which Mordecai Ledbury appeared before him concerned the interpretation of a contract between a literary agent and a well-known author, and it aroused considerable public interest. Mordecai represented the agent; Hayden Welsh, the author. During the trial, Mordecai made little effort to conceal his disdain of Mr Justice Traynor's lack of understanding of the literary life of London and with his wig perched crookedly on his enormous head, and the sweat running down the deep runnels which led from above the nostrils to beside and below the chin in the dark twisted face, he lectured the judge at length. Balanced precariously on his crippled legs, he thumped the desk of the bench in front of him on which he had laid his two sticks, one of which he would pick up from time to time when he decided to perambulate a few paces up and down counsel's bench, inevitably dropping the other. He did not, however, permit this to interrupt the flow of his argument as he ignored the obsequious attempt of the solicitor's clerk, who darted from his place and groped on the floor in an effort to retrieve it. Jack Traynor, remembering his friend John Williams's advice, kept his temper and sat, outwardly impassive, listening to Ledbury's lengthy final address. As he did so he forgave Patrick Foxley his Oxonian airs and graces in the case earlier in the week and when Mordecai at last concluded his protracted submissions it was with considerable satisfaction, which he could barely conceal, that he launched into his judgement almost before Mordecai had collapsed with a clatter into his seat. He made clear how little he had been impressed by the argument of counsel for the literary agent and how decisively he considered Mr Mordecai Ledbury wrong and Mr Hayden Welsh right. He ignored Mordecai's snorts as he awarded costs to Hayden Welsh's client and swept out of court, darting a look of triumph at Mordecai Ledbury as he disappeared.

'Roody prima donna,' he said in his Geordie accent when his clerk brought him a cup of tea as he sat in his room, his feet on the desk. 'Did you see the expression on his face?' The judge chuckled. 'He doesn't like losing, not before a Geordie judge. Like that young Foxley fellow last Monday.'

'But Mr Foxley won on Monday, Judge,' said his clerk.

'Aye, but Foxley's another prima donna of another kind, with a different style but he's still another prima donna. I can't abide either. We'd have taught them manners if we'd had them on the north-eastern circuit. They wouldn't have got far in Leeds.'

Mordecai had left the court, growling and thumping his stick, not stopping to talk to his disconsolate client, leaving that to his junior counsel and his resentful solicitor. As he limped down the stairs into the central hall of the Law Courts muttering to himself, his clerk at his side, Adams knew him well enough to keep silent.

It was only when Adams was helping him into his short coat that he dared to speak. 'Did you read in this morning's papers, sir, that the Minister for Defence Procurement has resigned?'

Mordecai shook his head. 'I don't read about the antics of those comedians.'

'He is to sue News Universal for what they published about him,' Adams went on. 'We have a retainer on behalf of the group. From Mr Goodbody.'

Mordecai sat heavily in the chair. 'So we have. You should never have let me accept it.'

Adams brushed the collar of Mordecai's coat with a clothes-brush. 'News Universal', he said, 'have insisted upon an immediate consultation and Mr Goodbody and the Managing Director are in your room waiting for you.' He put down the brush and handed Mordecai a copy of the *Sunday News*. 'Just to remind you, sir.'

Assisted by Adams, Mordecai struggled down the steps into the forecourt of the Law Courts to the taxi waiting for him. Even though his chambers were only a stone's throw from the Courts, a few hundred yards across the Strand, he always had a taxi to take him to the Temple after a day in court. Adams took a seat beside him and Mordecai began to read the extracts of the Richmond diary in the newspaper. To reach the Temple the cab had to make a lengthy, circular and expensive journey through heavy traffic down Fleet Street into Tudor Street and under the arch to King's Bench Walk.

They sat in the cab while Mordecai finished reading. Then, with a snort, he got out and Adams paid off the cab.

Goodbody, Spenser and Godfrey were in Mordecai's large room overlooking the Inner Temple garden, seated in a semicircle facing the big desk beneath the tall window. A fourth chair had been placed next to Spenser. It was, for the present, empty. Mordecai stumped in, acknowledging the presence of none except Goodbody, to whom he gave a cursory nod, before sinking into and his chair behind his desk, his back to the window.

'You've been in court all day?' Goodbody asked pleasantly.

Mordecai grunted. Goodbody could tell that he was in a temper. He must have lost. It would be a difficult conference. 'Well?' Mordecai growled. 'What's all this about?'

Goodbody introduced Spenser and Godfrey from the News Universal legal department.

Mordecai ignored Spenser and said to Godfrey, 'What kind of a lawyer are you?'

'A barrister,' Godfrey said.

'Have you done a pupillage? In whose chambers?'

'Patrick Foxley's.'

'Did he throw you out?'

Godfrey coloured. 'No, I decided to get a job.'

'Why?'

'Personal reasons.'

'Money, I assume,' Mordecai muttered. 'Starving wife, children tugging at the gown, obliged to take News Universal's shilling.'

'Mordecai!' Goodbody expostulated.

Mordecai switched his gaze to Spenser. 'You are the Managing Director?' Spenser bowed. 'Do you have any say in what is published in the newspaper?'

'Not specifically, only if there is, as it were, a business element.'

'What do you mean by that?'

Spenser cleared his throat. 'For instance, if there is a need for the authorisation of extra funds, such as to purchase a book or some feature which—'

'Did you authorise the publication about which this man threatens to sue?'

'No, the Chairman, Mr Digby Price, made the decision to publish.' Spenser pointed to the empty chair beside him. 'We're expecting him here at any moment. He's coming from Paris.'

'When the piece was published, didn't you realise that you ran the risk of being sued?'

'Yes.' Spenser nodded towards Godfrey. 'Lacey advised that there was a risk—'

'And you ignored that advice?'

'The Chairman', Spenser repeated, 'made the decision to publish.'

The door opened. 'Mr Digby Price,' Adams announced.

Price strode in: a squat, aggressive figure. He stood for a moment, looking around him. Spenser got to his feet and pushed the empty chair towards him. Price nodded briefly to Mordecai and sat down heavily. 'What have you been talking about?' he asked.

'The trouble you've got yourself into,' said Mordecai.

'You mean the trouble you are going to get me out of,' Price contradicted.

'The Managing Director was telling me that you personally authorised the publication. Is that correct?'

'I did. I authorised it because I thought it provocative and entertaining. I knew that some of the characters mentioned would object. I wasn't worried if any of the so-called society people issued a writ. I reckoned none of them would dare and I had reason to believe that two of the three politicians mentioned would not sue.'

'What was the reason?'

'That's my business,' Price replied. There was a silence.

Mordecai broke it. 'You don't wish to tell me?'

'No.'

Spenser knew. He knew Price had seen the Prime Minister on Sunday at Chequers.

'Well, one of them has,' said Mordecai.

'I hoped he would. For a long time I've waited for the chance to expose him. He's corrupt and dishonest, and I welcome his writ. I want the bastard ruined.'

Mordecai flung himself back in his chair. 'You've come all the way from Paris to tell me that?'

'No. I came because I want to hear your advice about defending any claim he might make.'

Mordecai studied Price under his bushy eyebrows; then he looked away. 'The routine in a claim for damages in an action for defamation', he began, 'is to plead that what was published was not defamatory but if it was, then it was fair comment. Finally, as a last resort you plead that what was written was true. When the other side is considering that, you get out your cheque-book and pay them off.'

Price leant forward in his chair. 'I'll get my cheque-book out to pay you, Ledbury, provided you stop being so bloody sarcastic and bloody well make sure I don't have to get out my chequebook to pay Richard Tancred.' He jumped to his feet and began to walk around the room, pacing to the window, then back to the door. 'Let me make this clear. I don't pay Tancred a penny, not now, not later and not ever. I've hired you, Ledbury, to make sure I don't. I'm the one in charge and—'

'You are in charge up to a point,' Mordecai interrupted. 'You can give your instructions, yes, but I'm in charge of the conduct of the litigation and I remain so unless and until you terminate the retainer.' He paused. ' If you want to reject my advice—'

Goodbody intervened, fixing Mordecai with his eyes. 'I think we're at cross-purposes. The Chairman misunderstood the way you answered him, Mordecai, about the form of defence.' He turned to Price, who was standing glowering, his hands on the back of his chair.

'What Mordecai meant was that usually at this stage a defendant lodges a holding defence, that is a formal defence until he's ready to file the real defence. Of course there's no question of paying the man off. Mordecai was jesting. It is true that it is sometimes cheaper to pay off a claimant than to fight him, even if you were to win but in a case like the present, the holding defence remains on the file only until we have assembled the evidence about what Tancred was up to with Oscar Sleaven. Then we plead justification, in other words we formulate our real defence – that what the words meant was true. That Tancred and Sleaven were up to something dishonest; that Sleaven was paying Tancred in order to get lucrative contracts. If, of course, your people can't come up with any evidence, then we can't succeed and you would have to pay up. If they do produce the evidence, what they have discovered will form the substance of a defence of justification and we shall win. Is that not right, Mordecai?'

Mordecai frowned, shifting in his chair.

'The Tancred–Sleaven relationship as described in the diary appears to me, as I believe it would to any fair-minded reader, very sinister,' Goodbody went on. 'The Minister and the industrialist, secret conversations, meetings in strange places. Richmond, whose solicitor I was for years, was no fool. He was a shrewd observer and he certainly formed the impression that there was something improper going on between them. And so would anyone who witnessed what Richmond described.' He turned to Price. 'But I'm sure you have your people looking into all of this.'

'I have an army looking into it, as you call it. They'll go through every second that man has ever breathed until we know more about him than he knows about himself.' He wagged a finger at Mordecai. 'This is war, Ledbury, I want to make that plain. War to the death and you're going to fight this war on my behalf because, despite all your offensiveness, I know you're the right man to do it. In fact, it's because you're so bloody rude that I've gone for you. You don't like me and I don't like you, but this is a professional job and I'm told that, if you're anything, you're a professional.' He stopped.

No one spoke. Mordecai was staring straight ahead of him.

Price went on, 'You're in charge of the battle when we get to court, I know that. One doesn't keep a dog and bark oneself, but my instructions are to fight, fight every inch of the way, with every weapon in the book and if you can't find one in the book, then use some that are not. It's no surrender and no chequebook. Is that understood?'

Again there was silence. Spenser had his head bowed, his hands together, the tips of his fingers against his lips as though in prayer.

When no one spoke, Price said, 'Well that's what I've come here to say. This is a fight. Understand?' He looked around the room. 'You got the message?'

Mordecai remained silent, still staring ahead of him. For a moment he caught Godfrey's eye and Godfrey thought he saw the glimmer of a wink. But it might have been a trick of the light.

Price turned to Spenser. 'I'm returning to Paris. Keep me informed.' He twisted on his heel and left, banging the door behind him.

Mordecai took out a large red bandanna handkerchief and wiped his face. 'You heard the man,' he said. 'Keep him informed. And you might as well keep me informed too. That also might help.' He looked at Goodbody. 'I don't think it would be profitable to continue this conference. Good afternoon, gentlemen.'

The three rose to go. Then Spenser said, 'May I say something?'

Mordecai nodded. 'If you wish.'

'The issue between the Chairman and the ex-Minister is personal. It originated in the past, over exactly what I don't know. All I do know is that he has a bitter hatred for Richard Tancred and that when he read what Richmond had written he thought it presented him with an opportunity to expose a man he has always believed was corrupt. My advice as the Group Managing Director was to avoid litigation but the Chairman was determined to go ahead and he'll go to any lengths to win. I assure you that Mr Price will never consent to any settlement.'

'Is that all you can tell us?' Mordecai enquired. Spenser nodded. 'Thank you.' Mordecai gestured to Goodbody to remain.

'I'll telephone later this evening,' Goodbody said to Spenser as he and Godfrey left.

When Mordecai and Goodbody were alone, Mordecai shook his great head. 'What have you let me in for, Oliver Goodbody? That man Price is unbalanced. He's obsessed.'

'Is he?' asked Goodbody quietly. 'I am not so sure. Perhaps he is right.'

Chapter Six

'I'm very glad we didn't bring the editor,' Spenser commented in the car taking him and Godfrey back to the office. 'It was a difficult enough conference as it was. I don't think she's the kind of lady Ledbury would have warmed to.'

'I thought that the Chairman and Ledbury were going to come to blows' said Godfrey.

'I don't mind how fierce Ledbury is with us, so long as he's fiercer with the enemy.'

'What kind of man is Richard Tancred?' Godfrey asked.

'Very little is known about him,' Spenser replied. 'He went into the Foreign Service after Cambridge, but I suspect it was really MI6.'

'He was a spy?'

'In the Special Intelligence Service world. Then he went into business. In my twenty years with News Universal I've always found someone able to tell me most things about most people. But not about Tancred.'

'There's a passage in the diary where Richmond describes him as monk-like, celibate.'

'If he is, that's rarely true of those who go into politics. Political power is an aphrodisiac. In any event this case will be about his honesty, his relations with Sleaven, not what he gets up to in bed. Which is why I have added accountants and financial experts to the team investigating him and his past. And Oscar Sleaven.' He paused.

'And I've provided them with a very, very substantial budget. You are off to Manchester tonight?'

Godfrey nodded. A contract problem with printers. He'd be back in the morning.

'Take the car on to the station after you've dropped me.'

Godfrey stared out of the car window and thought about the News Universal team of reporters and experts slipping into offices, chatting in City bars, searching through records, copying, analysing, if necessary stealing documents – the financial men in their smart suits, the reporters in grubby raincoats going from house to house, questioning neighbour, cleaning lady, colleague at the office, probing the present, dredging up the past. And always with the chequebook in their breast pocket. No one nowadays, he reflected, can keep a secret safe from those rich enough and determined enough to uncover it. Homes staked out, tradesmen bribed, trash cans rifled, so-called friends offered money. Money. Always money. Every man has his price, Robert Walpole had said three hundred years ago, but at least that was bribery for political power or influence. Nowadays it was bribery to discover private secrets, the secrets of sex – and then publish them to titillate the readers. Every lover, spouse, parent, even child had his or her price. Everyone was eager to tell and betray when the man with the chequebook knocked on the door. And who was there who hadn't something they wouldn't want exposed by a *News* hack, slanted by a *News* sub-editor and served up to millions over their cornflakes at breakfast on a Sunday morning?

But then he reflected that this investigation was not just to provide a juicy read at the breakfast table. This was a legitimate exercise – preparing a defence against a claim for damages. After all, it was Tancred who had started it. It was he who was demanding damages. News Universal were defending themselves. They were entitled to investigate him. But had Tancred started it? Had it not been started by Price's decision to print because he wanted to ruin Tancred? And before that had it not been the actor who'd hawked around the diary for sale? And before him, the diarist scribbling down the gossip and secrets about his friends?

But whoever had begun it, the machinery had now commenced to grind; the wheels were rolling, the cogs were turning – and he was one of the cogs. Or rather, he was more, for he was part of the team whose hands were on the levers, collating, tabulating the information dug up by the investigators, pointing them like bird dogs in the direction they should follow. He was a part of the scandal machine of the scandal rag. 'Do reporters', he asked suddenly, 'ever invent a story or pay someone to tell a false story?'

'They rarely have the need. People fall over themselves to reveal other peoples' secrets, especially if they're offered enough money. Most reports are basically true. The story, of course, may be slanted, made more exciting.' Spenser paused, then went on. 'And the journalists have to look after themselves. Their livelihood can depend on their ability to come up with a good story. If it looks good, it may not be gone into in great depth. Checks are made, sometimes even affidavits are taken but if the story is sensational enough and the corroboration is pretty thin, sometimes a risk is taken. If it turns out to be wrong, then we apologise and pay up.' He laughed. 'While making sure we put it about that the reason for paying up is that the story was true but it wasn't possible to get the proof needed for a court of law.'

For a time they travelled in silence. Then Godfrey said, 'This is going to be very different. They say Richard Tancred was the probable successor to the PM. The damages could be enormous.'

They would if Tancred succeeds, Spenser thought. And that, he knew, could spark a major crisis for the Corporation. For Spenser knew better than anyone how vulnerable at present was the financial position. The circulation war was costing News Universal millions and all the time circulation was declining, even if it had picked up a little on the publication of the Richmond Diary. But overall, News were losing the war. A massive award of damages in the Tancred case could have a devastating effect, whatever the Chairman might think. Vast damages and vast costs could bring the Corporation to the brink. Spenser knew the numbers even better than the Chairman. So if he decided that the defence of News Universal in the lawsuit was going to fail, he'd instruct his brokers to sell even more of his stock than he had already. He was not going to let himself be ruined by the obsession of the Chairman over his feud with Tancred. 'You are right,' he replied. 'If the defence fails, the damages and the costs will be enormous.'

The car was drawing up at the tower block of the management and editorial offices of News Universal. 'Which is why, young man,' Spenser added, his hand on the car door, 'we have to bust a gut, to use a vulgar phrase, to ensure it does not.' He got out of the car. 'Don't forget I want you to get a statement from Streatley when you get back from the north. We must be ready to prove he brought the manuscript to us. I want you to interview Streatley as soon as possible.'

Chapter Seven

In the late afternoon of the conference in Mordecai Ledbury's chambers in the Temple, Anna James was working happily in her studio. The evening before she'd got
a model from the agency, a man called Cosimo, middle-
aged, with an ugly, interesting face. She did a drawing
in chalk of his head and shoulders. When she came to
dismiss him he became difficult, pressing her to come
out with him for a drink. She refused. His breath stank
of gin. It had taken some time to get him down the stairs
and out of the studio.

She was working on a new still life when the telephone rang. 'I was a bit pissed last night,' Cosimo
mumbled. 'No offence meant. When do you want me
again?'

'No hurry,' Anna said. Never, she thought. She'd had
enough of Cosimo. 'I'll let you know.' That morning she
had taken the drawing off the easel and leant it against
the wall. Cosimo said he'd be happy to come again, any
time she wanted. 'I'll let you know,' she repeated and
hung up.

The light was fading and she switched on the spot-
lights as she worked for another hour on the still life on
the easel. Another bell sounded, this time the front door.
Oh, no, she thought, not Cosimo. The bell rang again, a
long, continuous ring. She went downstairs. 'Who is it?'
she called from the hall. 'If it's you, Cosimo, go away.'

'It's your landlord,' came a man's voice. 'Can we have
a word?'

Her landlord? Job Streatley. She had not met him

when Goodbody's, the solicitors, had given her the keys and she had moved in. The house beside the studio had been shuttered and dark. She opened the front door. In the dim light that came from the hall and fell on the doorstep she saw a man in his early thirties with a thin face and blond hair. Beside him was another man, larger, with square shoulders. In the half-light, the pair seemed faintly menacing.

'Job Streatley,' the blond man said, smiling. He held out a passport, open at the page with his name and photograph. 'Not my most flattering likeness, not the one I use in *Spotlight* for the theatre, but as we've not met and you're on your own, I thought I should identify myself – like the coppers or the gas man.' He smiled again, the smile flitting across his face, showing his white teeth, switching off abruptly. 'I haven't been around since you came and I thought we ought to meet. May we come in? I'd like to have a talk.'

Anna hesitated. 'About—' she began.

'Oh, just a friendly neighbours' kind of talk. I won't keep you long.'

She turned, leaving the front door open and stood at the bottom of the steep staircase to the studio, her hand on the banister. The two men came into the hall, the second shutting the front door behind them.

Streatley was quite short, his yellow hair, she saw, was dark at the roots. He was dressed in a kind of black Mao jacket buttoned to the neck and close-fitting black trousers. The other man had a shaven head and the face of a bruiser with a ring in one ear. He was in a T-shirt and she could see the tattoos on his biceps.

'I know this place well,' Streatley said cheerily, 'from when old Francis was alive.' He peered down the long passage which ran beside the stairs and led to the small kitchen and the sole bedroom and its bathroom. It was there he'd brought his friends – and had so troubled Francis.

Anna had imagined Francis's friend as someone

graceful and willowy, rather gentle. This man was hard.

'This is Taylor, my assistant,' said Streatley, pointing to the other who was standing behind him by the door. He's even harder, she thought. Assists at what? she wondered.

'Can we go somewhere where we can talk?' he added, smiling again.

'As you know, there's only the studio—'

'And the bedroom,' he interrupted, the same unpleasing smile flashing momentarily across his face. 'No, of course the studio. Just the place for a talk.'

Anna led the way up the stairs.

Streatley went to the canvas on the easel. 'Nice,' he said of the still life, 'very nice.'

Taylor leant against the wall under the tall north window. Anna pushed the trolley on which were her palette, her tubes of paint and the jars of turpentine and linseed oil up against the easel, obliging Streatley to stand back. 'Sorry.' He ran his hand through his hair and smiled again. But his eyes were not smiling.

'What do you want to talk about?' she asked.

'About this place, about the studio.'

'What about it?' She sat on the high painting stool near the trolley.

'I'm an actor and I'm often out of London, touring and so on. I've my own place in Islington and this is too big for me. So I want to sell. But the studio being an integral part of the property and—'

'It's not integral. It's separate.'

'Of course,' he agreed, 'but it adjoins the house and is in the grounds, and you can only get to it through the same gate from the gardens. No one interested would want to buy if someone were occupying the studio.'

'Why not? It's two separate dwellings. In New York, there are plenty of places like this. There must be the same in London.'

'Maybe there are,' he said sharply, while the smile came and went. 'But in a sale it'd be a disadvantage to have someone living on the property. So what I've come to ask is whether you'd agree to a deal.' He paused, looking at her under his arched eyebrows. They were plucked, or at some time had been plucked, she noticed.

'Because you want to sell the property?' she asked.

'Yes. The whole of it. And I've got somebody who is interested, really interested. I've the chance of a quick sale. They've seen the house – and the outside of the studio. I've described the inside and they only want to buy if the studio is included. They're from overseas, Hong Kong, and they're in a hurry. I don't want to lose the chance.'

'And I'm in possession of the studio.'

'I want to buy you out.' He was strolling around the room. 'At a reasonable price, of course. I've no firm ideas about price but we can discuss that once we've decided the principle.' He stopped, watching her.

'What principle?'

'That you agree to sell . . . And leave. Leave quickly.' Until then he had made an effort to sound pleasant, his voice light. Now it became harder. 'I don't want to quarrel. Nothing's more unpleasant than neighbours quarrelling.'

'Why should we quarrel?'

'We won't, not if you're sensible, not unless you turn me down or play silly buggers over the price. That'd make for bad feelings between us, real bad feelings.' He began to patrol again around the studio. 'To be strictly accurate, it'd make for bad relations between you and Taylor. I won't be here myself.' He turned to Taylor, who was leaning against the wall, his hands in his pockets. 'But Taylor will. Taylor'll be in the main house, won't you, Taylor?'

Taylor nodded. There was no mistaking, now, the menace.

Streatley continued, 'There've been a lot of burglaries around here so I can't leave the place unoccupied. I have to have someone here, someone capable of looking after it, of dealing with anyone who's a nuisance.' He grinned at Taylor who looked steadily at Anna. 'Taylor's the man for that. He'd be a match for anyone who makes a nuisance of themselves, wouldn't you, Taylor?'

'I should be,' Taylor said.

'He's trained, you see. He knows how to handle villains and nuisances – and not be too particular about how he does it.' Streatley turned back to Anna. 'He's just the man I need to look after my property.'

Anna said, 'I haven't seen anyone in the main house. There've been no lights since I moved in. I thought it was unoccupied.'

'You're right. No one has been here. Taylor came last night. I've been too busy to give the matter much attention myself but now that someone is so keen to buy I must.' He walked over to Taylor and turned. Both men were facing her. 'Buying the whole place, that is,' he added. 'That's what they want and I don't want to pass up the chance. We're talking about quite a bit of money.'

'I'm sure you are,' Anna agreed. Then she added, 'I heard you've been busy selling your friend's private diary?'

He stared at her coldly. 'I came here', he said, 'to discuss this property. Nothing else.'

'I should think that the publication of that diary might cause a lot of people a lot of pain. Did your friend ever think it would be published? And in a rag like the *Sunday News*?'

'That's nothing to do with you. I came here to discuss buying you out. You'd get what's fair.' He was angry now.

Anna's heart began to beat faster. She knew she shouldn't have said that about the diary and wished she hadn't. She got off the stool and pointed at Taylor. 'Why did you bring that man with you? What has he to do with a deal between you and me?'

'I told you. He's my assistant. What happens here concerns him because he'll be living here looking after

my property. You'll see a lot of him around the place . . .
If you stay.'

She looked from one to the other. Her heart began to
flutter. 'I'll get my lawyer to talk to you,' she said.

He broke into one of his ingratiating smiles. 'Do that,'
he said. 'I'll call him.'

He took a pad and a pen from the pocket of his black
Mao jacket. 'What's his name?'

'I'll tell him to call you.'

'All right.' Streatley wrote on the pad and handed the
sheet of paper to her.

'That's my number in Islington. What's his name?' he
repeated.

She hesitated. Godfrey Lacey was the only lawyer she
knew in London. But she also knew that he was not
what she needed. She'd require someone tougher than
Godfrey to take on Job Streatley. But there was no one
else. 'Godfrey Lacey,' she said, looking at the piece of
paper Streatley had handed her.

'Well, tell him to call me at that number. What's his
firm?'

'He'll call you.'

'Make sure he does. And soon. Just one word of
advice. Tell him you're going to be sensible, you're
going to be reasonable. Otherwise I don't think you're
going to be very happy if you stay on here. I don't think
your life would be very comfortable.'

'Is that a threat?'

'No, just an opinion. You do understand that the
garden is not included in your tenancy?'

'I never thought it was.'

'There's only a right of access.'

'I'm aware of that.'

'Then please make sure your boyfriends understand
it. Taylor found a drunk wandering round the garden
last evening. Isn't that right, Taylor?'

'I did,' Taylor said. 'He banged on the door of the
main house, shouting that he was looking for the studio.
He said he couldn't find it, it was too dark.'

Cosimo, Anna thought.

'Bloody drunk,' Taylor added. He picked up the board with the drawing of Cosimo she'd done the evening before. It was on the floor beside him. 'That's him,' he said. 'That's the bloody drunk.'

Streatley looked over Taylor's shoulder. 'Nasty-looking brute,' he observed. Taylor leant the board back against the wall. Streatley went on, 'It's not nice having someone like that wandering about my property at night, drunk, looking for his girlfriend. That's a trespass. That's the sort of thing that makes for bad relations, really bad. That could cause problems with you and Taylor living so close. And we don't want rows, do we? Not rows in public or in court about drunken boyfriends calling in the middle of the night and disturbing the neighbours. Particularly when the place is on the market.'

'He's not a boyfriend,' Anna said. 'He's a model and he wasn't drunk.'

'Taylor says he was. I've told Taylor to keep a sharp lookout from now on. He'll deal with any trespassers or nuisances.' He patted Taylor on the shoulder. 'But I don't want anything unpleasant, especially when someone's interested in buying. But if things do turn nasty, Taylor won't get the worst of it. Will you, Taylor?'

'I won't,' Taylor said, staring at Anna.

Streatley continued, 'So see your drunken pals don't wander about in my garden.' He paused again. 'It wouldn't be nice for you if there's trouble – not for a young woman living all on her own. Better make yourself a penny or two and move out. That way everybody's happy.' He walked to the studio door. 'Make sure your lawyer calls me.' He disappeared down the stairs.

Taylor came from where he'd been standing under the north window. As he crossed the room he managed to barge into the easel, which tipped over on to the painting trolley. The canvas fell to the floor, the palette on top of it. Pools of oil and turpentine flooded the floor; paints and broken glass from the bottles were scattered beside it. 'Sorry, love,' said Taylor as he too went down the stairs.

'All right, up there?' Streatley called from the stairs. 'I thought I heard a crash.'

'Just a little accident,' she heard Taylor say. 'No harm done.'

'By the way,' Streatley called, 'we're having a spot of bother over the electrics. I hope you have a torch.'

She heard the front door bang behind them and went to the top of the stairs to make sure they had gone. Then she returned to the studio. Tears came into her eyes as she stood looking at the mess on the floor and the ruined canvas. Suddenly the lights went out. She stood in the dark, frozen and silent, afraid. When she moved she felt the crunch of broken glass under her shoe as she groped round the room and made her way downstairs. In the kitchen she struck a match and looked for the telephone. When she picked it up the line was dead. She began to tremble. She must get hold of Godfrey, of anyone who might help her. In a panic she fumbled for her coat and bag. She would telephone Godfrey. She knew no one else.

She ran up the Brompton Road and found a call box. Shaking, she looked up the number of News Universal and got through to the legal department.

'Godfrey Lacey is in Manchester. He's due back late tonight,' the woman's voice said. 'I'll give you his home number. At least, it's the number where he's staying. He's moved. He's with a friend.'

Godfrey had indeed moved. He'd left Alice. 'Why all of a sudden?' Alice had asked. 'Why not before?' He'd replied that he'd said he'd go when she was settled. 'You're pathetic,' Alice had said. He had filled a suitcase and when he came downstairs she had the baby in her arms. He'd put half a dozen fifty-pound notes on the kitchen table that he'd drawn from the office to meet his expenses in Paris. 'I'll keep up the mortgage,' he'd said. 'The father will have to support the child.' As he left, she stood in the door and shouted, 'You'll have to pay, you'll have to pay a fucking sight more than that.'

He'd gone to a friend, Brian Reed, who had been his best man and lived in Fulham. They'd been in chambers together, Patrick Foxley's chambers. Brian had not been surprised when Godfrey had asked him. He'd known the marriage couldn't last. Godfrey and the foul-mouthed cockney. It was just sex, he'd supposed.

Brian let him have his attic room, reached from the hall by a built-in ladder. Godfrey could stay there until he found a place.

When Anna called asking for Godfrey, Brian answered. Godfrey, he informed her, was in the north and expected back late. Then he said, 'You sound upset. Can I do anything?'

Hesitantly Anna told him what had happened. 'I need a lawyer and he's the only one I know in London.'

'Where are you?' Brian asked. When she told him he said she was just round the corner from him. 'Come to my place. I'm a lawyer. We'll see what we can do.'

Brian, fresh-faced, tubby, was in the street outside the house where he had his flat, waiting for her. When he brought her upstairs and they entered the sitting room a tall dark man was standing with his back to the fireplace. 'This is Patrick Foxley,' Brian said. 'Now let me get you a drink. You look as if you need it.'

He brought her vodka on the rocks while Patrick Foxley watched as she sat, still trembling. 'I'm sorry to be a nuisance.' She nursed the drink in both hands. 'It's silly but I got rather frightened. I just wanted to get away from the studio.'

'Tell us exactly what happened,' Brian said.

When she'd finished, Patrick asked, 'Have you the telephone number?' She handed him the slip Streatley had given her, and he picked up the telephone and dialled.

'An answer service,' he muttered over his shoulder. Then Anna heard him say, 'This is Patrick Foxley QC, speaking on behalf of Miss James. She has reported your threats and your outrageous behaviour. Unless the light is restored the police will be informed and you'll be taken to court.' He slammed down the receiver and stood looking down at her. 'He may be keeping away from the telephone deliberately so there's probably little we can do tonight. Tomorrow we'll get him.' He looked at his watch. 'You seem exhausted. You need something to eat.'

'No.' She shook her head. 'I don't want anything.'

For a time no one spoke. At last Patrick said 'We won't be able to get the light on and he may not be back tonight. What will you do?'

She shrugged. 'I'll have to go back. I've nowhere else to go.' Again there was silence.

Then Patrick said, 'You had better come to me.'

She looked up, questioning.

'You can't go back to your studio. Brian has no room here. I live round the corner in Tregunter Road and I have a spare room. You can spend the night there. In the morning we shall deal with Streatley.'

'But I can't—' she began.

'Yes you can. You look all in. You'd better come now.'

Almost before she had time to consider he had her by the arm, walking her out of the flat and down the Fulham Road. As they went, he said 'I know about Streatley. He sold a diary to the *Sunday News*. They are Lacey's employers so Lacey mightn't be able to help you.' He paused. 'How did you meet Lacey?'

'In Paris. At least, on the train. I didn't know any other lawyer in England.'

'Don't worry. We'll see to Streatley.'

'Are you a lawyer?'

'I am, but I'm not the kind you need for this. I'll get you the right man.'

'How did you know about Streatley?' she asked.

'Through my work.'

'He's not very pleasant.'

'I imagine that he is not.'

'I'm putting you to a lot of trouble.'

'I have plenty of room,' he said shortly. He had taken his arm from hers. 'In case you're worried, you'll be quite safe.'

She stopped. 'I didn't think I wouldn't be,' she began angrily.

He took her by the elbow. 'We're nearly there.'

He was walking very quickly and he hurried her along. They turned into Tregunter Road and he led her into a ground-floor apartment in a tall house. 'The spare room is downstairs in the basement.'

He went ahead down some stairs and threw open the door of a bedroom. 'The bathroom leads off it,' he said. 'Would you like a hot drink?' She shook her head. 'I'll bring you some pyjamas.' He reappeared a moment later and handed them to her. 'I'll arrange for an alarm call for eight o'clock. The telephone is by the bed. The daily woman will be here soon after eight. Here's a sleeping pill.' He paused and looked at her seriously. Then he smiled. 'There's a lock on the door. Now I have to work. Goodnight.' And he was gone.

She wandered around the room. It was like a room in an hotel: no photographs, no books. Flower prints on the walls. Nothing to indicate the personality of its owner. There were soap and towels in the bathroom.

He's very cool, she thought. She held up the pyjamas. The trouser bottoms reached six inches beyond her feet. The jacket would be enough. She washed in the bathroom, swallowed the sleeping pill and got into the bed, deliberately not locking the door. In bed she thought about him. Soon she slept.

*   *   *

The telephone woke her with a start. She jumped from the bed, wondering where she was. Then she saw the note that had been pushed under the door.

You have an appointment with Max Wainwright, a solicitor, 2 Norfolk Street, off the Strand, 10 a.m. sharp. He is experienced and tough. He'll know what to do. I have suggested to him that you might be better off out of the studio but not to take a penny less than fifty thousand. Mrs Lane, my cleaner, will be here at 8.30. She will give you coffee or whatever you want. Good luck.

Patrick Foxley

Max Wainwright was bald and fat, but with a twinkle in his eye and she liked him. He asked her how well she knew Patrick Foxley.

'I only met him last night,' she replied.

'He's very bright,' Wainwright said. 'When you know him, you'll like him.'

She told him of the visit by Streatley and his so-called 'assistant' and he listened gravely.

'Monstrous,' he said when she had finished, 'perfectly monstrous.' He'd make sure that didn't happen again but it mightn't be very agreeable to go on living there. He wouldn't be able to stop every piece of harassment and unpleasantness. Streatley was obviously desperate to get her out. He probably did have a buyer for the whole property. So it'd probably be best if she left and the sooner the better. He'd get her a good price.

With Anna sitting opposite him, Wainwright telephoned Streatley. He put on the loudspeaker so that Anna could hear what was said. When Streatley came on the line, Wainwright told him that if there was any more harassment of Miss James he'd call in the police and take him to court. There'd be publicity and he'd be in trouble. He'd not be able to sell after that. Streatley began to make excuses. Wainwright cut him short, asking how much Streatley would pay for vacant possession. Streatley said fifty thousand, provided Anna left immediately. 'Having regard to your behaviour,' Wainwright replied, looking at Anna, 'the price will be a hundred and fifty.' And he put down the receiver. He told Anna he should be able to get her between fifty and a hundred, and suggested she look for another place straight away. 'I've nowhere to go. I don't know London.'

'I'd thought of that,' he replied. 'So had Patrick Foxley.'

'Patrick Foxley?' she asked. And to her annoyance, she coloured a little.

Wainwright smiled. 'He wants to make sure you are all right. You made a great impression. As I said, when you get to know him, you'll like him.'

He took from his desk the particulars of two flats he said he'd been instructed to sell. 'The best', he said, 'is the one in Clapham. It's not yet on the market and I'll hold it until you've seen it. If you like it, I can arrange a rental agreement and give you credit for the deposit against Streatley's payment. Provided', he added with a twinkle, 'you invite Patrick and me for a drink when you're settled.'

Nice, reassuring Mr Wainwright, Anna thought on the bus on the way to Clapham. And clever Patrick Foxley. He was not so comfortable as nice Mr Wainwright but it was about him that she thought the most.

Chapter Eight

Some weeks later, shortly after 8.30 in the evening, Oliver Goodbody arrived at the door of Mordecai Ledbury's apartment in Albany off Piccadilly. Mordecai, in his dressing gown and the legs of white silk pyjamas protruding from beneath it, opened the door.

'Only just risen?' Goodbody asked, amused.

'Taking things a little quietly today,' Mordecai replied, leading Goodbody into the drawing room, which overlooked the central Albany passage, bordered by the flowerbeds under the glass awning. It was an oddly feminine room for such a masculine man. Which of his women, Goodbody wondered, had supervised the decoration? Above the fireplace hung a Boucher, two pert and pretty women playing with a swing, the one on the seat revealing her thighs. Worth, Goodbody thought, around twenty-five thousand pounds?

On the table between two armchairs were a tankard and an open bottle of Dom Perignon, standing in an ice bucket. Mordecai limped over to the corner cupboard and produced another tankard.

'Have you any whisky?' Goodbody asked.

'No,' Mordecai replied, 'wine or nothing.' And he filled Goodbody's tankard before collapsing into a chair.

'I thought I should report progress. Price's people have produced plenty of information about the society women. Most of it amusing and some of it, incidentally, concerning you.'

'They were my friends. But thanks to you and what

133

you've got me into they are not now,' Mordecai growled, his face buried in his tankard. 'But why should Price be interested in them? They're not suing him. He should be concentrating on Tancred.'

'No one has seen Tancred since he walked out of Downing Street. They've come up with his background. Father dealt in antiques in Suffolk, mother French. Both dead. Privately educated, mostly in France; won a scholarship in modern languages to Cambridge, entered the Foreign Office, served in Bangkok and South Africa, before leaving to go into business with a firm in Birmingham making machine tools, eventually managing director, then chairman, and finally went into politics. No wife, no family, no mistress.'

'And his connection with Sleaven?'

'They are analysing all the contracts between the Ministry and Sleaven Industries while Tancred was the Minister. This'll take time.'

'If Price is unable to prove a financial connection between Tancred and Sleaven he'll have to settle.' Mordecai rose and, using the trolley on which stood the now empty bottle as a support, moved slowly towards the dining room. 'Richard Tancred saw his chance of getting a great deal of money out of Price by suing him,' he said over his shoulder, 'and if Price doesn't come up with some evidence that money passed between him and Sleaven, that's what Tancred will get it.'

'Price understands well enough. He has an army investigating Tancred. He's confident that he'll unearth what's needed.'

Mordecai disappeared into the small dining room, went through to the even smaller kitchen and opened the EuroCave, which comprised his cellar, and took out another bottle of Dom Perignon.

Goodbody remained in the drawing room looking at the Boucher. He had not told Mordecai, nor was he going to tell him, that in Price's latest instructions from Paris orders had come to target Tancred's solicitor, Cranley Burrows. As a result the investigators were now shadowing Burrows, noting wherever he went, to whom he spoke, recording what visitors he received and sifting through the waste-paper baskets and refuse bins at his office. They had even approached one of his women clerks and reported some progress. Goodbody knew that if Mordecai were aware that Price had ordered Tancred's solicitor to be targetted he'd be outraged. He'd not tolerate unethical conduct. He'd throw in the brief – and not be sorry he had. But Oliver Goodbody was well aware that he himself could not afford to do that. There was too much at stake for him. So he kept silent.

Mordecai returned with the fresh bottle, again using the trolley. 'We cannot go into court without some convincing evidence of a money link between Tancred and Sleaven,' he repeated. 'If Price can't provide that, then it's our duty to tell him he must settle and get what terms he can.' He opened the bottle. 'If he doesn't, the case will cost him a fortune.' He poured the wine. 'I cannot pretend that the loss of a fortune by that scoundrel would give me many sleepless nights. Provided he has paid you the fee you need.'

Goodbody made no reply. He had received from Spenser a payment on account but it had not been large. He had not demanded more for he'd feared that his anxiety to have more in advance might reveal the situation of his firm and Spenser would lose confidence in its capacity to handle the case. Anyhow, he comforted himself, there was no worry about fees. Not with a client such as News Universal. So he sat in silence, drinking Mordecai's champagne.

Later he spoke to Spenser and reported what Mordecai had said.

Next morning, in the rue Casimir Perrier in Paris, Digby Price took Spenser's telephone call. 'Tell Goodbody to stop fussing. I'll get the evidence,' Price said. Then he got angry and began to shout. 'And tell him

once again that whatever the lawyers say, I'm not paying that bastard one penny, not even if it brings the
whole of News Universal crashing down on my
head.'

Our heads thought Spenser.

Price, as he shouted down the telephone, looked
across the room to the woman who was sitting on the
sofa, her slim legs curled beneath her. She had a perfectly shaped Oriental face under short black hair; her
eyes were narrow and darkened with kohl, and her lips
bright-red with lipstick. The scent of *fracas* filled the
apartment. She smiled as Price went on. 'I'm paying out
a bloody fortune for my people to come up with something and that's what they're bloody going to do. I know
that man is a crook. That's all there is to it. So tell the
lawyers to stop whining. I'm never going to settle.
That's final.' He slammed down the receiver.

The woman put out her hand and he walked to her
and sat beside her, raising it to his lips. Then he rose and
went to the wall safe hidden behind a Modigliani above
the fireplace. He came back to her carrying a velvet case.
He sat and, opening the case took out a slim diamond
necklace. 'Turn,' he said. He fastened the necklace and
she rose and ran to the looking glass at the other end of
the room, looking at herself, twisting this way and that
so that the jewels shone in the sunlight.

She turned back to him and stretched out her hand.
'Come,' she said and he came to her. When he was close
she stood on tiptoe and kissed him. While her tongue
was exploring his mouth she slipped her hand down to
the front of his trousers, undoing the buttons. She took
hold of him and turning, led him into the bedroom.

He had first seen her outside the entrance to the
Crillon Hotel in the place de la Concorde. It was not
long after the Hungarian had been dismissed and he
had made the decision to publish the Richmond diary.
He had been giving luncheon to Spenser who had come
to Paris to report. Spenser had left for the Gare du Nord
but Price had been detained, approached by an

acquaintance. When he left the hotel it was raining and she was standing on the pavement, a short, slight figure holding above her dark head a red umbrella. The concierge was in the street, searching for a taxi. Price saw him turn and shake his head, shrugging his shoulders. The woman under the umbrella stamped her foot. '*Merde*,' she said; then she looked up at Price and smiled, and he smiled in return.

Price's car drew up with a spray of rainwater. '*Merde*,' she repeated stepping back.

'Can I give you a lift?' he said. Two days later she moved into his apartment. Ever since, he could not take his hands off her and he would not leave her alone. He took her to restaurants but rarely to friends. He kept her as if in purdah in the apartment, and when he was working she would come and sit near him in the office off the hall. So she was often beside him when he took and made the constant telephone calls to Spenser and Goodbody, or when he harried the team of investigators in London. She encouraged him and soothed him when, as happened frequently, he exploded with anger and frustration at the lack of initiative or progress by his servants. 'Don't worry so,' she would say, leading him to her bed. 'Have patience. You will succeed. I am sure that you will succeed – in the end.'

On the day that Spenser spoke to Price about the concerns of the lawyers he took Oliver Goodbody to lunch at the Savoy Grill, at the table in the alcove in the corner that was reserved for him on every weekday. 'You must understand that for the Chairman this is more than just a law case,' he said when they had ordered. 'It's a mission; an obsession. Nothing will ever induce him to settle.'

'Not even if we were able to fudge up some terms of settlement that would give each of them some kind of let-out?'

Spenser shook his head. 'He believes he has found the

chance to destroy Tancred and he's not going to let that chance slip.'

He sipped from his glass of Chablis and looked down at the sole that, with typical neatness, he had been filleting with such dexterity. 'And his new woman is encouraging him.'

'How new is she?'

'A few weeks.'

'Who is she?' Goodbody asked.

'Wilson, Price's PA, tells me that her name is Helena. She's in her early forties, looks ten years younger, Siamese or Chinese, at any rate from somewhere in the east. She had been living in Palm Springs, California before she came to France. Wilson says that she's a cut above the usual *poule de luxe* that Price goes for. Or at least she's a very superior one, intelligent, cosmopolitan and Price is besotted with her. Wilson has never seen him like this before. She's with him all the time, even in the office. Apparently he tells her everything and, at the moment, everything for Price is the campaign to get Tancred. Wilson believes that she encourages him.'

'How do you mean?'

'Wilson says she's very anti-British, quite open about it, violently against everything English and she's amused that he is taking on the British establishment. Perhaps she's just humouring him, playing up to Price's obsession, but Wilson thinks that she really does dislike England and the English. He never lets her out of his sight.'

'Never?'

'Except when he comes to London. She refuses to come here. Says she loathes this country. Wilson says Price told him she had some unhappy experience in the past with an Englishman – or with England generally. She's the reason why now he never stays overnight in London but returns to Paris. When he had to go to Beijing soon after they got together, he wanted her to accompany him but she wouldn't. She said she never went back to the East. He practically locked her in the apartment while he was away.'

'What has Price got against Tancred?' Goodbody asked.

'God knows. Something way back in the past that, I suspect, happened in South Africa. Tancred, you know, was once there when he was in the Foreign Service. Anyhow, ever since Tancred went into politics Price saw to it that his newspapers attacked him, especially when he was in government. They couldn't touch him personally because they didn't have anything on him, just criticised his Ministry and his appearances in the Commons, and generally denigrated him. So when Price read that diary there was no stopping him.' He signalled to the waiter for the check. 'Price believes he's already half ruined Tancred by the publication and by forcing him into court, and that whatever the result, the smear of dishonesty will remain. But he's also convinced he'll get the evidence about Tancred and Sleaven. He's sure it's out there somewhere, that there is something that'll prove there was corruption between Sleaven and Tancred; and he's determined he'll get his hands on it, however much it costs him. When he gets it and wins the libel suit he'll demand a criminal prosecution. Tancred ruined, Tancred in jail. That's what he wants.' Spenser paused. 'It's revenge, but for what I don't know.'

'According to Talleyrand,' said Goodbody, finishing his wine, 'revenge is a dish best served cold.'

'Well that's not for Price. His is white-heat revenge.' Spenser paused again. 'Added to his obsession for revenge over Tancred, he now has this obsession with this woman who is prodding him on. Women,' he went on morosely. 'They are always a complication. Especially in business. *Cherchez la femme*. It's as banal as that.' They got to their feet to leave. 'The result is that nothing will prevent Price having his day in court,' Spenser added, 'and there's nothing you and I can do about it.' Except look after myself, he thought, as the two walked to the door.

Outside, as they waited for a taxi, he said, 'By the way, what do you make of young Godfrey Lacey?'

'Quite sound as a lawyer but inexperienced. Not very forceful.'

'He's not – how shall I put it? He's not quite one of us. I don't believe he approves of his employers.'

'Nor, I should remind you, does Mordecai.'

'You must convince him. That young man does not matter. Ledbury does.'

A fortnight after these conversations Tancred's solicitor, Cranley Burrows, flew to Toulouse, as he had on three previous occasions. This time he was followed. He travelled business class in the front of the aircraft. At the back were two of Price's investigative team. At Toulouse airport Burrows was picked up by a car and driven north. A local driver in a black Citroën met Price's men. They followed Burrows's car at a discreet distance. After an hour and in the village not far from what turned out to be their destination, Burrows's car drew up and Burrows went into the small village shop. The Citroën parked at the far end of the village out of sight. When Burrows reappeared and was driven away, the Citroën followed, but they were blocked by a farm lorry as they left the village. So when they came to the fork outside the village, Burrows's car had disappeared. They decided to take the right fork but came into open country with no sign of any car ahead or of any habitation. They turned back and took the left fork. When the roof of a farmhouse came in sight the Citroën stopped and the two proceeded on foot.

In the late afternoon they saw Burrows leave. One of the London men followed him in the Citroën. The other remained, watching the farmhouse. When the Citroën returned, having seen Burrows on his way back along the autoroute to Toulouse, the watchers settled in, making an inn, the Lion Rouge about five kilometres away, their headquarters and reported to News Universal that it was believed that Tancred was residing in a farmhouse close to the village of Pontaix in the Alpes Dauphiné Massif, although he had not so far actually been sighted. The house, they reported, was the residence of a Madame Turville who had lived there, apparently alone, for the past two years. She was a French citizen, wore a wedding ring and was thought in the village to be a widow in her early fifties. She had kept herself very much to herself since she had come to the farmhouse, but three months before she had begun purchasing more groceries in the village shop than before and she had been seen unloading from her car a significant number of the plastic bags of the type provided at the *Supermarche* in the nearest town. Also, a 'foreign' car had been seen recently in the usually deserted lane near the farmhouse. Finally, Madame Turville was receiving a great deal more mail than she had when she first came, much from the Far East and Australia as well as London, including some large packages in sealed envelopes.

Two days later they reported that Tancred had been sighted. He'd been seen walking arm in arm with Madame Turville early one evening in the meadow behind the farmhouse.

Goodbody passed on this information to Mordecai, although he took care to say nothing about the surveillance on Cranley Burrows and his firm.

'So Tancred has a woman in France,' Mordecai said. 'What of it? So, I would remind you, has Price. How does that help prove that when Tancred was a minister of the Crown he was up to some corrupt financial dealings with Oscar Sleaven? I'm not interested in the man's private life. That's unimportant. I want evidence of some financial link and without it we haven't a chance.'

'I know, I know,' Goodbody said wearily. 'You'll get it. Price is certain you'll get it.'

Chapter Nine

Despite the location of Tancred, the surveillance in France was not thorough. The men from London were enjoying their time at the Lion Rouge, staying up late drinking marc with the proprietor and trying out their atrocious French on his daughter at the bar. As a result they did not rise early enough one morning to witness the start of an expedition undertaken by Tancred and Madame Turville. Very early they left the farmhouse and drove away in Madame Turville's small Chevrolet car, she soberly dressed in grey and Tancred formally in a dark suit and dark tie. They drove west to Valence, crossed the E15/A6 autoroute and proceeded along the banks of the Eyrieux river in the direction of the small town of Le Cheylard. Here they stopped, entered a café, drank coffee and ate croissants. After an hour they returned to the car and continued west towards St-Agrève. On the outskirts of the town the car pulled up outside the wall of the church of Ste Marie-Claire.

For half an hour Madame Turville and Tancred sat in the car. Then they got out and entered the building. Shortly after this a hearse drew up and a coffin was taken into the church. There appeared to be no other mourners except three nuns in old-fashioned habits who had apparently accompanied the hearse in a small Peugeot. After a quarter of an hour the coffin was borne from the church, followed by the priest, with an altar boy holding a receptacle with holy water – and behind them Madame Turville and Tancred walking side by side. The three nuns brought up the rear and the small procession made its way round the side of the church to a prepared plot in the graveyard. There the priest said the prayers over the grave, and before the coffin was lowered both Madame Turville and Tancred sprinkled it with earth. After the priest and altar boy had returned to the church, Madame Turville and Tancred spent some time in the graveyard talking to the nuns whom Madame Turville eventually embraced, before she and Tancred made their way back to the Chevrolet and drove away.

As none of this had been observed, no report of it reached Price's legal team.

Chapter Ten

At News Universal Spenser was no longer taking Godfrey to the conferences with Oliver Goodbody. The role of collecting and annotating reports from the investigating team had been handed over to the solicitors in Lincoln's Inn Fields.

A few days later when Godfrey arrived at the News building, the concierge at the front desk told him he was to report at once to Mr Spenser. Sprawled in a chair in Spenser's office was a stout, florid man, in his shirt-sleeves, his shirt bulging over the belt around his baggy grey trousers. Spenser was standing behind his desk. 'Ah, Lacey,' Spenser greeted Godfrey. 'This is Michael Waite.'

The man in the chair grinned up at Godfrey and waved a hand. 'From what used to be called the junior branch of the profession, old son, the solicitors' branch, the blokes you barristers wouldn't have a drink with.' He laughed, his stomach heaving under his shirt. 'How many years call?' he asked Godfrey.

'Three,' Godfrey replied. Waite chuckled.

'Michael was legal manager of *The Star*,' Spenser said. 'We're very fortunate to have secured his services. He's taking over, as Legal Manager so there'll be less pressure on you, Lacey. Well, I wanted to introduce you and now I have some further matters to discuss with Michael.'

'I'll pop in and have a chat when I'm through with the MD,' said Waite cheerily as Godfrey turned to leave.

The new Legal Manager had been allotted an office next to Godfrey, separated by a glass partition. Overnight all the Tancred libel papers had been removed into his office. Waite did not appear until after three. As he flopped into a chair, Godfrey caught the whiff of whiskey. 'I'm glad to be on board,' Waite began. '*News* pays a damn side better than *The Star*. How long have you been here?'

'About a year.'

'So you know the ropes. What I'll want from you, old son, is the office work, answers to the letters, complaints, references to the Press Council, all that crap. The MD says you're as bright as a button so we'll make a great team.' He got up and strolled round the room, picking up papers from Godfrey's desk and glancing at them. ' De-fam-ation,' he went on, spelling out the syllables. 'That's my line. That's why they've poached me from *The Star*. At, I'm glad to say, a handsome increase in salary.' He sat down again and took off his jacket. 'I gather they asked you to read the diary and advise before they published? Have you had any experience of libel?' Godfrey shook his head. 'How could you, with only three years call? The wig must be as white as a virgin's arse.' Waite chuckled. 'Unfair I call it, landing you with that. Anyhow I'll be in charge from now on. But why they've gone to that bloody old fraud Goodbody, I can't imagine. He's not the fellow for a contest like this. They must have gone to him in order to get Ledbury. They're pals, you know – that is if you could be a pal of Ledbury. Now there's a real four-letter man. He was pretty good in his day, I'll give him that, but in my opinion he's past it now. However, his reputation for being so bloody offensive may put the wind up the opposition. Better to have him than that young ponce, Foxley. I hear he's on the other side.'

This was news to Godfrey. Brian had not told him. Perhaps Brian had thought it would be awkward for him, Godfrey's old pupil master being against his present employers?

'Pity they didn't get hold of me earlier,' Waite went on. 'I've been at this game for years. It's the know-how, you see. Or rather the know-what. That MD seems a smart enough lad but if this case is not to become a right cock-up I'm the man they need.'

You certainly are, thought Godfrey. You're just right for News Universal.

Next morning Waite telephoned Oliver Goodbody. 'I'm the new Legal Manager at News Universal and I've taken charge of the Tancred case. I'd like a chat with Ledbury,' Waite began. 'He'll know of me, of course, from *The Star*. I want to talk tactics for court. Pass the word, will you old son, and fix it up?'

'The old son' fixed it up. When Waite breezed into Ledbury's room, Mordecai was seated behind the desk; Oliver Goodbody to his left. Waite flopped uninvited into a chair in front of them. 'Nice to see you Ledbury,' he began as he opened the file he was carrying. 'I expect you remember me from my days with *The Star*?'

Mordecai stared at him balefully. After a pause he said, 'I seem to have heard of you.'

Waite chuckled happily, 'Nothing too terrible, I hope. You and I had some rare old battles in the past, you on one side, me on the other. Anyhow this time we're on the same side, shoulder to shoulder eh?'

'What do you want?' Mordecai asked.

'Just thought I'd make my number now I've taken over. I thought you'd like a chat. Must keep everyone in the picture, don't you know.'

'You've seen the Defence?'

'I have, of course, but—'

'Then you'll know that the case for the defendants at present is that the words do not bear the meaning alleged by the plaintiff. When we are able to, we shall plead that the words are true. In other words that there were corrupt payments made to the plaintiff when he was a minister by Oscar Sleaven, the proprietor of a concern with whom the plaintiff's ministry was doing business. Anything else?'

Waite was not put out. 'The defence in the proverbial nutshell,' he said genially. 'Trust the old advocate to put it nice and succinct. But what I really came to chat about is the trial and—'

'That is a matter for me.'

'Oh, I know, Mr Ledbury, that you're the big boss for the trial.' He chuckled but not so convincingly as he had before. Mordecai continued to fix him with a baleful stare. 'At *The Star*, counsel always encouraged my input, seeing as how I've had so much experience. So I thought I'd come along to have a chat.'

'That is thoughtful of you but unnecessary.'

'No, I'm very happy to assist. Always wise to have a council of war with counsel, I always say.' He chuckled again. 'Now, as to the evidence—'

'There isn't any – as yet.'

'I gather that the News people haven't come up with much—'

'Much! So far they've come up with very little so if you want to make yourself useful, chase them instead of worrying me. When they do produce some evidence, you tell Mr Goodbody. So get busy and come back when you have something to give me.'

Waite chuckled, this time even more forcedly. 'You want what every counsel wants, Mr Ledbury? The smoking gun, eh?'

'When they find it, let me know.' Mordecai pressed the bell on his desk. 'Good day,' he said.

Adams showed Waite out of the room through the main door of the Chambers to the lift. As he got into the lift, Waite said loud enough for Adams to hear. 'Stuck-up old bastard. He'll make a balls of it.'

Back in his room, Ledbury lowered his head onto his hands. 'Don't ever let that creature near me again. What's happened to the young barrister?'

'Gone.'

'When?'

'Resigned this morning. Spenser told me.'

'And they've left us with that monster!' Mordecai lay

back in his chair. 'We've still nothing, Oliver. Where's that evidence that Price is so sure is out there?'

'There's still plenty of time. Price is certain he'll get his hands on it. And what Richmond wrote was not just gossip. Tancred and Sleaven were up to something. Price'll find the evidence. He's certain. So am I.'

'As certain as Price?' Mordecai lumbered slowly to his feet. He looked at Goodbody, shaking his head. 'All Tancred has to do is to lie low and come to court and he'll get a great deal of money. He'll get much more if we go into court accusing him of being corrupt and we've no evidence and we fail. That'll get him a fortune. Yet Price is still demanding I go in with all guns blazing when so far he has not produced a single round of ammunition.'

'Something will turn up.'

'Mr Micawber,' Mordecai said as he stumbled to the lift. 'You're as bad as Price.'

Chapter Eleven

Emerald Cunliffe lay in bed in her country house, her breakfast tray on her lap. It was a Saturday and she was engaged in the agreeable task of planning the *placement* for her dinner party before the ball that Sylvia Benedict was giving that evening at Wainscott.

It was over a year since Emerald had lain there, reading of the treachery of Francis Richmond. The *Sunday News* was never now among the newspapers brought to her with her breakfast tray. It was banned both at her house in Chester Square in London and at The Waves. Since that never-to-be-forgotten Sunday she read only the more staid broadsheets dipping, as was her habit, into the Arts and Book sections to become *au courant*, as she put it, for when she descended from her bedroom to join her weekend guests in time for a cocktail before luncheon.

Because of Sylvia's ball, this weekend was special. For on this Saturday evening there was to be the first real party either of the friends had held since the publication of Richmond's infamous diary; and Emerald was, of course, bringing her dinner guests to Sylvia's for the dance. She now pencilled in the places at table for dinner, after which they would drive the fifteen miles to Wainscott for the ball, whose arrangements the two friends had been planning with mounting excitement for several months.

Before the publication of the diary it had been the regular practice on most weekends for each of them to bring her house guests to the other for lunch on Sunday and the only time when this had been abandoned was during the six months immediately after the publication of the Richmond diary. During those six months Emerald and Sylvia had nursed their wounds in private and had abandoned their weekend house parties. The Waves and Wainscott had stood silent, emptied by the treachery of the man who had been entertained so often in both, the man who had betrayed his friends from beyond the grave.

But Emerald Cunliffe and Sylvia Benedict were tough. They could never have reached their position in the social world had they not been. So two days after the Sunday of the betrayal by the dead Francis Richmond and by Mordecai Ledbury who had refused to advise them because he had been retained by News Universal or been bought by News Universal, as Sybil Benedict had it – they had appeared together at lunchtime as usual at their favourite haunt in London, Harry's Bar in South Audley Street. They'd had lengthy discussions as to whether they should be seen in society so soon after the publication of the diary.

It was Emerald who had decided. 'If we don't make a public appearance,' she'd said on the telephone, 'we'll never be able to face anyone again. It will only be more unpleasant if we postpone it. I will not be driven out of society by that bitchy old queen now, I hope, roasting in hell.'

The lunch at Harry's Bar had not been enjoyable. They were not cut; acquaintances bowed or smiled as they passed but none came over to them, as so many usually did when they took their places at their usual table. They could not avoid observing the whispers behind hands nor, in some cases, the suppressed giggles.

'We are figures of fun,' Sybil hissed, close to tears.

Emerald was made of sterner stuff. 'It's been so long since any of them had a man,' she said loudly. 'They've forgotten what it's like.' She glared imperiously around the room as she ordered bellinis with an extra dose of champagne and only a dash of peach juice. Nevertheless they observed that none came to chat to them and, earlier than usual, they swept out.

They did not repeat so public an appearance for many more weeks. Dinner parties were cancelled and for several months neither had a weekend house party. During this time both were well aware, as Digby Price had made sure they would be, of the activities of his hacks who haunted their houses, trying to speak to their friends and servants. Eventually the attentions became so intrusive that they considered going to court to stop the pestering. Characteristically Emerald was the more bellicose and she forced her solicitor to take her to see counsel to obtain advice as to whether there was anything to be done to stop the harassment.

The counsel chosen was Patrick Foxley. He told her Richard Tancred had retained him in his suit against News Universal, which pleased her; but he advised her against going to law or writing letters of complaint. 'Price may want to provoke you into taking some kind of action,' he said, 'but you mustn't. It would be playing into his hands. He'd try to humiliate you by raking up all the gossip he could find about you and, and if he couldn't find enough, he'd invent it. You must treat what was published about you and his present harassment with the contempt it deserves. If it goes beyond what you've told me, we might complain to the Press Complaints Tribunal. As you have not brought proceedings against the newspaper, these people have no right to behave as they are doing.'

Emerald was much taken by Patrick and ten days after the conference he received an invitation to dine at Lady Cunliffe's London house in Chester Square. It was a small party. Patrick was placed between Emerald and Sylvia, and towards the end of dinner Sylvia asked him what he thought of Mordecai Ledbury. His hostess leant forward to catch his answer.

'He's a formidable advocate,' Patrick replied. 'But . . . he's not quite the force at the Bar that once he was.' He looked at Sylvia. She was disappointed. She had hoped for something more. 'Is he a friend of yours?' he added.

'He was once. Not since Price bought him.'

'I must say I was surprised when I heard he was representing News Universal. He's been very rude about them in the past.'

'Money,' she said, 'that's all it is. That man Price can buy anyone.'

More invitations to dine followed from both Sylvia and Emerald, and when house parties were resumed at Wainscott and The Waves, Patrick Foxley was now and then invited and now and then he accepted. On this Saturday, when Emerald was lying in bed engaged in settling her *placement* for her dinner that evening, he was among the guests she was expecting to arrive later in the morning.

Emerald's American friend, Dolly Partiger, who was paying her annual summer visit to England, had already arrived. When Emerald had discussed with her the party for the ball, Dolly had asked her to invite Anna James, a young friend of hers from Oldhaven whom she had not seen for over a year and who was now living in London. Anna was by then well settled into the flat Max Wainwright had arranged for her to rent and, when Emerald telephoned and she learnt that Dolly had suggested her, she accepted – although she expected she'd know no one at the dance. Then Emerald went on to say she'd see that a young lawyer, Patrick Foxley, would give her a lift down on the Saturday morning.

'I know him,' Anna had said.

'Good. He's very bright. And attractive.'

He is, Anna thought, as she put down the telephone. That first evening when he had given her a bed in his flat she'd been too upset by the encounter with Streatley and Taylor to take much notice of Patrick's looks. Except that he was tall and dark. She had just been grateful for the way he had taken control and found Max Wainwright for her. But twice since her move to Clapham she had seen him. A week after she'd moved in he had called and asked her to dine. She had hesitated but she could hardly refuse. When he had come to collect her she'd been struck by his obvious good looks. He must be very conceited, she felt, and she was unsure that she'd like him. But he had been very agreeable and correct, and he'd interested her. He took her to a local restaurant, made her talk about herself and her painting, saying little about himself and dropping her home early, excusing himself by saying he had to work when he got back. When, a week late, he repeated the invitation she was pleased. On this occasion he had kissed her lightly on the cheek before he drove away. So she knew he was attracted to her, as she was to him, but there had been no opportunity to get beyond the cool terms which he apparently had laid down for their friendship. When she heard that he was to take her to The Waves for the weekend she was glad. Not only would she now know at least one person at the ball; perhaps she might also even discover what, if anything, lay behind that cool exterior.

At eleven o'clock precisely he drew up outside her flat in Clapham in his silver Saab convertible. When she opened the door to him he stood on the doorstep, in an open blue shirt and pale trousers, the first time she'd seen him without his dark lawyer's suit and formal tie. As they made their slow way through the traffic to reach the M3 motorway to the south-west, he asked her how well she knew Emerald Cunliffe and she told him she did not know her at all.

'I've been to dine at her London house and once or twice to The Waves for the weekend,' Patrick said.

Anna replied that she'd only been asked because her aunt's friend, Dolly Partiger from New England, was staying with Emerald.

'And I've only been asked because I'm the lawyer in a case against her enemy, News Universal,' he commented, smiling.

'Is that the newspaper?' Anna asked.

'Yes. The *Sunday News* printed a diary that was very rude about her.'

'Of course. I remember. Streatley sold it to them.' She paused. 'Godfrey Lacey works for them.'

'He has left News Universal,' Patrick observed.

The mention of Godfrey's name made him think about the Tancred case, for it was now not long before the trial and the case was never far from his mind. He wanted something from Godfrey, since Godfrey would know the inside story of how News Universal had come to publish the diary. If he could be persuaded to help, this could be important. He might be able to reveal if there was anything personal or malicious behind the publication and if Tancred's team could get evidence of this the consequences for the scale of damages would be considerable.

'Godfrey's got a job with a merchant bank,' he went on. 'He spends a lot of time abroad.'

Anna thought of the scene in Paris when she'd been so angry and disappointed over the portrait commission and had drunk too much. It was not an evening she cared to remember. She glanced up at Patrick beside her, at the set look around his mouth. There is more to him, she thought, than just his film star looks.

They drew up at The Waves in time for lunch. Anna was greeted enthusiastically by Dolly Partiger before they were introduced to the ambassador, without whom no party of Emerald's would be complete; not, this time, the Italian Ambassador who had returned to Rome, but the Egyptian Ambassador and his striking, if fat, wife. The others were Elizabeth Wheatley, an elderly and rather dowdy novelist, and her sad but distinguished-looking husband, Christopher; and the Solicitor-General and his pretty wife. Two other guests, the painter Sandro Marini and his wife, were not expected until later. In the afternoon Patrick took Anna for a walk. They were away for two hours. When they returned Anna, rather flushed, went to her room to change. As she lay in the bath she decided she'd changed her mind about Patrick Foxley. He was not only interesting; he was nicer than she'd thought. And not nearly so sure of himself as he made out. He'd talked about his visits to the States, to the country around Charleston in the south; and New York which, he said, somehow always disturbed him. 'Why?' she'd asked.

'I don't know. Probably because I've never been there for long enough. I found it threatening. Silly, isn't it?

At dinner he was placed next to her but he was monopolised by Emerald and she talked principally to the dinner neighbour on her other side, the painter Sandro Marini. During the meal she overheard Emerald enquiring about the Tancred case and when it was due to be heard. In a few weeks, Patrick said. If she liked he would arrange for his clerk to get her a place.

'I would. Provided you promise you'll win.'

'I cannot do that.' He laughed. 'But I'll do my best.'

As they rose from the table he turned to Anna. 'May I drive you to Wainscott?' he asked.

It was a warm evening in early May and at ten o'clock the party got into their cars. Patrick and Anna were the last to leave so that when they got to Wainscott and the car parker directed them to the lines of cars on the lawn, the rest of The Waves party were already in the house.

It was a large, rose-brick mansion, floodlit for the occasion with lines of *flambeaux* with naked fire, which lined the drive leading to the entrance steps. Patrick took her arm as they climbed the steps to the great front door and entered the hall, from which rose a double circular flight of stone stairs, which a queue of guests were slowly mounting to the first floor. As they did so, Sylvia fluttered down the stairs, pausing now and then to embrace someone, including Patrick, smiling at those she didn't know who included Anna. 'Forgive me, darlings, but I have to be in the hall. I must be there when he arrives.' And on she went down the stairs.

'Who is "he"?' Patrick asked the man on the steps immediately above them.

'Her lion for the evening,' he replied. 'The Prime Minister. Personally, I can't see why she's making such a fuss.'

Anna looked over the banister and saw Sylvia at the door, greeting the silver-haired figure whom she'd often seen on television or in the press.

'We'd better move on,' said Patrick and when they had reached the top of the stairs he steered her towards the sounds of music in the salon.

'As you can see, I am, alas, alone,' the Prime Minister said to Sylvia in the hall. 'Joan has one of her wretched headaches so you'll have to put up with me by myself.' He stopped and stared up at the double staircase. He turned to Sylvia. 'It was from that landing above those stairs that Augusta greeted George Byron on an April evening in 1813 when, I am certain, even if some of the scholars are not, they consummated their criminal connection.'

'You know so much,' Sylvia murmured, taking his arm.

There were only a few people still on the staircase for by now the bulk of the queue had reached the top and, with no hostess to receive them, had disappeared into the four great state rooms which stretched in pairs across the whole of the south front of the house. A few, among them two women, one in maroon silk flared trousers, were still on the landing, looking down as Sylvia and the Prime Minister approached the staircase.

'I shall have to disappoint you and decline to join in the Lancers or execute the tango,' he said as they slowly mounted. 'I have a badly inflamed knee.' He had an ebony cane in his left hand. 'But I couldn't resist the chance of seeing you, my dear – nor this fascinating house.'

The woman in trousers, the journalist Julia Priest, turned to her companion, the Under-Secretary at the Home Office. 'Your boss is looking very old.'

'I'm told he's hurt his knee,' Patsy Oxborrow replied.

When the Prime Minister and Sylvia reached the top and came near to where the two women were standing, Sylvia said, 'You know Patsy Oxborrow, of course.'

'Of course,' the Prime Minister said cheerfully, quite unable to place her but with a vague recollection of having seen her somewhere before. 'How are you, how are you? You're looking splendid, a most fetching dress.' But he didn't linger. 'My dear,' he said to Sylvia, 'you must take me to where I can sit. Not too near the band so that I can't hear what is being said but not too far from all the gaiety.' They disappeared through the door to the salon.

'He had no idea who I was,' Patsy Oxborrow said. 'And I've been in his government for three years.'

'He can't go on much longer,' said Julia Priest, giving her hand a squeeze. 'He must retire soon and then he'll join you in the Lords and see you every day.'

'Perhaps then he might recognise me,' Patsy mumbled sourly. A man had come from the further salon and was approaching them. She switched on her fixed, brilliant smile. 'Perry,' she said. 'How nice to see you here.'

Sylvia had settled the Prime Minister in a gilt arm-chair in a small ante-room with the door open to the main salon where they could see the crowd talking and drinking – and the crowd could see them. In the room beyond was the dancing, and the music could be heard above the hum of talk. A waiter brought a glass of champagne. The Prime Minister waved it away. 'Whisky and soda, if you please.'

Sylvia saw Emerald in the distance. 'There's Emerald Cunliffe,' she said, 'talking to Ogilvy Grant.' She made frantic gestures signalling them to come to join the Prime Ministerial circle.

'Of all the media magnates he is the most personable,'

the Prime Minister said. 'His newspaper, the *Telegram*, although misguided over politics, is at least reasonably respectable.'

As they approached, Sylvia called out, 'The Prime Minister has a bad leg and can't circulate, so I'm bringing people to him.'

'Gout?' Grant asked the Prime Minister jovially.

'A twisted knee and very painful,' the Prime Minister replied equally jovially. 'And you must not tease me just because you and your newspapers haven't the wit to support my administration.'

'Unlike Digby Price,' Grant said.

'That creature!' said Emerald. 'Don't mention his name, not in the presence of Sylvia and myself.'

'He is certainly a man who makes many enemies,' said the Prime Minister. 'But I never permit the serious business of personal relationships to interfere with the triviality of public affairs. As you know, Ogilvy, I don't read the newspapers. I'm the author or the actor who never reads his notices.'

'It's rumoured, Prime Minister, that in fact you read the press regularly. Is that true?'

'Of course it is. I can admit it in the privacy of the private house for I was brought up to rely on that what is said at a country house party will remain inviolably confidential. Or is that too old-fashioned? My official position for public consumption is that I don't read the newspapers.'

'I suppose we'll soon be reading about Richard Tancred's libel action against Price. It can't be long now before it comes to trial.'

This subject was disagreeable to the Prime Minister and he was glad to be able to avoid making any comment by the approach of others whom Sylvia had lassooed and had brought to the ante-room. Soon more chairs were drawn up and quite a circle surrounded the Prime Minister, to his unfeigned delight. 'Ah, Peregrine,' he said, 'I am glad to see a colleague relaxing. Ballroom dancing is excellent for the liver. Or it was in my youth.

I used to enjoy it greatly and I'm sorry that, alas, age and infirmity prevents me joining in tonight. So I must sit and bask in the company of my enchanting hostess and her fascinating guests in the surroundings of this remarkable house. I was speaking with Lady Sylvia about Augusta Leigh who, as I am sure you know, often stayed at Wainscott.'

Peregrine McClaren was accompanied by Patsy Oxborrow whom he'd removed from Julia Priest, to that lady's irritation. She now hovered behind them. 'You remember Patsy Oxborrow, Prime Minister. She answers for my department in the Lords.'

The Prime Minister waved a gracious hand. 'Delighted to see you here. What a charming gown. Have you just arrived?'

Patrick and Anna came off the dance floor to which he'd led her as soon as they had entered the salon. He had danced, holding her very close and talking little. He performed well and Anna had enjoyed it, and for half an hour they had not left the floor. Now he brought her a glass of champagne and they were looking for somewhere to sit when Sylvia pounced. 'You two,' she said. 'It's your turn for duty.'

She led them through the crowd into the ante-room. There was a chair empty next to the Prime Minister, just vacated by Peregrine McClaren. Patsy Oxborrow attempted to secure it but Sylvia directed Anna to sit. 'Prime Minister, this is—' Sylvia began and stopped, looking at Anna.

'Anna James,' Anna said, 'from the States.'

'James.' The Prime Minister smiled with pleasure. 'From the States. You couldn't be his granddaughter as Henry was not that kind of man. A great niece? A cousin?'

'No relation,' Anna said, laughing. 'I'm sorry to disappoint you.'

'It would be impossible to be disappointed by you, my dear. But your namesake was a strange creature, was he not? He wrote about Trollope, you know, that

Anthony Trollope was at times vulgar. I suppose he was, perhaps in the early books. Do you read Trollope?'

'I do. My favourite is *The Warden*.'

'A failure when it was first published. Not until *Barchester Towers* had set the scene was *The Warden* acknowledged as the masterpiece that you, my dear, so rightly recognise.' He looked up at Patrick Foxley who was standing behind Anna's chair. 'Your dancing partner?' The Prime Minister took Anna's hand, patted it and held it. 'You make a fine couple,' he said.

'This is Patrick Foxley, Prime Minister,' said Sylvia. 'He's the QC representing your former colleague, Richard Tancred in his libel case against News Universal.'

The Prime Minister dropped Anna's hand sharply and his eyes became even more hooded than normal. He was not pleased to be reminded once again of the Tancred libel case. 'Ah, yes,' he said. 'A most unhappy business. Business usually gets unhappy when it gets into the hands of you legal gentlemen.'

It was Anna who replied, surprising herself by her fierceness, 'It's the legal gentlemen who often save people's skins. That awful newspaper is wicked in what it publishes about people.'

'Quite so, quite so,' the Prime Minister replied. He turned to Sylvia. 'My dear, I fear the time approaches when I must depart. But before I do, perhaps you'd permit me to walk through the salon among the remainder of your guests? And if I may, I should like to see the small green salon where I suspect Augusta first surrendered.' He got to his feet and took Sylvia's arm. Without a glance back at where Anna was still seated in the chair next to that which he had just vacated and equally pointedly ignoring Patrick Foxley, the Prime Minister and Sylvia left the ante-room.

Anna rose.

'Let's dance again,' Patrick said.

On the floor Dolly was dancing excitedly with Emerald's painter, Sandro Marini. She waved at Anna and laughed; and Anna remembered the ball at Oldhaven when Dolly had made a spectacle of herself dancing with Clarissa Stoneley's gigolo and caused Clarissa to get so cross. That was before the old man had been taken ill. If he had not, she thought, I would never have been here. She looked up at Patrick and smiled.

After five minutes he led her back again into the salon and then, with glasses of champagne in their hands, they wandered down the stairs and on to the terrace at the south façade. It was a velvet late-May night, a freak, early-summer night. They leant on the stone balustrade overlooking the rose garden. 'England at it's rare best,' he said. 'It's very romantic.'

'It's because everything is so old,' she replied, turning and looking back at the rose brick of the house behind them lit by the floodlights. 'Where I was brought up, or at least where I used to visit, the houses, some as large as this, were all so much younger.'

He took her glass and put it and his own on a white iron table. 'Let's walk in the rose garden,' he suggested.

They descended the stone steps, her arm through his. When they had turned a corner he stooped, broke off a white flower and handed it to her. She put it to her face, inhaling the scent. He took her wrist and gently moved it aside from her face. With his other hand he tipped up her chin, bent and kissed her. She had known he would; and she had wanted him to. He put his arms round her and held her against him. For some time they stood there; then she broke away and they walked once more, stopping every now and then to embrace. 'Let's dance again,' she said. And she danced with the flower in her hand. When they finally left the floor there was no sign of their party. They had left for The Waves long ago.

It was three in the morning before they went to his car, now standing almost alone in the empty paddock. 'Shall I lower the roof?' he asked. 'Or will you be cold?'

She shook her head.

He drove with one hand on the wheel, the other clasping hers. Soon she lowered her head on to his shoulder. They got into the house as they had been directed, through the side door. On tiptoe they crossed the hall and walked up the stairs to her room. Outside her door he paused, looking at her, but she took his hand and led him inside.

She was surprised by the gentleness of his lovemaking, the time he took before he was above her and then the look of wonder and triumph at the moment of culmination. When eventually he lay on his back beside her, she turned on her side towards him, her chin in one hand, looking down at him. 'You are a strange man,' she said.

'Why do you say that?'

'You're not quite what you look.'

'None of us is.'

'Why did you say that New York disturbed you?' she asked.

'It alarmed me,' he replied.

'You don't look like a man who's easily alarmed.'

'Don't I? But I am, by quite a lot.'

'Such as?'

'Things that wouldn't frighten other people.'

'What things?'

'I get nerves, especially over my work. Each time I go into court I feel ill. If you saw me you wouldn't think it. At least, I hope you wouldn't.'

'In every case? Or just the important cases?'

'Usually the big cases.'

'The case against the newspaper will be a big case?'

'It will. I thought it was going to be my big chance. But it's not turning out as I expected.'

'Do you think you'll win?'

He sat up. 'I'm up against Mordecai Ledbury and he's very formidable. And my client, Richard Tancred, is—' He broke off, then went on, 'If you think I'm strange, you should meet Richard Tancred!'

'What's so strange about him?'

He lay back again. 'I'm not sure what to make of him. He's very hard to fathom. And he's not making it easy for me. He's taken complete control of how the case is to be run.'

'Should you let him?'

'I can't stop him. Either I let him, or I hand back my brief. But I don't want to do that. It's still an important case, a good case to be in. I have the feeling there's much more to the whole story than he's telling me.'

'Does that matter?'

'It makes it very difficult for his advocate. As a result I'm very uncertain about my role.'

'When I first met you,' she said. 'I imagined you were very sure of yourself. That's the impression you give.'

'It's an act.'

'You were sure enough of yourself to make love to me. Was that an act?'

He pulled her towards him. 'No, no, no,' he said. 'Of course not.'

Next day the party from Wainscott descended upon The Waves for lunch. When it came to seating people around the lunch table, Emerald said to Anna, 'I'm removing you from that young man.' She looked knowingly at her, almost jealously, Anna thought. 'You spent quite enough time with him last night, glued together on the dance floor.'

So at lunch Patrick was between the Egyptian Ambassadress and Sylvia. Before lunch he had been cross-examined by Dolly Partiger. 'Are you married, young man?' Dolly had begun.

He smiled and shook his head.

'That's something,' she went on. 'I have to report to Anna's aunt on how she's behaving.'

'You must report that she's behaving beautifully.'

'A lawyer's answer. You are a lawyer, aren't you?'

'I am.'

'Successful?'

'Fairly.'

'The only lawyers I've known are very grasping and very lecherous. Are you like that?'

'Of course.' He caught Anna's eye across the room. Dolly saw it. So that's it, she thought.

Sylvia asked him about the progress of the Tancred case.

'It's due to come on later in July,' he replied.

'And will you win?' What Anna had asked a few hours earlier.

'We hope to. But it will not be easy. Do you know Richard Tancred?'

'I've met him. I don't know him. You have that false friend of ours, Mordecai Ledbury, against you,' Sybil said. 'But you told me he's not what he was.'

'If I did, that was rather brash of me. It's not wise to underestimate Mordecai.'

'But you have right on your side,' Sybil concluded.

'In the law courts you often need more than that. And one never knows what Digby Price and his people will come up with.'

'Will Oscar Sleaven play any part?'

He looked at her. 'I really shouldn't say anything about the case.'

Later in the afternoon Patrick drove Anna back to London.

They made love again in her bedroom in the flat in Clapham.

Chapter Twelve

It was early June and Goodbody was in his office in Lincoln's Inn Fields when a large package, in a jiffy bag postmarked London E1, was brought to him by his chief clerk. Pasted on the package was a label in typescript: 'Personal and Confidential. To be opened only by Mr Oliver Goodbody.' Mystified, Goodbody laid it on his desk and for a time hesitated before opening it, thinking of stories about unsolicited packets and letter bombs. But when he did bring himself to do it he found that, although it did not contain actual explosives, the contents in their own way were explosive enough. Waite's 'smoking pistol', he thought excitedly to himself. Ten minutes later he was in a cab.

Spenser was on the telephone when Goodbody arrived. He waved a hand and pointed to the mustard-coloured leather sofa at the end of the office. It was a pleasant room, except for the hideous colour of the leather sofa and chairs. As Goodbody lowered himself on to the sofa and laid his briefcase on the low glass table in front of him, he glanced up at the prints on the walls, a series of architectural drawings, rather fine, he thought, tasteful decoration for an office. He wondered who was responsible for hanging them. Not Spenser, of that he was certain.

Spenser replaced the receiver and came to sit in an armchair of matching yellow leather opposite Goodbody.

'I have received a package through the post,' Goodbody began, opening his briefcase, 'addressed to me, only to be opened by me. It contained' – he looked hard at Spenser – 'the evidence we need.' He remembered his first meeting with the man. He'd only been hired as bait to catch Ledbury. Now it was he who was producing the evidence that could be decisive and he was determined to make the most of it.

Spenser leant forward in his chair, his eyes fixed on Goodbody's hands as the latter took a bundle of documents from his briefcase.

'With these,' Goodbody went on, 'we can now go into court and prove Tancred was corrupt.' He tapped the bundle with the flat of his hand.

Spenser brushed aside Goodbody's hand in his eagerness and, pushing his horn-rimmed spectacles up to his brow, held the documents close to his eyes.

'No covering letter, no indication of who sent them,' Goodbody added.

There was silence as Spenser turned page after page. Then he sat back and gave a great sigh of satisfaction. 'Only someone with access to Tancred's most private and personal affairs could have got hold of these,' he said. They exchanged glances but neither man said more.

Together they went to see Mordecai Ledbury in Albany and Goodbody laid out the documents triumphantly on the dining table.

After a few minutes Mordecai grunted and closed the file. 'At last, at last.'

'This will make the Chairman's day,' Spenser said.

'And so it should,' Goodbody agreed.

As it happened, on that same evening Digby Price flew into London from Paris. He had been invited to see the Prime Minister at Downing Street but on the way he called in at the newspaper offices and spent two hours with Spenser who was busy copying the documents Goodbody had received. For once he did not visit the editorial floors to bully the staff and when Spenser saw him off in the car he was smiling grimly.

As instructed, he entered the Cabinet offices through the door in Whitehall at 5.55 p.m. A private secretary led him through the connecting door into No. 10. He was not kept waiting but was ushered up the staircase lined with the photographs of the PM's predecessors and into the small study.

'Mr Price,' the PM greeted him warmly. 'A whisky and soda?' He poured the drinks from a side table and waved Price to a chair. 'The last time we met,' he went on, 'you were concerned lest two of my ministers took legal action against your company. In my thirty years of public life I have always told colleagues that they must ignore what is said or written about them in the public prints. Insult is one of the penalties of public service, but it has to be put in the balance against the prizes and privileges.' He sipped his whisky. 'Unless, of course, what is written or said is sheer make-believe about their private life.' He paused again. 'You indicated that you'd welcome any influence I might have to dissuade them from going to law.'

Price nodded.

'I was glad to be able to do what you asked,' the Prime Minister continued.

'I thank you for it. On that occasion I also thought it right to warn you, Prime Minister, of parts of the diary that were not published,' Price reminded him.

'So you did.' The Prime Minister examined his long, graceful fingers in his lap before he went on, speaking quietly, almost to himself, 'Give me a grain of truth, said John Wilkes, and I will mix it up with a great mass of falsehood so that no chemist will ever be able to separate them.' Price remained silent. 'An untrue personal canard is a terrible thing,' said the Prime Minister. He lounged back in his chair. 'You reside in France, I believe?'

'I do.'

'The French think, and behave, rather differently from

us. I am reminded, Mr Price, of Madame Caillaux who shot an editor who had disparaged her husband, the French Finance Minister.' The Prime Minister smiled sadly. 'Only an editor, mind you, Mr Price, not a proprietor, but as one of my predecessors, Stanley Baldwin, said, "Not the sort of support you want from a wife."'

Digby Price grunted and the Prime Minister watched him closely, as he had at Chequers, hiding once again his distaste with a white hand delicately raised to his brow. 'Richard Tancred, of course, decided to take things into his own hands. You expected that, I understand?'

'And welcomed it. Now I shall destroy him.'

'I told him how ill-advised he was to go to law. One should make it a rule to avoid lawyers – while always, as Lord Melbourne had it, remaining on good terms with them.' The Prime Minister waved his hand. 'However, let us move on to the reason why I asked you to visit me this afternoon. I have in mind, Mr Price, submitting your name to the Sovereign for appointment to a life barony in the New Year Honours list. I must confess that a peerage nowadays is not what it was, for the company in the Lords is not what it was, but in your case a barony would acknowledge your service to the country and—'

Price interrupted him. 'No. I don't hold with any of that twaddle and I don't live in this country. I live in Paris.'

'Ah, yes,' the PM said. 'Paris, the scene of the Terror. The Parisians are an excitable people.' He paused, then added, 'A knighthood, perhaps?'

Price smiled grimly. 'No. Nothing. It's all nonsense.'

The Prime Minister smiled in return, disguising his disappointment. But at least he'd made the offer. 'You may be right. To quote one of my predecessors once again, Lord Melbourne said of the Garter that there's no damned merit to it. But some people enjoy it. At any rate I trust you will appreciate that the offer was intended to demonstrate my genuine esteem for your public work and your place in—'

Again Price interrupted. 'News Universal will continue to support your administration, all the more enthusiastically now that Richard Tancred has left it.' He rose. 'You and I, Prime Minister, we understand each other, and that's good. I like that. We won't make trouble for each other, will we? Although we both know we could – if we wanted, don't we?' He grinned at the Prime Minister, slouched in his chair. 'A nice touch, the lordship offer, but it's not for me.' He made as if to go but then turned back and smiled another of his grim, humourless smiles. 'But see your lady don't shoot me, won't you?'

Alan Prentice showed Digby Price downstairs and out through the Cabinet offices to where his car was waiting in Whitehall.

When he reappeared the Prime Minister sighed. 'That is a most unpleasant man. The more I see of him, the more unpleasant I think him.'

'And he owns some very unpleasant newspapers, Prime Minister.'

'So they tell me. As you know, I don't read them, except when you force me to. However, he assures me that he intends to continue to support the present policies of Her Majesty's Government, more especially now that the former Minister for Defence Procurement has gone. He was also very confident that he would make our former colleague regret that he is suing.'

'Mr Price believes he will win?'

'He appears to.'

'That must mean, sir, that he thinks he can prove the former Minister for Defence Procurement was corrupt, which could be a grave reflection upon the reputation of your administration.'

'I am aware of that, Alan. I can only pray that in the end the case may never come to court, that one or other may see sense and withdraw. That, at any rate, is my hope.' He rose from his chair. 'Now, as to my weekend plans. I have to pay another visit to my constituency.'

'Of course, Prime Minister.'

'I plan to visit this Saturday, arriving in the early afternoon. I shall go on from there to Chequers. Warn, if you please, my constituency.' Then, as Alan Prentice was leaving the room, the Prime Minister added as if it were an afterthought, which it certainly was not, 'Perhaps you should also warn Mrs Wills, as tea might be agreeable.'

Was it bearable, he thought as he climbed the stairs to the small flat, to go on with this performance week after week, when he could retire with his books to his comfortable library in his house in Somerset? No more performances, no more attendance on the whims of fools. Peace, quiet, leisure. He'd be especially glad to be done with his Cabinet colleagues and their intrigues. The hidden dagger in politics, Robbie Bruce Lockhart had said, was to remember that the friend of today was the enemy of tomorrow. He himself had been wielding the dagger very effectively for thirty years. It was time to give it up. But, as he had thought so many times since Price's visit to Chequers, he did not wish to leave with the whiff of scandal about him.

As he settled down in his armchair in the flat and picked up *The Last Chronicle of Barset*, he pondered on what he'd miss in retirement. If anything, he thought with a smile, it would be the captive audience that had been obliged to listen to his soliloquies. But then, he reflected, the world is not altogether unamused by tales of times past and battles long ago. So *La commedia* might not be altogether *finita*. He laid his book in his lap. But Penny Wills would. There'd be no excuse to visit her after his retirement to Somerset. He would no longer be able to see much, if anything, of her.

Penny Wills! It had been a long romance, starting when he had first been elected. To begin with it had been passionate. Aidan, dear Aidan, he reflected complacently, dear Aidan had been very good, very good indeed. Then, as the years passed, so had passed the hurly-burly of Penny's sofa and it had become . . . comfortable. That was it exactly. She had been a great comfort, so different from the blue-blooded, tweed-garmented Joan, smelling, not altogether disagreeably, of lavender and garden loam. Penny had been a romp: warm, vulgar, sensual and wholly delightful. And loyal. That was rare nowadays. Even when he retired she could, if she wished, make money. The ex-PM's mistress. Her story. The newspapers would buy it and print it, quoting extracts from his speeches to the Party Conference on marriage and morality. But Penny would never betray him, not loyal Penny. So the loss of her would be the only real loss when he went, as soon he would.

But not quite yet. The court case might never come to trial. Then it might all blow over. A new political crisis would arrive, the Richmond diary would be forgotten and he could depart with grace. So long as Price kept his word and Penny stayed loyal. Unless, of course, Richard Tancred defeated Price in the courts. Then Price's malevolence might have no bounds.

Chapter Thirteen

When News Universal disclosed to Richard Tancred's lawyers, as they were obliged to do, the documents Goodbody had so mysteriously received, Tancred immediately returned to London. He made no secret of his departure from France, crossed under the Channel through the Tunnel, sped up the M20 and parked the Jaguar in the lock-up garage in Clapham. For a few hours thereafter the watchers lost him but later he was seen to arrive at his flat in Chelsea.

The following morning they saw him take a number 11 bus to Fleet Street and then walk to Patrick Foxley's chambers in Paper Buildings. He remained there for an hour and a half before he returned to Chelsea. He made some purchases in the King's Road, collected his car in Clapham and set out again for the Channel Tunnel on his way back to Pontaix. He'd been in England for less than twelve hours.

When Tancred departed from the conference in the Temple, he left all three of his lawyers, Patrick Foxley, the junior counsel Ian French, and Cranley Burrows, grave and uneasy.

'We do nothing, say nothing and leave it to them to prove their case,' said French at last, shaking his head.

Patrick rose from his desk. 'He's told us what he wants.'

'Will he get away with it?' French asked.

'He's relying on his performance in the witness box.'

'And that depends on Mordecai's cross-examination,' said Burrows quietly.

'All we can do is warn him,' said Patrick looking out of the window at the Temple garden far below. 'And that we have done. Now we must do as he instructs us.'

He could not conceal his disappointment. The case was not going to turn out as he had thought and hoped. It would not now be a battle royal between Mordecai, the veteran whose weapon was the bludgeon, and him whose weapon was the rapier. Because of what Tancred had laid down, all would now turn upon his client and his performance under cross-examination. And, worst of all, Tancred had not provided him, his counsel, with any explanation. He had simply declared that this was to be the strategy, these the tactics.

Patrick knew he could refuse to be used in such a way but that would mean withdrawing from the case – and this he would not do. He could not. It was still an important case to take part in. But when it came to the trial it would be Mordecai against Tancred. Only if Tancred survived that cross-examination might it later become Foxley against Price. If Tancred did not, if Mordecai triumphed, they would be finished.

Since Sylvia's dance in May Patrick had been seeing Anna regularly. He couldn't see enough of her. Anna knew that the case on which he had set such hopes was approaching and tried to dissuade him from taking her out so often, but he refused. 'Will you come to court?' he asked her.

'Of course, if you would like me to.'

'I would, very much.'

She laid her hand on his face. 'I couldn't stay away. I know how much it means to you. And as I watch I shall think of the angst under that icy exterior.'

'I'm not now very confident,' he admitted. 'News have got their hands on some pretty damning evidence and Tancred won't explain it, not even to me, his counsel.'

Perhaps he can't, she thought. And for the first time she, too, began to worry that he would lose and News Universal would win.

By now it was being widely rumoured around the Temple that the News people were supremely confident. Why, it was wondered, had Richard Tancred taken such a risk in suing News Universal? Presumably, it was said, because he had never suspected that News Universal would obtain the evidence against him. Tancred had gambled – and lost. He would not have been the first to do that. There were always those who believed they were smart enough to deceive the court and were eventually found out. Tancred was just another.

Lunching one day at the centre table in the Garrick Club, Patrick himself had been told by a journalist acquaintance that Digby Price was now telling everyone that he was going to strip Tancred of every penny he possessed and every shred of reputation. Then he'd call for the Director of Public Prosecution to prosecute and Tancred would end up in jail. 'Mind you, he'd better be right,' the journalist added, 'for word is also going around that the News Universal Group is pretty shaky. The *Telegram* is murdering them over circulation. If News is hit for heavy damages and costs that, with the blow to their prestige, could bring them down.'

'You can't be serious,' Patrick protested.

'I am. Before News got this new evidence there were rumours of influential investors selling stock.' He paused and chuckled. 'But even if News Universal goes down, Digby will be all right. Illegal diamonds, probably in South Africa.' The journalist pushed back his chair. 'But it won't come to that. The bookies are laying odds against Tancred. You're on to a loser, Patrick,' he said as he went to the desk to settle his bill.

*   *   *

Tancred heard the news on his car radio when he was fifteen kilometres short of the Tunnel on his way to London. It was BBC Radio 4 at midnight, thirty-six hours before the start of the trial. The car swerved violently to the right as he pulled it into a lay-by with a squeal of braking tyres. He turned up the volume and listened. When the announcer moved on to another item, he switched off the radio and sat silently in the dark, lit every now and then by the lights of the *camions* as they thundered past on their way to Calais. After half an hour he drove on.

Patrick was in the study of his flat when he heard the news, working on his note for his opening statement at the start of the trial. Earlier he had been with Anna but she had sent him home. 'The Italians', he'd grumbled, 'believe that sex before a game is good for their foot-ballers.'

'You're not an Italian.' She had kissed him and led him to the door.

He had got up from his desk, stretched and gone to the bedroom. He'd switched on the radio, Classic FM, Midnight Classics, while he undressed, music to take him to bed. Instead he got the news. He listened, standing rigid. Then he sank abruptly into a chair and he put his head in his hands.

Mordecai was asleep. He was woken by the telephone. 'Yes,' he growled angrily. 'Who is it?'

'It's Oliver. Sleaven is dead. I'm coming round.'

Mordecai greeted him in his pyjamas beneath his flamboyant black dressing gown. Goodbody thrust a paper into his hands. 'The PA report,' he said. 'Read it.' He flung himself into a chair.

Mordecai began to read. 'English couple die in Aca-pulco.'

'Couple?' he questioned, looking up at Goodbody.

'Read on,' Goodbody urged.

And Mordecai did, aloud.

In a luxury apartment just behind the famous Acapulco beach, the bodies of Oscar Sleaven and his wife, Ethel, have been discovered, dead of gunshot wounds. The servant found them when he came to work in the morning. An automatic pistol lay beside the bodies. There was no sign of any break-in and foul play is not suspected. The police say that the woman, Ethel Sleaven, died first with a shot to the heart that killed her instantaneously. Her husband, the police are confident, fired the shot. Oscar Sleaven had then put the barrel of the gun into his own mouth, pulled the trigger and blown off his head.

Mordecai lowered the newspaper. 'Go on,' said Goodbody.

Until eighteen months ago when he resigned, purportedly on the grounds of ill health, and left the country seeking, it was said, medical treatment, Oscar Sleaven was the Chairman of Sleaven Industries which, among its other activities, manufactured arms and equipment supplied to the Ministry of Defence. Since he left England for France, no one has known of his whereabouts. He and his wife disappeared from New York shortly after their arrival on a flight from Paris when, it was suggested by Mr Sebastian Sleaven, the brother of Mr Oscar Sleaven, Oscar Sleaven was to attend the Mayo or some other prestigious clinic for treatment. However, enquiries at the Mayo Clinic and other similar establishments have been met with a denial that any person of that name had been a patient at any of them.

It has now been ascertained that Oscar and Ethel Sleaven had come to Mexico from Rio in Brazil and had been living in a luxury flat in Acapulco for the past three months. Oscar Sleaven's next of kin, Sebastian Sleaven, is presently on his way to Mexico.

Oscar Sleaven is named in the proceedings in the libel action being brought by the former Minister for Defence Procurement, Richard Tancred, who is seeking damages from News Universal for allegations in the *Sunday News* that when he was a minister he was receiving money in exchange for favours granted to Sleaven Industries in respect of contracts for defence equipment. Oscar Sleaven denied this in a statement issued just after he left England. The case is due to be heard in the Law Courts in the Strand on 20 July.

Mordecai laid down the paper.

'He must have thought it better than prison,' said Goodbody grimly.

'Why the wife?' Mordecai asked softly. 'Why kill her?'

'Perhaps she didn't wish to live when she realised he was intending to kill himself? But the significance for us is that Tancred's co-conspirator has killed himself thirty-six hours before everything comes out in court.'

Mordecai nodded gravely.

Goodbody went on, 'Now you have what Waite describes as the "smoking gun". First the documents, then this suicide—'

'And murder,' said Mordecai quietly.

Goodbody got to his feet. 'I'll leave you.' He shook his head. 'If I brought you Tancred's confession, signed, sealed and witnessed, I don't believe it would satisfy you. I think you dislike Digby Price as much as he dislikes Tancred.'

'Price is my client and I shall do my best for him. But it's my job to keep a cool head,' Mordecai replied as he limped in front of Goodbody to the door. With his hand on the latch he said, 'It must have been something very grave to have driven Oscar Sleaven to do what he did.'

Goodbody stared at him, then shrugged his shoulders

and walked down the short path to the central alleyway. Mordecai watched him, before closing the door and returning to his drawing room. For several minutes he stood by the open window, before limping back to the bedroom and his bed.

Part Four

Chapter One

At the start of the Easter term that year Mr Justice Holyoak, the judge in charge of the jury list in civil actions to be tried in the Royal Courts of Justice in the Strand, fell ill. He would be away until the autumn. Normally actions in the civil divisions of the High Court were tried by judges sitting alone without a jury, and juries were only retained in cases affecting personal liberty, such as claims for false imprisonment or wrongful arrest by the police; and cases affecting reputation, namely libel cases. There were always many libel cases in the jury list each term but few ever came to trial. At some stage the parties settled.

The Lord Chief Justice now had to find another judge to preside over the civil jury list until Mr Justice Holyoak returned. Judicial business at the time was unusually brisk, especially in the provinces, while several judges were away from the courts presiding over official enquiries and he was hard pressed to find a replacement. Eventually he settled on Mr Justice Traynor. When the Chief told him, Jack Traynor complained that his experience with juries was limited to criminal cases in the north of England. Was the Chief certain he was the right man for the task?

The Chief was irritated. Traynor provided a neat solution to his difficulties. 'Juries', he replied testily, 'are all the same. What is needed is common sense.' He did not add 'and the ability to make the jury understand what you are saying'. Personally, he found Mr Justice Traynor's 'Geordie' or north-east accent so pronounced as to be, to his ears, sometimes almost unintelligible, but he reflected that those who served on juries might not. In any event there was no one else.

'I've never even appeared in a libel case as counsel,' Jack Traynor went on.

'Nor had I before I tried my first libel,' the Chief replied airily. 'In fact, I had never addressed a jury before I became a judge.' Indeed he had not. With a distinguished academic record and a Fellowship of All Souls, he had been marked out for early promotion to the Bench. After a few years he was appointed the Junior Counsel to the Treasury, 'the Treasury devil', as it was called, acting on behalf of government departments engaged in litigation. After six years in that post he had been made a judge of the High Court and, for the first time in his life, found himself in a court with a jury. When he summed up in the first criminal trial in which he'd ever taken part as either counsel or judge, the jurors had not the slightest idea what the clever gentleman on the bench was going on about, retired to their room shaking their heads and returned with a verdict quite contrary to what the clever judge thought was right. He was, however, soon plucked away from such mundane matters and appointed to the Court of Appeal where he could analyse and theorise about law to his heart's content. From there he had been made – a controversial appointment – Lord Chief Justice.

'You'll pick it up quickly enough,' the Chief went on. 'Most cases in the jury list settle, while the law of defamation is basically judge-made law. It's all in Gatley, an excellent textbook, and you'll get good help from the libel Bar. You'll do it splendidly.'

In his room a dispirited Mr Justice Traynor sent for the clerk of the civil jury list to bring him the printed jury list for the forthcoming term. The clerk produced the list and immediately pointed to the case '*Rt Hon Richard Tancred v. News Universal, Ms Shirley Eaton (editor of the* Sunday News) *and Digby Price*.' 'This is a libel action set down to last five working days, due to commence on 20 July,' the clerk of the jury list said. 'It will be the only case in the list likely to "stand up". All the others would almost certainly·settle.' He paused, then added, 'It is a case that will undoubtedly attract great public interest. The claimant used to be a Cabinet minister and the defendants are the publishers of the *Sunday News*.'

'What is the libel?' asked the judge.

'The newspaper claims that the plaintiff was taking bribes,' the clerk said with satisfaction. He was not a supporter of the government in which Tancred had served and he and his wife were regular readers of the *Sunday News*, which they much enjoyed.

The following Sunday, on his Sunday morning walk, Jack Traynor bought a copy of the *Sunday News*. When he had glanced at it he quickly thrust it into a dustbin. His sister Agnes would not have been amused to have him bring a newspaper into the house featuring a gang rape on a housing estate and the reflections of a transsexual drum major.

But as he marched home up the hill from the village, he gloomily reflected that his very first libel case was to be an action between a politician, probably corrupt, and a scandal rag. No wonder there would be public interest. In his room on the following day he told his personal clerk to find out who were the counsel retained in '*Tancred v. News Universal*'. In the evening his clerk reported. Counsel for Richard Tancred was Patrick Foxley QC and Mordecai Ledbury QC would act for the newspaper. The judge put his head in his hands and groaned. The too-clever-by-half Foxley and the offensive Ledbury. The prospect of what lay before him filled him with dread.

Chapter Two

The crowd queuing or struggling to get into the court
was immense. All London seemed anxious to attend
what the press were calling the libel case of the decade.
The suicide of Oscar Sleaven in Acapulco less than two
days before the start of the trial had made sure that
interest would be intense. Even before the sensational
news from Mexico, Digby Price had seen to it that News
Universal's publications had kept the forthcoming trial
well before the attention of the public. When it was
reported that Oscar Sleaven had killed himself and mur-
dered his wife, News headlines had whipped up the
story into a frenzy.

His rivals, the Telegram group, were naturally,
anxious to see News Universal lose – and crippled by a
vast award of damages. Over the previous months the
Telegram had printed several paragraphs about Richard
Tancred, his talents and record, describing him as the
most successful minister in the present administration,
referring to him as the Prime Minister-Who-Never-Was,
the man whose glittering political career had been
destroyed by the *Sunday News*. At the announcement of
Oscar Sleaven' s death the *Telegram*'s reaction was more
muted, but between them the two newspaper groups
with the largest circulation in the United Kingdom had
made sure that the Tancred libel case was more than
merely the cause of an ex-minister attempting to vindi-
cate his reputation in the courts. It had become yet
another battle in the long-running war between the
Telegram group and News Universal.

As the queue for places in the public gallery lengthened, a mass of people and photographers gathered around the railing of the forecourt of the Royal Courts of Justice in the Strand to await the arrival of the principal actors in the drama. Spenser had made sure that a crowd of supporters were stationed at the entrance to the Law Courts to acclaim Digby Price when he arrived. The *Telegram* management had also organised a claque and when Price stepped out of his stretch limousine with the darkened windows, they jeered loudly. But the cheers of the News Universal contingent drowned the jeers. Price stood in the forecourt, waving gaily and chatting to his supporters, before he gestured at those who were jeering him and disappeared into the central hall. A reverse cheer and counter-cheer greeted Tancred, who arrived in a taxi with his solicitor, Cranley Burrows. He acknowledged neither cheer nor counter-cheer. He spoke to no one and, without a single glance to right or left, ascended the steps into the building.

Inside the court, the gallery in the balcony was soon filled and many were turned away. Below, in the body of the court, the rows of seats for witnesses and representatives of the parties were also filled with privileged spectators who had obtained their places by being escorted to them by the clerks of counsel engaged in the case. The front row nearest the raised judge's bench was reserved for the actual parties and their respective solicitors, the second for the QCs on both sides and the third for the junior barristers. Into this row, however, there had also crowded briefless barristers in their pristine white wigs who had come to listen to what was forecast as the most exciting libel case in recent years and which, they hoped, would provide some days of excellent forensic sport.

Tancred and Burrows made their way across the central hall up the stone stairs along the corridor and took their places on the left side of the court facing the judge's bench. In his grey suit, white shirt and dark tie, Tancred cut a distinguished figure but with his mottled complexion and dark hair he looked foreign next to the fresh-faced, auburn-haired Cranley Burrows. Some in the gallery leant dangerously over the rail to look at the scene below until ordered by the usher to resume their seats as Tancred, with an air of indifference and ease, chatted to Cranley above the noise and clatter of the people taking their seats behind them.

Patrick Foxley QC and his junior, Ian French, slipped into their respective rows and Patrick leant forward to join in the talk between Tancred and Burrows. The legal team for the claimant was now in position. However, the comparable places on the right of the court reserved for the newspaper's lawyers remained empty. There was no sign of them or of any of News Universal's senior executives when the prospective jurors filed into the jury box. Of the jury, seven were men, one of whom was a large black man whose bulk made him uncomfortably squashed in his seat; one stood out by his smart appearance, an elderly, military-looking man in a dark-blue blazer with brass buttons; and one, red-faced and tieless, was soon talking loudly to anyone who cared to listen. Five were women, two middle-aged, one a decided and bewildered-looking spinster and two who might be young mothers. The fifth was a young, light-skinned Asian in a bright-orange sari. When she was settled in her seat she stared interestedly around the court, a half-smile on her face.

Patrick stood to arrange his papers on the desk in front of him, then turned and faced into the body of the court. His legal uniform of grey wig, immaculately starched wing collar and linen bands, and black silk's gown over his well-cut swallow-tailed black court coat suited him. His eye settled on the person he'd been looking for – Anna James, sitting four rows behind him. She was hatless, the recalcitrant lock of black hair as ever falling in front of her eyes, dressed simply in a white shirt above dark, close-fitting trousers. Patrick smiled and she grinned back, raising her eyebrows, puckering her lips and indicating how quaint she found the whole scene in the court and the sight of Patrick in a wig. She saw, however, that his face was pale and he looked drawn and strained. She knew how greatly the news of the death of Oscar Sleaven two days ago had unsettled him. 'It's a terrible blow,' he'd told Anna; and she knew that now he was really anxious. She, too, feared that the case, difficult as it had been, was slipping away beyond hope of retrieval. His anxiety had made her all the more determined to be with him in court.

Thomas, Patrick's clerk, had taken her to her privileged place. With her had come Emerald Cunliffe and Sybil Benedict, also the recipients of Patrick's favour, both hoping to witness the defeat and downfall of Digby Price and the discomfiture of their former friend, Mordecai Ledbury. Both were dressed in smart, well-cut linen suits but, as had been decided after prolonged debate, hatless. When Thomas had conducted the three across Fleet Street through the mob at the forecourt entrance, they had been greeted by a non-partisan cheer that Emerald and Sybil enjoyed. The crowd, of course, had recognised none of them.

When Patrick turned to smile at Anna there was as yet no sight of those whose longed-for humiliation Emerald and Sybil had come to witness. Their places were still empty. News Universal was at present represented only by Wilson, Price's PA, and Spenser's secretary who had been placed at the back of the court. But their principals were not far away; they were in a conference room in the corridor behind the court.

Mordecai was seated at a small table, his wig, blackened by wear and age, askew on his large head and his white linen bands already crumpled beneath his drooping wing collar. Beside him stood Walter Morrison, his junior counsel, a plump, good-humoured man with a red face, in his late thirties; next to him was Oliver Goodbody looking, Walter thought, more like an archbishop in mufti than usual. Behind them stood Waite in his baggy suit, holding in his hand a large folder, trying to appear important but only succeeding in looking, to Walter at least, like a bookies' clerk. He was flanked by

Spenser, as neat and tidy as ever. They were waiting for Digby Price.

The door was flung open and he burst into the room. 'Mexico,' he announced triumphantly. 'What about that!'

Mordecai nodded gravely. 'As I said on the telephone, it could be very significant.'

'Significant? It's devastating! One crook down. One to go.'

'We have two minutes,' Goodbody said hastily, glancing at his watch. 'The judge will take his place in exactly two minutes.'

'He'll have to wait,' Mordecai growled. He pushed back his chair and addressed Spenser. 'I want to be quite clear about this. Did you or did you not receive a memorandum written by Lacey on his return from Paris after the decision had been taken to publish?'

'I have no recollection of receiving any such memorandum. I've gone through all the files and I can find none.'

'You will swear to that?'

'In court? In evidence?' Spenser asked nervously.

'Of course, from the witness box. Will you swear you never received any memorandum from Lacey?'

'If that is necessary, I shall.'

'When did the request come from the other side for us to produce this memorandum?' Mordecai asked Goodbody.

'Last evening. No one knew anything about it. We immediately instituted a search of the files.'

'All I can repeat', said Spenser, 'is that I saw no memorandum from Lacey.'

Mordecai's clerk, Adams, came into the room and announced loudly, 'The judge is taking his seat.'

'What's all the bother about this memorandum?' Price asked.

Mordecai rose. 'I anticipate they'll apply to call Lacey to say that he wrote a memorandum when he got back from Paris and that it referred to what you said at the time when you decided to publish. I assume it will refer to your determination to expose Tancred.'

'Correct. And I have.'

Mordecai looked at him. 'It is this evidence they need for punitive damages. To demonstrate your malice.'

Price laughed. 'Malice, you call it? Balls. You mean my determination to expose a crook.'

Mordecai walked towards the door.

Digby Price caught him by the arm. 'Remember, Ledbury,' he said. 'You know how I want the case handled.'

Mordecai looked at Price's hand on his arm. Price dropped it. 'I remember the riding instructions,' Mordecai said. 'And when it's all over, I hope you will too.'

In the court the door behind the bench opened and Mr Justice Traynor, in his bobbed wig and blue gown crossed by a scarlet sash, entered. This coincided with the throwing open of the side door in the body of the court and the passage of Mordecai, limping noisily to his place, followed by Goodbody and Digby Price. The judge reached his place first. He stood waiting, looking grim as Mordecai struggled into his row, dropping one of his sticks with a clatter and acknowledging the judge with only a slight droop of his head. The judge took his seat and, when all in the court had resumed theirs, Mordecai subsided into his with a resounding crash. Spenser slipped into a place behind junior counsel. In front of Mordecai were Oliver Goodbody and Digby Price.

Mr Justice Traynor surveyed the crowded court. It was, as he had expected, full to overflowing, every seat taken and even the side aisles to the swing doors blocked now by spectator barristers' and solicitors' clerks. Trust Ledbury to stage an entrance and keep him waiting, he thought. But he'd not start a row. Not now. He knew there'd be plenty of occasions for that in the days that lay ahead. He forced himself to look genial, remembering he had to make his mark with the jury as his clerk placed his notebook on the desk in front of him and, with this assumed air of benignity that he did not feel concealing the twinge of apprehension, he prepared for the ordeal – his first libel trial with a jury, assisted, if that was the right word, by counsel he could not abide.

The associate from his place directly beneath the judge's dais turned to him. He nodded and the associate turned back to face the court and announced, 'Tancred against News Universal and Others.'

The usher proceeded to swear in the jury. There were no objections from counsel. One after the other the jurymen and women took the oath, holding the testament in their right hands, except for two men and one young woman who elected to make an affirmation. The judge noted that the young Asian woman had sworn on the Bible. For a moment he considered asking her if she realised what she had done but soon thought better of it. Why shouldn't she be a Christian?

The speed and lack of fuss with which the jury had been selected and its members accepted without objection from counsel, surprised Anna James. In the States she knew that jury selection was a lengthy and important part of a trial. She'd read of the woman in California who was paid enormous fees to assess prospective jurors on their appearance and advise on those to accept or reject. So she was taken aback by the swiftness with which the jury were assembled and sworn without objection or question from counsel, even though Patrick had told her that the so-called *voir dire* played little part in the English courts. 'It is said', he had told her jokingly, 'that with us the case begins when the jury is sworn. With you, the case is over.' Even so, she had expected some exchanges. Instead, the jury had filed into the box and taken the oath or affirmed and no one had said a word.

'Aye, Mr Foxley,' said the judge.

Patrick rose. 'Before I open the case to the jury,' he began, 'I should tell Your Lordship that it came to the attention of myself and my solicitors yesterday that there existed a relevant memorandum, which had not been disclosed by the defendants. When this was raised with the defendants they denied any such memorandum existed. Accordingly I shall be applying to Your Lordship to permit the service out of time of a witness statement by a witness I shall call who will prove the existence of the memorandum and its contents. That statement is presently being prepared and I shall raise it at the appropriate time—'

'Which is not, I fancy,' interrupted the judge, 'now.'

'No', Patrick replied, 'but I thought it right to say this in the presence of my learned friend, so that he and his instructing solicitor and clients may not be taken by surprise.'

Mordecai rumbled to his feet. 'Nothing that happens in these courts ever surprises me and I have been practising in them for over thirty years at a time when my friend was hardly out of short pants.'

Patrick flushed. 'There is no call to be personally offensive,' he expostulated.

'A joke, a statement of fact. My friend should not be so touchy.' Mordecai turned to the judge. 'I'll have something more to say about this when the appropriate time comes.' Before the judge could reply he had clattered back into his seat.

'Then we'd better await the appropriate moment,' the judge said, trying to sound good-humoured. He spoke with his pronounced Geordie burr, which the spinster-looking middle-aged woman on the jury, who lived in Surbiton and who had never in her life been further north than Watford, found difficult to understand.

'The name of the witness I wish to call', Patrick went on, 'is—'

'I know who it is,' growled Mordecai.

'The name of the witness I shall ask leave to call', Patrick repeated coldly, 'is Godfrey Lacey, a former employee of the defendants.'

'Aye, aye, Mr Foxley. You've had your say about that

and we'll consider it when you've submitted the witness statement. Now perhaps you will get on with it and open your case to the jury.' Squabbling already, Jack Traynor thought. Roody prima donnas!

When Patrick spoke the name Godfrey Lacey none of the defendants' team was surprised; they had known the application would at some time be made. To others in the court the name meant nothing. It did, however, to Anna. Godfrey had drifted from her life. The memory of that evening in Paris, of how she had drunk too much in the restaurant and the nightclub after her rage over the portrait commission still embarrassed her. She had not told Patrick what had happened. After she'd moved to Clapham, Godfrey had telephoned once, to ask if she was all right but really to tell her that he'd left News Universal. She knew that he had, because Patrick had told her when they were driving down to The Waves, and she had not heard from Godfrey again. When she heard Patrick announce that he proposed calling Godfrey as a witness – which meant a witness against his old employers, News Universal – she wondered what it was that Godfrey could say.

Patrick, tall and elegant, now faced the jury to make his opening statement. He began by reminding them of Richard Tancred's prominent position in public life and he recited the details of his client's distinguished career. Then he turned to Francis Richmond, referring to Richmond's 'insignificant' achievements in literary circles and his snobbish delight in the social world, which he masked by his malicious and feline comments on those who thought they were his friends. When he read aloud some of the extracts from the diary to illustrate this Emerald, in the row at the back of the court, stretched out her hand and took Sylvia's.

'It may have been,' Patrick went on, 'indeed one hopes it was, the diarist's intention that what he was writing would never be read. We do not know. All we do know is that the diary was sold in its entirety to News Universal by Richmond's literary executor and extracts were published in the *Sunday News*. I shall read some of them to you so that you may assess the kind of man the diarist was from what he wrote. It will be for you to judge what reliance you can put on the accuracy of his observations and the validity of his judgements.'

Then his tone changed and he became grave. 'I turn now', he said, 'to those extracts which refer to Richmond's reports of sightings of Richard Tancred, the Minister for Defence Procurement, in the company of an industrialist, Oscar Sleaven, whose company was at that time engaged in negotiating contracts with Richard Tancred's ministry, contracts which involved millions of public money.' Patrick read the entries in the diary about the meetings between the two men and the diarist's dark hints at the strange relationship between them. 'In these extracts,' he declared, 'you may have little doubt that Francis Richmond was making plain to any who read his diary his suspicion that something improper was going on between the Minister for Defence Procurement and the industrialist.'

It was these references, published in the *Sunday News*, Patrick told the jury, that amounted to the libel; they were 'the words complained of' because they raised the 'innuendo' that they meant nothing less than that there existed an improper, a corrupt financial arrangement between Richard Tancred, the Minister, and Sleaven, the businessman. Those passages were intended to create the impression that Richard Tancred was favouring his friend Sleaven in the award of contracts and that Richard Tancred, to use common jargon, was getting a 'back-hander', 'a cut', a commission on the profits Sleaven received out of contracts arranged with Tancred's ministry.

Here Patrick paused, looking steadily at the jury. Then he went on, 'The accusation is totally and utterly false. There was no such corrupt arrangement between the two whatsoever; not a penny was ever demanded by Richard Tancred, not a penny was ever offered by Oscar

Sleaven in respect of any contract entered into between Sleaven Industries and the Ministry for Defence Procurement. The contracts that were agreed between the Ministry and Sleaven Industries were decided in the same manner as every other contract with a department of state – upon an official assessment of the terms and conditions in the tender submitted and whether acceptance of the tender conformed with the national interest.' The publication in so widely read a newspaper of these extracts from the Richmond diary, Patrick continued, had inevitably brought Richard Tancred' s political career to an end. The only way he could clear his name was to bring an action for libel. He had no alternative.

While Patrick was addressing the jury, the judge kept his eye on them, noting the tieless, pugnacious-looking man who was continually shifting around in his seat and muttering to himself. He'll be troublesome, Jack Traynor thought. There was always one on a jury like this. But his eye in particular rested on the young woman in the sari who had sworn on the Christian testament. She was staring fixedly at Patrick, listening intently and she reminded him of Lois all those years ago. She had the same cast of features as Lois, the same dark beauty. It's the sari, the judge thought. Perhaps it's only the sari, and he turned back to his notebook to record Patrick telling the jury that the newspaper in their defence accepted that the words meant that there was a corrupt relationship between Tancred and Oscar Sleaven; above all, the defence claimed brazenly that the words were true. So the defence was saying, yes, Richard Tancred, Privy Councillor, Minister for Defence Procurement, was corrupt; he had been accepting money from an industrialist with whom the Ministry was doing business. A graver accusation could hardly be levelled against a public man, one who some thought might well become the next Prime Minister.

This defence by the newspaper, Patrick said, was known in the law of defamation as 'justification' – that the newspaper was justified in publishing the words because they were true. But under the law of defamation, Patrick went on to tell the jury, the burden of proving what the defendants claimed was true lay not upon the claimant, Richard Tancred, but upon the defendants, News Universal. The burden was heavy, because for the defence to succeed, News Universal, must prove – not hint, not suggest, not imply but actually prove – that the former Minister was corrupt. There was no obligation on Richard Tancred to prove he was not. If the newspaper failed to discharge that burden then the claimant, Richard Tancred, must succeed. 'And if News Universal does fail,' Patrick repeated, 'then Richard Tancred is entitled to receive from your hands massive damages to compensate for the libel that had, in effect, ended a great political career.'

There were two kinds of damages in the law of libel, he said: first, general damages to compensate Tancred for ruining his life and his career, and for exacerbating the libel by coming here to this court and repeating the lies about him; and second, punitive damages to punish a greedy, irresponsible organ of the press, which printed falsehoods with the intent of swelling its circulation and increasing its profits. 'Never has there been so wicked a falsehood published about a public man.' Patrick paused, before concluding with a flourish, 'The only way justice can be done and the reputation of Richard Tancred can be restored is by a massive award of general damages to demonstrate his innocence of the foul charge levelled so recklessly against him, plus a further massive award of punitive damages to punish the conduct of an irresponsible newspaper that dares to publish so gross a libel on a distinguished public servant in order to increase their circulation, swell their profits and fill the pockets of the proprietor from the broadcast of lies.'

And he sat down.

It had been generally expected, as it was indeed expected by the judge himself, that the opening by

Patrick Foxley would last some time. In fact, it was surprisingly short.

As he listened, Goodbody had noted that Foxley said not a word about the suicide of Oscar Sleaven. Why? he wondered. The jury must have read or heard about it. Why hadn't Foxley referred to it? Goodbody was not to know that Tancred had expressly forbidden it. 'Raise it with me when I'm in the witness box,' Tancred had said. 'I shall deal with it.'

'So will Ledbury,' Patrick had replied and Tancred had nodded.

Apart from no mention of the death of Oscar Sleaven, the judge also noted that there had been no mention by Foxley of any documents. The jury had so far seen none, although Jack Traynor knew they existed for the defendants had disclosed certain documents and they were among his papers. To Jack Traynor they appeared very significant. Yet Foxley had made no mention of them. He realised he was resting his case on a blank denial of any corruption and leaving it to the defendants to prove it if they could. But what those documents revealed when the jury eventually saw them, as at some stage they must, would come, the judge reflected, as a considerable shock. The documents could have a decisive effect. The course Foxley had taken, the judge considered, was surprising. Was Patrick Foxley, he wondered, once again being too clever by half? But he, like Oliver Goodbody, was not to know that this high-risk strategy had been laid down not by Patrick Foxley but by his client, Richard Tancred himself.

Mordecai understood well enough what the other side was about. The burden of proof of dishonesty, of corruption between Richard Tancred and Oscar Sleaven, was being left to him fair and square. Much, perhaps all, would turn upon his cross-examination.

The judge turned towards Mordecai. 'Yes, Mr Ledbury. Your opening statement, if you please.'

Without rising from his seat, Mordecai said, 'I do not choose to make a statement at this stage.'

There was a moment of stunned silence in the court. It was unusual for the defence not to take the opportunity of making an opening statement. Both Price and Goodbody turned to look at Mordecai, surprised.

'Why not, man?' Price asked, loud enough for the jury to hear him.

'Because I do not choose to,' Mordecai growled. 'The jury will understand what is my case soon enough when I start to cross-examine. It will come across better then.' And Mordecai stared back at him, looking grimmer than ever.

'Very well,' said the judge and, with Price muttering at Goodbody as he turned back in his seat, he went on 'Yes, Mr Foxley.'

Patrick rose again and called for Richard Tancred to enter the witness box.

Tancred took the oath, speaking quietly yet clearly; then turned to face his counsel. His evidence began with the story of his background and early life, and his entry into politics after a few years in the diplomatic service and then business.

Anna's attention wandered. She was still thinking about Godfrey. What was it he could he say? It must be something about his former employers and it must be important; otherwise Patrick would not have announced it so early in the case and with such a flourish. Patrick had mentioned a memorandum that had been written after Godfrey's return from Paris. That must have been about his meeting in Paris with the Chairman. What had Price said that could be so important?

But Spenser knew. He had listened to Foxley very attentively, especially to the passage about punitive damages and the claim that the extract from the diary had been published wilfully to harm Tancred – and to swell the profits of News Universal. If that was established and the defence failed, he knew that the damages could be enormous. His anxieties about the precariousness of News Universal's financial position had not abated. If the defence failed, the price he'd get for the balance of his stock would be minimal. All he could do now was to pray that the defence succeeded.

Tancred was continuing with his evidence, speaking clearly in a light voice, answering Patrick's questions about his birth – he was now forty-six – his education, his time as a diplomat, which he dealt with very shortly, his business career, entry into politics and rise to Cabinet office. Then he spoke of the publication of the diary extracts in the *Sunday News*, of how it was brought to his attention and of his realisation that to clear his reputation he had no alternative but to sue. 'Public men and women,' he said, 'have to accept insult and criticism but this publication affected my personal integrity, my reputation for honesty. I knew I had to clear my name and I did not wish to embarrass the administration of which I was a member. So I decided that I must resign and take this matter to the court.'

'Did you know Francis Richmond, the author of the diary?' asked Patrick.

'Slightly. I had encountered him many years ago. I knew of his books and articles in art magazines.'

'Would you call him a friend of yours?'

'No. I saw him sometimes at social functions. We had mutual social acquaintances. I rarely spoke with him.'

'The late Oscar Sleaven,' said Patrick. 'Who was he?'

'He was the chairman of Sleaven Industries, which is a conglomerate manufacturing vehicles and including, I believe, property interests.'

'Was he a friend of yours?'

Tancred paused before answering, then he said, 'No. He was not a friend. I have heard about his recent death.'

'Did that distress you?'

Again Tancred paused. 'I am sorry for anyone who meets such a violent end and at his own hand. I had heard that he was ill. But I cannot pretend that I am grieving for him.'

There was a stir in the courtroom. Price nudged

Goodbody. 'Nor am I,' he whispered. Goodbody ignored him.

'Did you do business with Oscar Sleaven when you were Minister for Defence Procurement?' Patrick asked.

'I did. He was one of the industrialists with whom I had to deal. His company was developing a new light armoured personnel carrier in which the Ministry was interested on behalf of the Armed Services. So I had many dealings with him. I had to in the course of my public duty.'

This time it was Patrick who paused. Then he asked, 'In the course of your ministerial dealings with Oscar Sleaven did you ever ask for or receive from him a bribe?'

'Never.'

'In the form of money or in any other form?'

'No.'

'Did he ever offer one?'

'No, he did not.'

'In short, was there anything corrupt or financially improper in your relationship with him?'

'Certainly not. The Ministry entered into certain contracts with him when I was the Minister. Those contracts were negotiated in exactly the same way as were any other contract. He never offered – he would not have dared to offer and I don't think he ever for a moment considered offering – a bribe either to me or to anyone in my Ministry. That he did and that I accepted a bribe from him is totally and utterly false.'

'Then why did he kill himself?' Price again whispered to Goodbody, who again ignored him.

'What was your reaction when you read the extracts of the diary of Francis Richmond that were published in the *Sunday News*?' Patrick asked.

'Anger, fury at the implication of what Richmond was hinting: that I was corrupt, dishonest. And I knew that with this publication in the *Sunday News* my political career was at an end, for I had no alternative but to deal with it.'

There was a moment of silence. Eventually Patrick turned to the judge. The judge looked up at the clock. It was just before one. 'That completes my examination-in-chief, My Lord,' Patrick said. 'I have no further questions for the witness.'

Still no mention of the documents, the judge thought, even in the examination-in-chief. 'You have completed your examination of the witness?' he asked, trying to conceal his surprise.

'I have,' said Patrick.

Jack Traynor played with his pencil, debating to himself whether to enquire why the witness had not been asked about the documents. But he thought about his inexperience over the technicalities in the law of libel. Should he raise it with Foxley? But what if there were good reason not to refer to them at this stage? It would be unwise to be caught out should he be shown to be wrong. No, the less he interfered at this early stage, he decided, the better. After a pause he nodded. 'Very well. I shall rise for the midday adjournment.' Now was his opportunity to get on good terms with the jury so he took it. 'Ladies and Gentlemen,' he said in his broad accent, smiling jovially, 'I can release you now from what, I fear, are those hard and uncomfortable seats in which you've been imprisoned for the morning.' He smiled again. 'These courts were built over a hundred years ago and our ancestors must have been midgets.' He had once heard a judge say similar words many years ago in York and he thought he would repeat them. He grinned at the large black man. 'I'm afraid they are mighty uncomfortable but I can do nowt about that and you'll have to be imprisoned in them again this afternoon and until the case is over. Meanwhile, dinner. So stretch your legs as the jury bailiff takes you to your room. But before that, a word of warning. Don't talk to anyone outside your own number about the case. It might be better if you didn't even talk among yourselves until you've heard all the evidence and you retire to consider your verdict. But that's a matter for you. What is a matter for me is to make sure you don't talk with anyone else – not even tonight when you go home. That is very important. In other words, mum's the word.' He smiled genially, rose, bowed and disappeared.

The jury were led from the court to their luncheon room.

'What was the old bugger on about?' the pugnacious red-faced man said as they went.

'I couldn't understand a word he said,' the middle-aged spinster complained.

'He's a Geordie,' a juryman behind her chipped in. 'From Newcastle, from the north-east. All he said was don't talk about it to anyone who's not on the jury.'

When they were seated at the table eating their lunch the older man with short grey hair wearing a blazer with brass buttons and a tie said to his neighbour, the large black man, 'What did you think of the witness?'

Before the black man could reply, the red-faced juryman leaned across the table to help himself to salt. 'He's a politician, ain't he? He'll have been up to something. They all are.'

'I thought he looked quite nice,' said one of the younger women on the jury.

She was rather pretty, in a flowered dress, with blonde hair. Dyed, though, thought the man in the blazer. 'What did you think of him?' he asked the woman in the sari.

She thought for a moment. 'I'm not sure,' she said.

The black man nodded.

Chapter Three

A pot of coffee, plastic cups and sandwiches were laid out on the table in the defendants' conference room. Mordecai flung off his wig and subsided into a chair. Adams produced a leather case from which he took a quart bottle of champagne and a glass. He opened the wine and handed it to Mordecai. Goodbody looked on disapprovingly but he knew better than to say anything. Digby Price glowered. Walter Morrison helped himself to the sandwiches and coffee.

'Why didn't you make an opening statement?' Price demanded.

'Because he didn't refer to the documents. I wish to leave the disclosure of our case to my cross-examination. That, I judge, will have the greatest impact on the jury.' Mordecai peered at Price over the rim of his glass before he added, 'Let me remind you that I am in charge of the tactics in the courtroom.'

Oliver Goodbody intervened hurriedly. 'I have reserved a room for you for lunch in the Wig and Pen Club across the road,' he said to Price. 'My clerk will show you the way.'

'You understand what is happening?' Mordecai asked Price.

'I understand that now's your chance to go for him. All that sickening, sanctimonious crap about service and government. Not a word about screwing a fortune out of Sleaven. Bloody humbug!'

'That was quite deliberate,' Mordecai replied.

'How do you mean?'

'They're waiting for me. That's when we'll hear the explanation.'

'An explanation? There can't be any! If he tries, then it's up to you to demolish it. I am relying on you, Ledbury.'

'That, presumably, is why you are paying me.'

Oliver took Price gently by the arm and steered him to the door. Spenser followed them.

Waite began. 'Would you like me—'

'No,' Mordecai interrupted. 'Just counsel and solicitor.'

Mordecai, Walter and Oliver were alone. For a time no one spoke.

'Well?' Mordecai began.

'Very risky not to say a word about the documents either in opening or examination-in-chief,' said Walter.

'They've left proof of corruption to us. They're entitled to.'

'They've also left you with the first word to the jury about the documents and that could have a damning effect. There are always those who are ready to believe politicians are corrupt and there'll be some of those on this jury.'

'Tancred will have some explanation, but whether it's true or false is another matter. What is certain is that he's deliberately keeping it for me. So I thought I'd keep what I've got for him.' Mordecai emptied his glass and pushed back his chair. 'How does he come across to you?' he asked generally.

'Rather sinister,' said Oliver Goodbody quietly.

'And to me,' Walter added, 'plausible, but sinister.'

'But is he dishonest? That's the question,' Mordecai mused.

For a time there was silence. Then Walter said, 'I suppose Lacey will say that he wrote a memorandum about his meeting with Price and that Price showed his animosity about Tancred and decided to publish because he thought it a good story that would stimulate circulation.'

'Yes. That's for the punitive damages.'

'Can we stop it getting in evidence?'

'Unlikely.'

'But you'll try?'

'Of course I'll try,' Mordecai answered testily. 'But even this country bumpkin of a judge can't be so stupid as to exclude it. He'll let them call Lacey.' He shook the last drops from the bottle into his glass and drained it.

'We're going to win,' Goodbody stated. 'I am quite sure. You'll do fine with him. You have all the cards.'

'Except the joker,' said Mordecai as he moved slowly to the door. 'Now I need the loo. The down side to champagne is that in my old age it makes me need the loo.'

Tancred was alone in the other conference room with Cranley Burrows and Burrows's clerk. Tancred refused food and coffee, and drank a cup of water.

'Technically the cross-examination has not yet begun,' Burrows said, 'so we can still discuss the case if we wish.'

'There's no more to say,' Tancred replied.

Burrows turned to the clerk. 'Check that Lacey's statement has been prepared. When it has, bring it to me and have copies ready for the other side and for the court. I want it served this evening.' The clerk left.

Tancred paced up and down the room. 'Is Elspeth Turville being looked after?' he asked Burrows.

'Yes, she arrived in London this morning on the early train from Paris.'

'She's not in court. Where is she?'

'At the Aldwych Hotel. With one of my articled clerks.'

'I can see her tonight, I suppose?'

'Better not. I expect you'll still be under cross-examination. You said we might need her as a witness.'

Tancred kept up his patrol across the room. 'I keep imagining,' he said suddenly, 'that Francis Richmond is watching us.'

'Looking up or down?' Cranley wondered.

Tancred smiled. 'Looking,' he answered. 'Just looking.'

'How do you feel?' Cranley enquired.

'Have you ever ridden in a point-to-point? Tancred asked.

'Never.'

'Well, it's like waiting for the Off.'

Cranley shrugged his shoulders. 'Perhaps Ledbury feels the same.'

'It'd have to be a very large horse,' said Tancred. 'No, Ledbury's too old a hand. To him this is just another brief. He may win or he may lose. I don't expect he cares very much. To him it's just one more day in court. But for me—' He shrugged and continued pacing across the room.

Foxley and French were eating sandwiches in chambers.

'How do you think it went?' Foxley asked.

'Not too bad, but the documents will produce a shock.'

'They will. But what kind of an impression do you think he gave?'

French hesitated. 'He sounds and looks what he is – clever. But not wholly candid. I didn't altogether like what he said about Oscar Sleaven. Pretty cold and dispassionate.'

Patrick put his head in his hands. 'As he has been cold and not very candid with us. It's the first time I've appeared for a client who refuses to tell me what he's going to say.' He stood up. 'All I do know is that it had better be bloody good.'

Mr Justice Traynor crossed the Strand to lunch in the hall at his Inn. He slipped into a seat at the end of the table, next to his friend John Williams, a judge in the Court of Appeal.

'Have you started your big case?' Williams enquired.

Jack nodded and ordered sausages and mash.

'That'll make you go to sleep,' Williams said when the dish arrived.

'Nay, it'll aid me keep my wool on. Ledbury and Foxley have already started squabbling.'

'All the better for you. The more they squabble, the more the jury will rely on you.'

'I don't want the jury to rely on me. I want to leave it to them fair and square with no spin from me. Politics, money, newspapers! If ever a case demanded a jury, it's this one. No, I aim to keep my trap shut. And on top of it there seem to be some pretty funny tactics by the claimant. But then, he's a politician.'

Williams rose. 'Well, don't make a balls of it, Jack. We don't want it turning up in the Court of Appeal.'

'Thanks,' Jack replied as he shook the Worcester sauce bottle over his sausages. He thought of the old, uncomplicated days when he was still at the Bar on circuit in Leeds, perhaps doing some easy, straightforward criminal case, prosecuting a bank robbery or a GBH; something, he thought in his present mood, with plenty of blood. To be followed by an evening in the Bar mess when he'd play his trombone. But that would have to have been in the old days. He'd not played the trombone in the mess for a long time, not since Lois had made such a fool of him. The young Asian woman in the sari on the jury, he thought. She was very like Lois to look at. But she seemed brighter. What would she make of all this skulduggery in high places? A far cry from the tobacconist shop in Ealing? But perhaps this was what she expected. In India, the politicians were all up to a spot of bribery and corruption. She's a pleasant-looking lass. He went to have coffee in the ante-room and thought gloomily of the afternoon that lay ahead with Ledbury and Foxley.

* * *

Emerald and Sybil had taken Anna to the Aldwych Hotel for lunch. 'All that listening to all that talk has made me hungry,' said Emerald as the three took their places in the dining room.

'We've not much time,' Sybil replied. She looked around the room. 'No one here we know.'

Elspeth Turville was at the table next to theirs, accompanied by Cranley Burrows's articled clerk, a young man in a dark suit and spotted tie. Elspeth noted the three women, the two older of whom were so smartly dressed.

'We have until two, the judge said,' Sybil went on.

Elspeth pricked up her ears.

'I find him very hard to understand,' said Anna.

'He's from the north.' Emerald ordered a carafe of white wine. 'I thought he looked rather nice. Robust. Manly.'

'Quite your type,' said Sybil.

'Miaow!' But Emerald was not offended.

'Tancred looks good,' Anna went on.

'As good as Patrick?' Sybil asked slyly, looking at Anna. 'But Patrick is so much younger than that old brute Mordecai. I hope he knows what he's doing.'

'Of course he does, my dear,' said Emerald. 'He's very clever.'

And very handsome, Anna thought. I like him in his funny wig. It suits him. But he does look very anxious.

Elspeth wished the young clerk would stop talking about a trip he'd made last summer to Antibes so that she could overhear more.

'Did you see the odious Price looking so pleased with himself?' Emerald asked Sybil.

Sybil sighed. 'How I wish that old pansy Francis were alive so that he could see all the trouble he's caused.'

'He'd enjoy it,' Emerald replied.

'I'll never get over him keeping a diary and writing all that beastliness about the friends who'd been so good to him. I still don't understand how he could.'

'My father told me that when he was in the old

Cavendish Hotel talking to Rosa Lewis, she once said,
"No letters, no lawyers and kiss your baby's bottom."
I wonder what she'd have said about writing a diary.'

Both Emerald and Sybil had ordered scrambled eggs
and smoked salmon; Anna a salad. She watched them
eat and drink their wine. For all their protestations of
outrage, she saw that at bottom they were enjoying
themselves. For them it was a show, a spectacle. For
Patrick it was a job, a step in his career. For Tancred, she
thought, it was life or death.

From the Wig and Pen Club Digby Price telephoned
Helena in Paris.

'How's it going?' she asked.

'It's only just begun. The fun will start this afternoon.'
He paused. 'I wish you were with me.'

'Now, none of that. You know I wouldn't go there.'

'What'll you do tonight?'

'Oh, go to the movies, I expect. Then come home and
dream of you.' He heard her giggle. 'Call me at eleven,'
she added.

'I shall.'

'And win. Don't forget that you have to win.'

'I shall,' he replied grimly. 'I shall.'

Chapter Four

Mordecai clambered to his feet. He made a great show of it, clutching the desk for support as he laid his sticks along it, pushing aside his papers, hitching his gown around his shoulders, then picking up one of the sticks from the desk and leaning on it.

Mr Justice Traynor waited, irritated. Finally he could not restrain himself. 'Mr Ledbury, we are all waiting. Are you ready to start your cross-examination.'

Mordecai did not reply immediately. Instead, he looked at the jury, then up at the judge on the bench above him. He shook his head. 'I find great difficulty getting to my feet,' he began in a low, sad voice. 'Nature has not endowed me with the graces enjoyed by Your Lordship and many others, so I must ask for the patience that has hitherto been extended to me by the very highest courts in the land.' He paused, then went on loudly, 'I am, as perhaps you can observe, much crippled.' It was a ploy he regularly used in front of a jury whenever a judge tried to hustle him.

The two middle-aged women on the jury looked at each other sympathetically.

Jack Traynor's already healthy complexion turned almost scarlet. 'What I said was not meant as any reflection on you, Mr Ledbury. I observed that you were on your feet and I was merely waiting for you to begin.'

Mordecai nodded. 'Then I shall,' he said 'I shall.' He turned from the judge to face Tancred in the witness box. His voice, which at first had been low, almost sorrowful in his rebuke to the judge, now became strong and forceful. 'So that from the outset there can be no misunderstanding, I suggest you are a rogue.'

Tancred half smiled and bowed.

Mordecai went on, 'I suggest that when you were a minister you corruptly accepted money from an industrialist, now dead, in exchange for granting him government favours. Do you understand?'

Tancred bowed again.

Mordecai said, even more loudly, 'Do you understand what I am suggesting? That you are corrupt? Please answer.'

'I understand very well,' Tancred said. 'That's your job.'

'My duty, you mean.' Mordecai spoke roughly. 'I am suggesting that you accepted bribes. Is that clear?'

'Quite clear. And quite untrue.'

Mordecai concluded, 'Now there can be no misunderstanding between us, can there?'

'None.' Tancred leant against the side of the witness box. His face was very pale but his hands with the long fingers, Anna noted, were quite steady as he folded them on the ledge. Mordecai began to pace along the row in which he stood. From where she sat Anna could only see his distorted back in his black gown and occasionally his profile. He looked to her like a misshapen raven.

'Oscar Sleaven made a run for it, didn't he?' Mordecai's voice was savage.

'I don't know what you mean.'

'I think you do. When the scandal broke, your pal, your fellow conspirator Oscar Sleaven, fled the country and now he's blown his brains out. Isn't that right?'

'Oscar Sleaven is neither my pal, as you put it, nor is he a fellow conspirator. He left England, I understood, to get medical treatment abroad.'

'Why did you understand that?'

'I believed that because Sebastian Sleaven, his brother and solicitor, made a statement to that effect.'

'When?'

'After Oscar Sleaven had left for the States.'

'Eighteen months ago?'

'Yes.'

'The morning after the diary was published in the *Sunday News*?'

'Some time like that.'

'Did you believe that statement?'

'I had no reason not to.'

'You thought it true, that he had resigned his chairmanship and gone abroad because he was ill?'

'As I said, I had no reason to doubt it.'

'Hadn't you? Wasn't it merely an excuse to escape from the scandal that had been unearthed by the newspaper?'

'If that is the interpretation you wish to put on it, that is a matter for you.'

'It will be a matter for the jury. For Oscar Sleaven ran away just as the *News* published the diary that referred to you and him – and what you were getting up to. Isn't that right?'

'He left the country, I understand, about the time of the publication.'

'And now he's dead. How did you learn of his death?'

'From newspaper reports.'

'Not from Sebastian Sleaven?'

'No.'

'Why not? You know Sebastian Sleaven, do you not?'

'I have met him.'

'You have more than met him, haven't you?'

'I do not know what you mean.'

'You have visited him in his apartment, where he lives. And very recently. Isn't that correct?'

The muscles on Tancred's face tautened. His hands now gripped the ledge in front of the witness box, the knuckles showing white. Mordecai swung round and faced the body of the court. He gestured and a slight, grey-haired man in the third row rose. Mordecai turned back to the witness. 'Do you know that man?'

Tancred leant forward, peering.

'Answer me. Do you know that man?'

At last Tancred said, 'I do'

'Who is he?'

'He is John Meadows, the political editor of your clients' newspapers.'

Another gesture from Mordecai and the man resumed his seat. The barrister went on, 'You knew each other from your days in politics, isn't that so?'

'Yes.'

'Do you consider him a trustworthy man?'

'As far as any journalist is trustworthy.'

'That is very amusing, but you may not find it so amusing when Mr Meadows tells the court that one evening four days – I repeat, four days – before your fellow conspirator Oscar Sleaven committed suicide, you made a secret visit to his brother Sebastian Sleaven at his residence in Portland Place. If Mr Meadows were to say that, would it be true?'

Tancred moved slightly in the witness box, as though shifting his weight from one foot to the other. 'Yes,' he said finally. 'It would be true.'

'On that evening, 14 July last, six days ago, at about ten o'clock,' Mordecai went on, 'after making a broadcast at Broadcasting House, Mr Meadows happened to be in Portland Place walking north in the direction of the underground station when he saw you descend from a taxi and slip hurriedly into the block of flats where Sebastian Sleaven lives. If he were to tell that to the court, would it be correct?'

Tancred wanted to take a sip of water from the glass beside him but he knew that he shouldn't. His lips were dry. He stood very straight, remembering. He'd known that Price's men were following him when he returned to London from France to see Patrick Foxley. He knew they would locate him at his home in his flat in Chelsea and follow him to the Temple, and he intended that they should. What he had not intended was for them to see whom he visited before he went to Chelsea. He had taken steps to make sure that after parking his car in the lock-up in Clapham he had given them the slip. He knew how to do it. He had been trained to watch for surveillance and to shake off a tail, and that was what he had done on that evening. When he picked up a taxi in Piccadilly to take him to Sebastian Sleaven in Portland Place, he was convinced that he was clear of them. But by sheer chance he had been observed. Because Meadows had been doing a broadcast and happened to be in Portland Place – and Meadows knew him and had seen him enter the flat.

'Answer, if you please,' Mordecai demanded loudly. 'Did you visit Sebastian Sleaven on 14 July, four days before Oscar Sleaven shot himself?'

'I did.'

Cranley Burrows half turned to look behind him at Patrick who sat rigid and grim-faced.

'Why?' Mordecai raised his voice. 'Why did you visit Sebastian Sleaven?'

'It was business.'

'What kind of business?'

'It was private business.'

'Your private business, Mr Richard Tancred, is now the business of this court. Did your private business with Oscar Sleaven's brother involve talk about this case?'

'It did.'

'Was that the purpose of your visit?'

'I did not say that. I said we did talk about the case.'

'Did you go to Sebastian Sleaven to warn him, Oscar Sleaven's brother and lawyer, that when this case came to trial in six days' time, Oscar Sleaven would be publicly exposed for giving – and you exposed for receiving – bribes?'

'No. Both Sebastian and Oscar Sleaven knew as well

as I that the accusation about giving and taking bribes is false.'

'Is it so false? So false that two days after you visited Sebastian and talked about this case, Oscar Sleaven was driven to murder his wife and blow his brains out?'

'I said. The accusation about the bribes is wholly false.'

'When you made that secret visit to Sebastian Sleaven, did you or did you not warn him that his brother was going to be exposed for paying you money in exchange for you granting him favours?'

'Both Sebastian and Oscar Sleaven knew what you were going to say about us.'

'Did you discuss that with Sebastian on that evening?'

'I did.'

'And two days later Oscar Sleaven blew his brains out. Are you asking the jury to believe that his suicide had nothing to do with your talk with his brother? That it was pure coincidence that shortly after you called on his brother and before this trial commenced Oscar Sleaven killed himself?'

'No, it may not be pure coincidence. I don't know what was the state of his mind or of his health when he shot himself. For all I know he may have been ill, terminally ill. I don't know. But what I am quite sure of is that his death was ultimately due to the poison your clients have spread about him and about me, and that you are still spreading here today.'

'By the poison, do you mean what you call a libel and I call a truth?'

'Yes.'

'Are you trying to suggest, then, that the newspaper is responsible for Oscar Sleaven's death?'

'I suggest that without this publication by your clients I do not think Oscar Sleaven would have died.'

'Because he wouldn't have been found out?'

'No. Because he wouldn't have been falsely accused.'

There was a moment of silence while Mordecai stared at the tall figure in the witness box. Tancred stood very straight, but his face was paler than before. He had not known that they knew of his visit to Sebastian Sleaven and he had not been ready for it.

'Are you seriously saying to the jury that the newspaper is responsible for the death of Oscar Sleaven? Yes or no.'

'Yes, in the way I have suggested. You, however, may put it in whatever way you wish. I am telling you and the jury that Oscar Sleaven and I are not guilty of giving and taking bribes.'

'So you say.' Mordecai paused. 'You like money, don't you? You are particularly anxious to get money for yourself, are you not?'

'Not particularly.'

'You've always wanted to get money for yourself, haven't you?'

'I repeat. Not particularly.'

'Then let me give you a "for-instance". Why did you leave the government of which you were a member?'

'In order to bring this case,' Tancred replied.

'What has that to do with it?'

'Everything. As I told my counsel, I resigned to be free to sue your clients for the libel they printed about me.'

'That is no answer.'

'It is my answer.'

'You could just as well have sued while still remaining a minister.'

'I did not think it proper to remain a member of the administration and at the same time sue for libel.'

'Why not?'

'Since the publication of the diary extracts by your clients, I was under a cloud. To remain in government would have embarrassed my colleagues.'

'Why? Others in public life have remained ministers and sued for libel.'

'They may have. I do not know. All I know is that

because of your clients' accusation of a corrupt financial relationship I had to clear my name. It would not have been fair to my colleagues, nor to the department I was administering, to have remained in office. That was my reason for leaving.'

'The only reason?'

'Yes.'

'Let me suggest another reason, the real reason. You thought you'd get more money in damages if you came before a jury – as you are now before this jury – and claimed that what the newspaper published forced you out of government. That these wicked people, who you also apparently say are responsible for the death of Sleaven, have ruined your great career and, to recompense you, the jury must give you a very great deal of money. Wasn't that the real reason why you resigned from the government?'

'No. It was not.'

'But it's money that you are after here, in this court, isn't it?'

'I am claiming damages.'

'You certainly are. You are asking for general and punitive damages. General damages for ruining your career; punitive damages to punish the newspaper. Money to end up in your pocket. Isn't that what you are after?'

'I was advised that it was necessary to ask for damages as only an award of damages would demonstrate the falseness of what your people published about me; and secondly to teach them a lesson for their irresponsible and reckless disregard for the truth.'

Mordecai paused, his eye still fixed on Tancred. 'I shall return to the question of money as I shall to your mysterious visit to Sebastian Sleaven, but would you agree that if what the newspaper published about you was true,' he said more quietly, 'they were only doing what a responsible newspaper should do? Namely, exposing a corrupt minister. Isn't that the public duty of a newspaper in a democracy?'

'If it were true, perhaps. But it isn't true.'

'So you say. So you keep saying. But as this case progresses we may learn otherwise.'

Patrick Foxley said from his place, 'That is a statement, not a question.'

Mordecai turned towards him and snarled, 'If you wish to object, do it standing – not skulking in your seat.'

Patrick got to his feet. 'I certainly shall interrupt if counsel makes statements and does not ask questions when his duty is to cross-examine.'

'I do not need to be taught my duty by young—'

'Mr Ledbury, Mr Foxley,' the judge intervened. 'There's no need to squabble. Let us get on with the cross-examination.'

'Exactly,' Mordecai agreed. 'And without unnecessary and childish interruptions.'

'That is also unnecessary, Mr Ledbury,' the judge said. 'Please let us get on.'

Mordecai glared at the judge but said nothing. Oliver Goodbody swung round in his seat and looked up at Mordecai. 'Don't quarrel,' he whispered. 'It's going too well.'

Mordecai glared back at him before turning once more to Tancred. 'Let us return to the subject of money. You have a great interest in money, have you not?'

'No more than most.'

'But like the money that you are after here in this court today, money you want the jury to award you, it was also money that you were after when you were in government. Isn't that true?'

'As for the second part of your suggestion, it is untrue. As to the first, I said that I am asking for damages for the wrong that your people have done me. I had to leave the government in order to fight this case.'

'As I said, others who believed they had been wronged have remained as ministers and brought actions for libel. I suggest you left government only because you thought that it would make your position more sympathetic to the jury and swell the damages. Isn't that so?'

'No, it is not.'

'So that you could plead that the newspaper had ruined your career. Isn't that it?'

'No, it is not.'

'For how long were you in politics?'

'Ten years.'

'How long in the Cabinet?'

'Five years.'

'For half a decade you were at the top of the tree, in the Cabinet, the pinnacle sought by every ambitious politician.' He looked at the jury. 'Not the most highly regarded trade, politics, is it?'

'No more than the trade of lawyer.'

A titter arose in the court. Good for Tancred, Anna thought, from the back row. She'd seen that he'd been troubled by the earlier questions and the jury would have, also.

Patrick half smiled. Tancred's visit to Sebastian Sleaven had come as a shock. Why had he gone to see Sleaven the night before he had come to the conference and before he'd driven back to France? It could only have been to warn him. Patrick was relieved that they had moved on. From now on at least Tancred would be ready for it.

When Tancred made that reply about lawyers, Mordecai turned away from the jury and almost faced Walter Morrison, his junior counsel sitting in the row behind him. Walter saw, although the jury could not, the hint of a wink before Mordecai turned back to the witness. 'Before you became a politician you were a diplomat?'

'I was.'

'Did you give up diplomacy so that you could make money?'

'I wanted somewhat more than I was receiving as a salary in the Foreign Service.'

'So you moved on into business. That was to make more money?'

'Yes.'

'And did you?'

'Yes, more than I earned as a diplomat.'

'Next you left business and moved into politics. Was that because you thought you'd make even more money?'

'Certainly not,' Tancred replied. 'There's no money to be made in politics.'

'You mean no money to be made in honest politics?'

'Of course.'

'But if to make more money was not the reason for your previous career moves, what was your reason for going into politics?'

Tancred was silent for a time. 'To contribute, to serve,' he replied at last.

'Contribute to what?'

Again Tancred paused. Then, 'To the country,' he said.

'Contribute to the country!' Mordecai's stick banged on the floor. He bent forward. 'You went into politics to contribute to the country.' He swung round towards the jury. 'You wanted to contribute service for the sake of the country?'

'That's what I said.'

'What do you mean by contributing to your country?'

'I thought that if I entered public service I might be of some use.'

'To whom? To yourself?'

'No, although I admit that I liked the idea of serving.'

'This sounds very fine, very public-spirited,' said Mordecai sarcastically. 'Giving service to your country?'

'Yes.'

Mordecai bent forward again, leaning with both hands on the desk. 'I suggest that the public service you now describe so high-mindedly meant nothing more than self-service.'

'No.'

'Looking after yourself?'

'No, certainly not.'

'But this service of which you speak in such a high-falutin way – Mordecai paused, then went on more loudly – 'was it honest service?'

'Of course it was.'

'Or is the truth that you were and always have been driven by ambition, vanity and greed – and a determination to find an opportunity to feather your nest?'

'Ambition, yes,' Tancred replied, 'I suppose I had ambition. Vanity, yes, a little vanity. Because I thought I could be of use. But to feather my nest, no.'

'Getting money, greed for money. Hasn't that been your lifelong preoccupation?'

'No, it has not.'

'You had no money when you left university and went into the diplomatic service, had you?'

'No.'

'And you didn't make much money from the trade of the diplomat – going abroad and lying for your country – did you?'

'No.'

Mordecai paused. 'Or was it spying for your country? Was that what you were really doing?'

For a second Tancred hesitated. But Walter Morrison had tugged at Mordecai's gown and handed him a piece of paper. Mordecai looked at it and nodded, his attention distracted from the witness.

'I was a diplomat,' Tancred said. 'I did what a diplomat had to do.'

The moment passed.

'Did you get much money out of business?' Mordecai went on.

'A little. Enough to make a political career possible.'

'And you thought that politics would bring you more?'

'I did not.'

'Were you not anxious – no, I must choose my words

carefully – were you not determined to get money out of politics?'

'I was not.'

Mordecai held the sheet of paper Walter had passed to him. 'In the extract of the diary published by the *Sunday News* there's a passage about a conversation in a house at Oldhaven in the States when you are reported as saying that you'd stay in politics only as long as it afforded you some chance of *getting some money*. Do you remember that?'

'I remember something to that effect in the diary.'

'To that very effect. You were overheard talking about *getting money* from politics. What did you mean by that?'

'I didn't mean anything.'

'*Getting money* from politics,' Mordecai repeated. 'How do you *get* money from politics?' Mordecai rapped the desk. 'Honest politics that is.'

'You don't.'

'No, you don't. But you were heard to say that you were going to *get* money out of politics. That can only mean, can it not, *getting* money out of corrupt, crooked politics?' Tancred shrugged as Mordecai went on quickly, 'Money out of politics? *Getting money* out of politics? That was what you were in politics for and that is exactly what you have done. You've *got money* from politics?'

'No. I have not. That is what your newspaper accuses me of doing but it is untrue.'

'We shall see about that.' Patrick stirred as if he were going to object again but Mordecai gave him no opportunity. 'I ask you for a last time. What did you mean when you said that you intended to *get* money from politics?'

'I did not say that.'

'The diarist records that you did. He wrote down what you said.'

'The diarist is wrong.'

'How was he wrong?'

221

'Because I never said what he claimed I said.'

'Why do you think that the diarist should have written in his journal that he heard you say you wanted to get money from politics if you never said it? Was Francis Richmond such an enemy of yours that he'd invent that?'

'Francis Richmond was not a friend but I did not regard him as an enemy.'

'Then why should Richmond in his private diary—'

'It's not turned out to be very private since you circulated it to millions of readers.'

'No, it's not private now, but when Francis Richmond wrote up his journal, he might have thought that no one would ever read it. So why should he write down what you now say is false? Why should he have solemnly written in his diary that he heard you say you were out to get money from politics?'

'I have no idea. All I know is that I never said it.'

'Can you think of any reason why Richmond should have recorded that you said that if you had not?'

'No, I cannot – except that he was mistaken.'

'So you say now, when the world has read what Richmond wrote about you. But I suggest the truth is that he accurately recorded what you said. That you were out to get money from politics – and that is exactly what you have done.'

'Is that meant to be a question?' asked Tancred.

Mordecai waved his hand angrily. 'You know very well what I am suggesting. That one evening in Oldhaven, New England, when you did not know you and your friends were being overheard, you said you intended to get money from politics. That is what you said then and that is what you have done. Got money by accepting bribes from Oscar Sleaven. Isn't that the truth?'

'No, it is not. I did not say that. For one thing—'

Mordecai interrupted. 'I'm not interested in your one thing or your next thing. I'm—'

Patrick was on his feet. 'My learned friend must allow

the witness to give his explanation. Counsel is bullying the witness and interrupting him quite improperly.'

Mordecai turned on him angrily. 'I will not be called a bully—'

Jack Traynor tapped loudly with his pencil. 'Mr Ledbury, Mr Foxley. It does not assist the jury if counsel lose their tempers with each other and squabble like schoolboys. Mr Foxley, please sit down. If the witness needs protection I shall give it to him. However, Mr Ledbury, you must allow the witness to answer and give what explanation he wishes.'

Patrick sat.

Mordecai glared as the judge. 'Schoolboys!' he hissed.

'You wish to explain?' the judge asked Tancred.

'I do, My Lord. As I have tried to make clear to Mr Ledbury, I did not say what the diarist claims I said. At the time Francis Richmond was eavesdropping, he was trying to overhear a conversation between three persons sitting on the veranda outside the room he had entered. He could not have been sure which of the three said what and shortly after he left the room he was taken ill with a heart attack. He must have written that entry in his diary some time after the event. His account is not reliable and I repeat that I never said that I intended to get money out of my service in politics. And I never have.'

There was a pause. While Tancred had been speaking Mordecai had stood with his head bowed, leaning on his stick. Now he raised his head and glared at Tancred. 'Who was with you on the veranda the night Richmond overheard you?'

'Lester Chaffin, who is in the US government.' Tancred paused. Then he said, 'I don't now recall who was the third.'

'I didn't think you would. Was it an Englishman?'

Tancred shook his head. 'I don't now recall.'

'Richmond, you see, heard the voice. He writes that it was an English voice. An English voice talking about getting money out of politics. That means it was your voice. And now you are swearing that it wasn't you?'

'If anyone said it, which I doubt, it wasn't me.'

'So it was someone else who said it, someone with an English voice, someone who was in politics – and who it was you can't remember! Is that what you are asking the jury to believe?'

'All I can tell you is that I didn't say what Richmond wrote I said and I very much doubt if anyone did. Richmond was a malicious gossip and he wrote this after he'd been taken ill.'

'What do you understand from the expression, getting money from politics? It can only mean, can it not, that a person uses his office to line his pockets?'

'Perhaps.'

'And the explanation you offer the jury is that the diarist, when he wrote that, was ill and got it wrong?'

'Yes.'

'Well, the jury has heard your explanation. They will make up their own minds.' Mordecai pushed his wig back from his forehead; then pulled it down again. It was still askew. He went on, 'Had you made any money when you were in business?'

'I told you. Some.'

'More than you got out of politics?'

'Of course. I say once again, I never got anything out of politics. When I was a minister I had my salary and I had a few private investments from what I had saved when I was in business. Basically I lived off my salary. I did not need much. I have no family.'

'None?'

'No. I have no family alive.'

'Do you own any property?'

'No. I have a flat in Chelsea, in Consul Road, a ground-floor flat in quite a large house that I hold on a seven-year lease. There are three years of the lease to run.'

'Do you own property abroad?'

'No.'

'The day you resigned from the government you left this country and went to reside in France?'

'Yes.'

'Why?'

'Because I wished to.'

'For eighteen months you lived at La Ferme Blanche near to Pontaix in the Alpes Dauphiné Massif, isn't that so?'

'It is.'

'With a Madame Turville?'

'Madame Turville lives there. I was a guest.'

'Of hers? Is she the owner of La Ferme Blanche?'

'No.'

'Who, then, is?'

'I believe the property is in the name of some local *avocat*. The real owner is a friend of mine.' Tancred paused. Then he said slowly and emphatically, 'Mr Harry Cheung.'

When he said the name Digby Price, who had earlier been shifting about in his seat, grinning happily and nudging Oliver Goodbody, suddenly looked up at Tancred, startled.

'Mr Cheung lives in Hong Kong,' Tancred added.

'Then let me ask you about this gentleman, the real owner of the place where you have been hiding out,' Mordecai went on.

Tancred looked down directly at Price. 'Mr Price will know that name. Mr Harry Cheung from Hong Kong. Cheung.'

Mordecai was bent over the documents on his desk. When Tancred repeated the name, Price half rose from his seat and turned to Mordecai.

'What is it?' Mordecai asked.

'Don't go into this,' Price said. 'Not until I've made a check.'

'Why?' Mordecai lowered his voice so that neither the judge nor the jury, nor Patrick Foxley to his left could hear.

'Leave it until I've checked it out,' Price repeated. 'I don't want her brought into this.'

'Her? Who is "her"?'

The two were facing each other, Price with his back to the judge. 'Move on to the money,' he said.

'You instructed me to ask about the woman he was living with in France. You insisted I should.'

'Not now, not until I've checked. Move on to the money,' Price repeated.

The whole court was witnessing, even if they could not hear, the exchange between Mordecai and Price who was still standing facing his counsel with his back to the judge. People in the gallery had stood and craned over the rail to see what was happening. A noise had arisen in the court, a hubbub, like the sound of the sea.

The judge tapped with his pencil. 'Mr Ledbury. We are waiting. Are you going on with your cross-examination?'

'I am taking instructions,' Mordecai replied abruptly. He motioned to Price to resume his seat. Then he shuffled some of the papers in front of him, swung round and looked ostentatiously at the clock at the side of the court. He turned back to the judge and said more politely than he had when he had addressed the bench before, 'It's approaching the time for the adjournment and I wonder if Your Lordship would oblige me by rising for the day now? It is only a few minutes before the normal time but I need to speak further with my client.'

The judge remained silent, staring fixedly at Mordecai. Why should I help him? he thought. He comes on all polite because for some reason he's suddenly in trouble. 'We mustn't waste the jury's time, Mr Ledbury,' he said. 'We must stick to the hours laid down for the sitting of the court.'

'I appreciate that, my Lord, but I believe that if I can have an unhurried talk with my client, in the end it will save time.'

'Can't you move on to another part of your cross-examination? The witness had just mentioned the name of the owner of the farmhouse in France, a gentleman from Hong Kong.' He looked down at his note. 'A Mr Harry Cheung.' He was pleased to repeat the name that had for some reason led to the scene between Ledbury and his client. 'Is it about that you want to take instructions?'

'It is, My Lord.'

The judge looked at the clock. There were less than three minutes before the regular time for adjourning. It wasn't worth having more of a row, but he'd make Ledbury pay. 'Very well,' he said slowly, making obvious his reluctance. 'I shall rise now but I shall sit tomorrow morning five minutes earlier, at ten twenty-five, to make up the time lost because of your request for an early adjournment.'

Mordecai bowed, this time more politely than the perfunctory nod of the head with which he had saluted the judge at the start of the case.

Jack Traynor turned to the jury. 'Remember what I told you when we broke for your dinner. Don't chat about the case with anyone, even with the family when you get home. It won't be easy but please try.' He paused. 'Just have a quiet evening in front of the telly.' He smiled at them, the smile of the genial man of the world, the impartial arbiter taking his fellow arbiters into his confidence. 'An earlier start, then, tomorrow morning because of Mr Ledbury. Be in your places, please, at ten twenty for a ten twenty-five start.' He turned to Tancred. 'You're under cross-examination, Mr Tancred, so you too must keep mum.' Another grin at the jury, and he rose from the bench and disappeared through the door behind his chair.

The jury, mystified, filed from the jury box and out of the court. 'What was that about?' the middle-aged jurywoman asked the pugnacious juryman when they were in the corridor.

'Lawyers' fiddles,' he replied. 'Ten minutes earlier tomorrow. Bloody lawyers.'

In his room, Jack Traynor's clerk helped him off with his robes. 'Polite, all of a sudden, weren't we?' the judge said. 'Quite a different Mister Ledbury, eh?'

'He certainly wanted you to rise, My Lord,' the clerk answered, putting the judge's wig in its box.

'Ay, his client got excited over the name of the China-man from Hong Kong. I was tempted to tell Ledbury to get on with it but then I thought that as there was only five minutes to go I'd accommodate the fellow.' He sat at his desk. 'I enjoyed the bow!'

In the conference room Mordecai confronted Price. 'By that interruption you succeeded in ruining what up to then had been a pretty good session.' Walter, Oliver, Spenser and Waite were assembled by the door. 'What the devil was all that about?'

'Cheung is Madame Helena's family name,' muttered Spenser.

'What of it?' asked Mordecai. 'Is it an uncommon name?'

'I didn't want you to go into it until I've checked if there's a connection,' Price said. 'That's all. I don't want her involved.'

'All Tancred has said is that the farmhouse is owned by a Harry Cheung.'

'He said I'd know the name. He was getting at some-thing, I know he was.'

'Who is Madame Turville?' enquired Mordecai.

'His woman, I suppose. But keep off Cheung until I know. I'll find out tonight,' repeated Price.

'Tancred only threw it out to trick us, to startle Mr Price,' said Spenser.

'That's right. Move on to the Sleavens' money. That's what we want to get to,' Price insisted.

Mordecai looked at him steadily, then got to his feet. 'You've done your best with your antics to ruin the end of a not unsuccessful day. The jury will have seen you get excited. They'll want to know why. It's never wise to leave unanswered questions in the mind of a jury.' He moved towards the door. 'I'll see you all here tomorrow morning before court. Ten o'clock.' He turned to Walter and Oliver. 'You two. In chambers in half an hour.' When they had gone he began his slow process to the robing room.

In the taxi back to the Temple Mordecai looked out of the window. Adam heard him mutter to himself, 'Cheung. Why did he bring up that name?'

Anna shared a taxi from the Law Courts with Emerald and Sybil.

'What did you think?' Sybil asked.

'I thought Mordecai Ledbury was horrid,' Emerald replied. 'I can't think why Patrick didn't stop him from asking all those nasty questions and making those wicked suggestions.'

'Perhaps he's not allowed to,' said Anna.

'What was going on at the end?' Sybil wondered.

'It was when Tancred spoke that Chinese name,' Anna replied.

'Price has a Chinese woman in Paris. Before her it was a tart from Budapest. He collects tarts. This one is the latest.'

'It wasn't as I expected.' Sybil looked out of the window of the taxi. 'Court, I mean. I don't think I liked it very much.'

'Won't you come tomorrow?' Emerald wanted to know.

'Oh, I couldn't miss it but I didn't really enjoy it. Not this afternoon with Mordecai being so horrid.' They arranged to meet at Patrick's chambers again the next morning.

Patrick was in his chambers with Ian French and Cranley Burrows, none of them looking particularly happy. Cranley said that a difficult day had at least ended with some embarrassment for Mordecai.

'Yes,' Patrick agreed. 'Thank God for Price's interruption. It had been pretty rough before. That visit to
Sebastian Sleaven which he never told us about!' He got
up and wandered to the window, leaning on the wall
and looking down at the Temple garden. 'What was he
up to, going to see Sebastian Sleaven?' he muttered
almost to himself. He turned back to the others. 'And
why the hell won't he take us into his confidence?'

'He never has and he never will,' said Cranley. 'And
there's nothing we can do about it.'

'Perhaps he really has nothing convincing to say,'
suggested French gloomily. 'Perhaps he gambled
because he thought they wouldn't be able to come up
with proof. That's what's being said in the Temple. The
documents, Sleaven's suicide and the visit to Sebastian
Sleaven.' He shook his head. 'It doesn't look good.'

In the Cabinet Room at Downing Street the Prime Minister said to Alan Prentice, 'I see that the Tancred case has
started in the High Court.'

Alan smiled. 'So you've been reading the evening
paper, Prime Minister? You're not meant to read the
newspapers.'

'Just a glance. Only on this special occasion. How is it
going?' He knew that Prentice had sent a junior secretary to attend and report.

'Not very well for the former Minister, I understand.
He is being cross-examined by Mordecai Ledbury. There
was an incident at the end with Price talking to Ledbury
and the court adjourned early.'

'Price was there?' the Prime Minister mused. 'Of
course. He had to be there. Such a very disagreeable
man.'

'There's been a message from your constituency
office, Prime Minister,' Prentice said.

'From Aidan Wills?'

'From Mrs Wills, actually.'

'On behalf of Mr Wills, I suppose.' The Prime Minister

got to his feet. 'I'll return the call from the flat upstairs.'

Alan Prentice watched him shuffle out of the room to the stairs. He's suddenly looking much older, he thought. Four years as Prime Minister and for all his pretence of being above it he keeps his finger on every pulse in government. The strain is beginning to tell. And he's too conscientious about his constituency. No wonder he looks all in.

Later in the evening Price at last got through to Helena in Paris on the telephone. 'I've been trying to get hold of you since five o'clock.'

'I told you to call at eleven.'

'I know but this was urgent. Where've you been?' he asked.

'I've been to the movies as I told you I would and—'

'Who did you go with?'

She laughed, a seductive, mocking laugh. 'A handsome young man, half your age.' She laughed again. 'Whom do you think? By myself, of course. Don't you believe me?'

'I suppose so,' he grumbled. 'I miss you.'

'I hope you do. How did the afternoon go? You sound rather agitated.'

'Something came up at the end of the day. Until then it was going all right. I have to ask you. Who is Harry Cheung?'

'Harry Cheung? I've never heard of him. Why?'

'Tancred brought it up in court at the end of the day. It gave me a shock. He went out of his way to say I'd know the name.'

'Of course you know the name. It's my name, isn't it?'

'I know that. But do you know a Harry Cheung?'

'No, I don't. But Cheung's quite a common name in Hong Kong. I've never heard of a Harry Cheung.'

'No one in your family?'

'No, certainly not.'

'No connection to you?'

'I said. I've never heard of a Harry Cheung. Why are you going on about it?'

'I had to check. I don't want you involved.'

'Because someone has the same name you think I'd be involved? I'm not involved and I won't be. The only way I am involved is in pleasing you. Don't worry about me.'

'I can't help worrying about you. So there's no connection?'

'No, of course not.'

'I had to check. I suppose it was just one of his tricks, trying to get at me through you, or rather through your name.'

'That's absurd. If he really tried to do that, he must be getting desperate.'

'He is. He's in trouble and he knows it.'

'I'm glad,' she said simply.

There was a pause. 'I do miss you,' he repeated. 'I wish you were here with me.'

'Among the beastly English? No, thank you. I'm better here. What stage in the trial have you reached?'

'He's being cross-examined. And being knocked about. And we haven't even got on to the money yet, not touched the details nor the documents. That'll come tomorrow. That's when he'll be finished. He won't be able to get out of that.'

'When will it be over?'

'Oh, some time yet, but we'll know what's going to happen by tomorrow evening when he's confronted with the money. Perhaps the day after. In effect, it should be all over by then.'

'Let me know how it goes. But I shall be at the movies tomorrow.'

'Again?'

'I like the movies. What else have I to do? You're having all the fun.'

'Then come and join me.'

232

'Certainly not. I'm not coming near that horrid country. Good luck, my darling.'

He heard her laugh as she replaced the receiver.

Tancred had returned to his flat in Consul Road. He made himself some coffee and drank it black. From a locked briefcase he took a thick, heavy ledger and various documents. He began to make entries in the ledger, extracting figures from the documents. At half past seven the bell rang and he opened the door to Elspeth Turville. Even though Burrows had warned him. After all, she might be a witness.

Chapter Five

Half an hour before the start of the second day of the trial the News Universal team met in the conference room. Mordecai was again at the small table, Walter Morrison behind him. Oliver Goodbody led in Price, Spenser and Waite. Price flung himself into a chair opposite Mordecai, thrust out his legs and buried his hands deep in his trouser pockets.

'The Chinese name, yesterday afternoon—' Mordecai began.

Price interrupted, waving a hand, 'Forget it. I shouldn't have let it get to me but hearing it in court gave me a jolt. Not to worry about it. Just leave it. Move on to the money.'

'In my experience,' Waite said, 'juries always enjoy hearing about money.' He chuckled. Mordecai glared at him. Waite stopped chuckling and looked away.

Mordecai turned back to Price. 'He must have had some reason for mentioning that name.'

'It was just an offhand—'

'Nothing that man says or does is offhand,' Mordecai growled.

'Then let's hear what he has to say about the money. He can't be offhand about that. Let's hear how he explains the money.'

Mordecai said, 'He threw out that name yesterday afternoon quite deliberately.'

'Of course he did. He must have discovered that my friend in Paris has the same name and he was trying to rattle me. He did it to get at me – to get himself out of the hole you'd got him into.'

Mordecai looked at Oliver Goodbody, who looked away.

Price got to his feet. 'I didn't like the name of my friend being brought up in court, that's all. But I've checked it out. It's not in any way connected with her. So for God's sake, man, leave the name alone.'

Before Mordecai could reply Spenser said hastily, 'He can't deny about the money.'

'I don't expect him to,' Mordecai replied.

'We know about the money,' said Waite, 'because we've seen the documents. So has the judge. But the jury hasn't. When they see those documents they won't like it. They won't like it at all.'

Price strode towards the door. 'All you have to do is to make the jury understand that he took money from the bugger and that the bugger has shot himself. That's enough, isn't it?' He opened the door. 'I'm going into court.'

Oliver Goodbody, who had remained silent throughout the meeting, followed Spenser and Waite from the room, leaving Walter alone with Mordecai. When the door had closed behind them Mordecai picked up his sticks and gathered himself together for his entrance into the court.

'Why does the name trouble you?' Walter asked as he held open the door.

Mordecai stopped. 'I don't know. But it does.' Then he growled, 'What were those lunatic suicidal Japanese called who flew their aeroplanes into the ships?'

'Kamikaze,' Walter replied.

'Well, that's what you and I are.'

'Why? What's worrying you? You'll get him all right. He can't get round the money.'

'It's just what I feel – in my bones, in my gut,' said Mordecai.

Usually, when there was a jury, he staged an entrance very late as he had the day before, taking his place noisily with a perfunctory nod to the bench. But today he entered the courtroom in time to precede the judge and he got to his place just as Jack Traynor reached his. Mordecai bowed politely and remained standing, ready to resume his cross-examination. To those in the court hoping for a good day's sport, he looked as threatening as ever. Yet as he stood there looking so formidable he had a sense of foreboding. Something wasn't right. He gave a great shrug, shaking his whole head and body like a dog and letting out a grunt.

Jack Traynor looked at him with distaste.

The clerk called out 'Tancred versus News Universal and Others, part heard', the judge nodded and Mordecai began.

'Who was Oscar Sleaven?' he asked Tancred loudly, not looking at him but at the jury.

'The Chairman of Sleaven Industries.'

'Is that a conglomerate that trades in property and manufacturing, including the manufacture of trucks and military vehicles?'

'Yes.'

'And you had dealings with Oscar Sleaven when you were the Minister for Defence Procurement?'

'I did.'

'Many dealings?'

'Yes.'

'In October three years ago, when you were the Minister, did Sleaven enter into a contract with your ministry to supply the Army with a new armoured personnel carrier, or APC for short?'

'As far as I can remember, I believe that he did.'

'Did the contract for the manufacture and supply of those vehicles involve millions of pounds of public money?'

'It would have, certainly.'

'So whoever got the contract could anticipate making hundreds of thousands of pounds of profits?'

'Yes.'

'And a contract for the manufacture of those APCs

was entered into between the Ministry and Sleaven Industries?'

'I have said I believe so, yes.'

'Before the contract had been signed had tenders been sought by the Ministry from a number of manufacturers?'

'Of course.'

'Was the Sleaven tender the lowest of those submitted?'

'I'm not sure.'

'I suggest it was not. Not by many thousands of pounds.'

Tancred shook his head. 'I cannot quite remember after all this time. But you may be right.'

'I suggest that you know perfectly well that I am right. October three years ago. The Sleaven tender for the APC contract. It was not the lowest tender, yet the Sleaven tender was the one your ministry accepted. Why?'

'I expect it was because we judged that their tender had other important advantages – better performance of the vehicles and sooner delivery dates.'

'The unsuccessful manufacturers whose tenders had been lower were resentful, weren't they? They complained bitterly, didn't they?'

'I do not know. But manufacturers who fail to win a contract usually are bitter and do complain.'

'And why should they not complain if they had submitted a lower tender and yet failed to win the contract?'

'As I said, I think the advantage of Sleaven Industries was that they offered better terms and conditions.'

'Was that the reason they got the contract?'

'It was.'

'The only reason?'

'Yes.'

Mordecai waited. Then he said, 'Or was the real reason because the Chairman, Oscar Sleaven, was paying you money?'

'That is totally false.'

'Is it? You knew Oscar Sleaven. He was a friend?'

'I knew him. Not well.'

'You were often in his company?'

'Sometimes.'

'More than sometimes. You were continually meeting outside the Ministry. I take an example. Richmond records that he saw you and Oscar Sleaven at the Italian Embassy on 27 April two years ago; then three weeks later at a dinner given by Lady Sylvia Benedict in London on 18 May; and again later that same month at a weekend party at Wainscott, Lady Sylvia's country house. Three occasions within the space of one month.'

'That we were fellow guests on those occasions was a coincidence.'

'On each of those occasions you were seen to engage in private conversation with Oscar Sleaven.'

'As I said, we were fellow guests.'

'Why, on each occasion, did you talk privately to him?'

'Out of politeness. By chance we had both been invited as guests.'

'Was it chance that later in that same summer you were observed meeting Oscar Sleaven at the Tate Gallery?'

Tancred was silent.

Price looked up, smiling his grim, self-satisfied smile.

'No,' said Tancred, 'that meeting was by arrangement.'

'At the Tate? You arranged to meet at the Tate? The Minister arranges to meet the industrialist he's doing business with at a picture gallery? Wasn't that an odd place for a minister of the Crown to meet one of the industrialists with whom his ministry was negotiating million-pound contracts for the supply of military vehicles?'

'It would have been, yes, if that meeting had had anything to do with the business of the Ministry.'

'Did it not?'

'No, it did not.'

Anna, beside Emerald and Sybil, both in smart but different outfits from those they had worn yesterday, leant forward in her seat. She expected Mordecai next to ask what, then, the meeting at the Tate had been about? So did Walter Morrison, sitting behind Mordecai; so did Digby Price in front of him. But instead Mordecai turned and gestured as he had the day before when John Meadows had stood and been recognised by Tancred. This time it was a middle-aged woman, with dyed, burnished hair, heavily made up, dressed in a brightly flowered dress who rose from the seat next to Anna. As she stood she simpered and looked about her, apparently delighted at the attention she was receiving.

'Do you recognise this lady?' Mordecai asked.

Tancred nodded. 'I do. It is Mrs Lane. She owns the house in Consul Road in which I have a flat.'

'If Mrs Lane were to go into the witness box where you are now standing and say on oath, as you are now on oath, that she remembers Oscar Sleaven coming to see you in your flat late at night on two occasions two years ago, would she be right?'

'She would not. She would be mistaken. Oscar Sleaven never came to see me at my apartment.'

Mordecai handed a photograph to the usher. 'Show that to the witness. Is that a good likeness of Oscar Sleaven?'

Tancred inspected it, then handed it back to the usher. 'It is.'

'If the lady were to say that she recalls seeing the man in that photograph coming to your flat on two occasions late at night after you had returned from the House of Commons, would she be wrong?'

'Quite wrong.

'Are you categorically saying she would be wrong?'

'I am.'

Mordecai gestured and Mrs Lane resumed her seat. 'Then we shall have to wait to hear her evidence – and when we do, we shall remember your denial,' said Mordecai looking at the jury. 'In any event I suggest that, as well as secret meetings in picture galleries and elsewhere, Oscar Sleaven also visited you in your flat, secretly and late at night.'

'I deny it.'

'If she were to say he did, Mrs Lane would be lying?'

'She would be mistaken.'

'Just as Francis Richmond was mistaken in recording he overheard you speak of your desire to get money from politics?'

'Yes.'

'Their word against yours.' Then Mordecai added quietly, 'And you with so much to lose.'

Patrick half rose. 'That is not a question,' he said.

Mordecai waved his hand dismissively but went on quickly before the judge could intervene, 'The meeting at the Tate. You agree that meeting took place? Richmond was not mistaken about that, was he?'

'No. That meeting was by arrangement.'

'And it had nothing to do with the business of your ministry?'

'No.'

'Why meet, of all places, at the Tate?'

'I thought it was a discreet place to meet but it was observed by Richmond and misconstrued.'

Mordecai looked at the jury. 'You wanted to have a discreet meeting with Oscar Sleaven, so you chose a picture gallery. And when your meeting was observed, you say that meeting was misconstrued?' he asked quietly.

'Yes, it was. Because that meeting was observed, it has led, in part, to this case.'

'Oh, yes it has certainly helped to lead to this case. For did not that secret meeting, like your other meetings with Oscar Sleaven, have to do with money?'

After a moment Tancred said, 'No, it did not.'

'Not to do with money? Are you telling the jury that this meeting in the Tate, this secret meeting in the picture gallery, between you, who had the power to award contracts worth millions of pounds, and the man eager to win such contracts, had nothing to do with money?'

'Not directly, no.'

'Indirectly?'

'Not exactly.'

'Not directly?' Mordecai repeated, 'not *exactly* to do with money? What does that mean?' He paused. 'I have observed, Mr Tancred, that you use words carefully and with precision, as we would expect from so experienced and skilful a politician. So you must forgive me if I wonder what that means. "Not exactly". What does "not exactly" or "not directly to do with money" mean?'

'What it says. That meeting was not exactly to do with money.'

There was a lengthy pause. Then Mordecai said, 'As you claim that your secret meeting with Oscar Sleaven was not, to quote you, *exactly* to do with money, perhaps the time has come for the jury to look at these.' He held up a bundle of documents. 'Do you know what these are?'

'I believe I do.'

Mordecai motioned to the usher who took the bundle to the witness box. While he did so, Mordecai said to the judge, 'You have these documents, My Lord.'

Jack Traynor nodded. And about time too, he thought.

In the witness box Tancred turned over the bundle page by page rapidly, almost cursorily. Then he laid it on the broad ledge in front of him.

'What are those documents?' Mordecai asked.

'Copies of my personal bank statements,' Tancred replied.

'Do you have the originals here in court?'

'My solicitor has.'

'Would you care to compare the originals with the copies?'

Tancred shook his head. 'No, they are accurate copies.'

'Are you interested to know how we got our hands on your personal bank statements?'

'No. I was aware that you had them.'

'Of course you were. They were disclosed by us and are among the documents prepared for the trial. But these are very personal documents, your private records. Are you not interested to learn how they came into our possession?'

'Not particularly.'

'It is said that there are four ways to lay hands on another's bank statements.' Tancred shrugged and Mordecai went on. 'By computer hacking, by tricking someone on the bank staff to divulge their details, by bribing the staff or by bank staff leaking them malevolently. Which do you think this was?'

'I do not know. All I know is that you have them.'

'Well, despite your unconcern, real or feigned, may I tell you that we received them in the post, with no accompanying letter, no indication who had sent them?'

'That is of no interest to me.'

'So you say. But these documents will be of great interest to the jury. That they were sent to us anonymously would indicate, would it not, that you have enemies?'

'I expect I have. Your clients, News Universal, are certainly an enemy. Perhaps I have others. Most people who have been in public life do.'

'The person who sent them to us must have had access to your private affairs. Are you not concerned about that?'

'No. You have described the various ways that your informant could have got them. All I can say is that you have possession of accurate copies of my private bank account. You disclosed them on discovery so I have

known about it for several months. There is nothing
I can do about it.'

'Have you any bank account other than this one with
Coutts?'

'No.'

'So the court can see from these statements exactly
what monies were received by you during your last two
years as a minister?'

'It can.'

The jury began examining the bundles, some of them
at first looking a little bewildered, others turning over
the pages and pointing out items to those with whom
they were sharing a bundle.

'Does that bundle of documents consist of photostats
of monthly statements of your bank account at Coutts &
Co., Lower Sloane Street in London?'

'I have already told you. It does.'

'Extending over a period of twenty-four months, dat-
ing back two years from April last year?'

'Yes.'

'Then let us examine them together. First, let me ask
about some regular monthly credits. Do these represent
the payments of your ministerial salary?'

'They do.'

'Quite modest sums?'

'If you say so. But not everyone would agree with that
description of a ministerial salary.'

'Possibly not, but compared with other credit items in
the account, they are modest. There also some irregular
credit entries from what appears to be a finance
house?'

'Yes. Those are the receipts from my investments.'

'Even more modest sums. Now let us turn to the debit
entries. Are there regular debit entries consisting of a
monthly sum paid to Mrs Maria Lane by direct debit. Is
that for the rent of your flat?'

'It is.'

'Do you own or rent any other property anywhere
else in the world?'

'No.'

'Not in France?'

'No.'

'Apart from the regular debit entry for the rent of your flat, are there many debit entries referred to as cash?'

'There are.'

Mordecai turned away from Tancred and looked at the jury. 'So much for the payments out of your personal account and what I suggest are the legitimate payments in. Let us now turn to other credit entries that figure in these accounts. Look at the entries that have been high-lighted on the statements, credit entries on the first day of each month and the last day of each quarter.' He stopped. The juryman in the blue blazer with the brass buttons was whispering to his companion and looking up at Tancred. The young Asian woman was sharing a bundle with the spinster jurywoman who found it so hard to understand the judge's northern accent. She was pointing at various entries. Jack Traynor watched her, and his gaze never left her for long. He noted her long, slim fingers and polished nails as she drew attention to the items in the documents, guiding the confused spin-ster jurywoman beside her. She's more beautiful than Lois, he thought. And more intelligent.

Mordecai satisfied that he had the attention of all members of the jury, went on, 'Throughout those two years, is there a similar credit entry on the first day of each month?'

'Yes.' Tancred laid the documents on the ledge of the witness box. 'This all appears quite clearly in the bank statements, Mr Ledbury.'

'It does, but the jury have not seen these documents before. Disquieting though you may find it, I propose to take you through them one by one. What do the entries highlighted in yellow show?'

'A monthly credit of one thousand pounds – as the jury can plainly see.'

'Paid into your account on the first day of each month?'

'Yes.'

'Twenty-four of them?'

'Yes.'

'Regular payments of the same sum paid at regular intervals?'

'Yes.'

'Twenty-four credits of one thousand pounds each during the two years covered by these bank statements?'

'Yes.'

'There are also other entries that have been highlighted, not in yellow but in red. Do they appear on the last day of the third month in each quarter of each year?'

'They do.'

'Are they all for a similar sum?'

'Yes. The jury, Mr Ledbury, can surely see all this for themselves.'

'They can. But answer my questions. What is the sum that is paid into your account every quarter?'

'Ten thousand pounds.'

'Over the space of two years does that amount to eighty thousand pounds?'

'Eight tens invariably add up to eighty, so your mathematics, Mr Ledbury, are quite correct.'

'Sarcasm', Mordecai growled, 'won't divert the jury from noting, as I intend they shall note, that over a period of two years a very substantial sum of money was paid into your bank account – your personal account that fortunately came into our hands. Twenty-four thousand pounds from the monthly payments and eighty thousand from the quarterly payments, all received by you in the space of two years when you were a minister. Isn't that correct?'

'Your mathematics, Mr Ledbury, are, as I have said, impeccable.'

Mordecai glared at the witness. Tancred's hands

remained folded over the documents on the ledge of the witness box. 'The bank statements also reveal, do they not, from whom you received that money?'

'They do.'

'I direct the jury's attention to the column headed "Description" against these credit entries. That indicates, does it not, the source whence each of these sums had come?'

'Of course it does.'

'In the description column is there a name?'

'There is.'

'Tell the court what is the name recorded against these payments.'

'As the jury can again plainly see with their own two eyes,' Tancred said wearily, 'the name is Oscar Sleaven.'

'Yes,' Mordecai agreed. 'Oscar Sleaven. The late Oscar Sleaven, who got the lucrative contract for the armoured personnel carriers even though he'd not put in the lowest tender and who last week blew out his brains shortly before the start of this trial.' He waited, watching the jury turning the pages, several of them nudging the companion sharing the bundle, then looking up at Tancred, the young Asian woman in particular, with a half-smile on her face. Mordecai turned back to face Tancred. 'So from your own personal bank account records – which so fortuitously came into our hands – we can see that during these two years you were receiving scores of thousands of pounds from Oscar Sleaven?'

'You can.'

'Let me try on you a little more of my simple arithmetic on which you have so complimented me. First, there are the payments of a thousand pounds on the first day of each of twenty-four months. Total twenty-four thousand pounds. Correct?'

'Quite correct, Mr Ledbury,' Tancred replied.

'With a further eighty thousand, making a hundred and four thousand pounds. Isn't that correct?'

'It is.'

'All received by you from Oscar Sleaven in two years and at a time when you were a minister of the Crown?'

'Yes. It is all very clearly set out in the statements.'

Price who had been sitting with his hands folded and head lowered, turned to look at Mordecai, nodding his head and smiling grimly.

Mordecai went on, 'So you don't deny, you cannot deny, that while you were a minister of the Crown and Sleaven Industries was one of the commercial enterprises with which your Ministry was contracting the Chairman, Oscar Sleaven, paid you personally in excess of a hundred thousand pounds?'

'I do not deny it. There was no need, Mr Ledbury, to go through such a prolonged exercise—'

'Whether the exercise was prolonged or not is a matter for me,' Mordecai snarled. 'I need no lecture from you on how I choose to conduct this cross-examination. Do you admit that Oscar Sleaven paid that sum into your personal account?'

'I do.'

Walter Morrison leant forward and handed Mordecai a document. Mordecai examined it and said, 'Yes, let me remind you again what Richmond recorded you as saying. That you intended to *get money from politics*.' He let slip the paper, which fell to the floor in front of his desk. The usher came to pick it up. 'Leave it,' Mordecai commanded and turned back to face Tancred. 'You have done just that, have you not? You have succeeded in getting a great deal of money from your position in politics, from your position as a minister?'

'No, I have not.'

'In the face of those documents alone, how can you stand there in that witness box and swear under oath that you did not get money out of politics – as Richmond claims you said that you would?'

'First, as I told you I did not say what he recorded me

247

as saying. He was wrong about that. Second, I was not getting money through politics.'

'How can you dare say that? You were getting a great deal of money from Oscar Sleaven. And no one would ever have known about this money' – Mordecai picked up the file and wagged it at the jury – 'if some public-spirited person had not sent these documents to the newspaper. Is that not right?'

'Probably.'

'And we can also see from the bank statements that as quickly as the money came into your account, it went out again. The money didn't remain long in your account, did it?' Mordecai was still holding up the bundle, looking now at the jury. 'A great deal of money was being received by you, but your account was only ever marginally in credit at the end of each month. You were drawing it all out in cash. Isn't that correct?'

'It is.'

'All this money coming in and going out. You must have been living pretty well, Mr Tancred, to have spent so much money?'

'No. I was not.'

'Not what?'

'I was not living particularly well. I had my flat in Chelsea. That was all.'

'Were you salting it away offshore so that when the time came you could retire to some place where you could enjoy it and not be reached by extradition?'

'No, I was not.'

'Tell me,' asked Mordecai, 'is the money still flowing in from your friend, Mr Oscar Sleaven – or rather, was it still flowing in until his death?'

'He was not my friend and the money ceased in April last year.'

Mordecai paused. 'April?' he said ruminatively. 'April last year? Was that shortly after you had ceased to be a minister of the Crown?'

'It was.'

'So it ceased when you were no longer of any use to

him? It ceased after you'd been shown up by the *Sunday News*. Was that the reason the payments from Oscar Sleaven ceased? Because you were no longer a minister of the Crown and had been exposed?'

'No. The payments ceased because the reason for them had ceased.'

'Certainly, the reason for them had ceased. It ceased because you could no longer give your friend the help for which he was paying you. Isn't that right?

'No, it is not right.'

Mordecai said nothing. It had, of course been easy. The bank statements revealed it all, the sums of money, the name of the person who had paid them. He had only prolonged the questioning so as to make sure that the least numerate of the jury could grasp the extent of the large sums Oscar Sleaven, a man whose contracts with the Crown would bring him in many millions, had been paying regularly into the personal account of the Minister for Defence Procurement. Those were undisputedly correct records and there was at least one contract when a Sleaven tender had been accepted by the Ministry although other tenders were lower. And Sleaven and Tancred were meeting mysteriously, secretly. And just before the trial when all this was certain to come out into the open, Tancred had gone to visit Oscar's brother, Sebastian Sleaven. And four days after that visit Oscar Sleaven had killed himself. What could all that mean? What did it point to if it was not a guilty and corrupt association?

With Mordecai momentarily silent, the court waited for the final answer to the final question. If the monies paid to Tancred were not corrupt payments, what were they? The spectators leant forward. Tancred, ivory pale, stood erect in the witness box. Still Mordecai waited.

'Yes, Mr Ledbury?' said the judge.

Mordecai turned so that he had his back to the witness box. Something held him back. But he knew that he could not avoid the final question. He took a stumbling pace or two away from the jury, his stick thumping on the floor. All that the jury could see of him was the humped back and the rear of the grey, almost black, wig. At last he said quietly, over his shoulder, almost to himself, 'Then tell us what you say was the reason that Oscar Sleaven's payments to you ceased.'

Tancred did not reply, waiting for Mordecai to turn and face him.

Mordecai swung round. 'Tell the jury why the payments ceased,' he repeated loudly.

'Because the child had died,' Tancred said.

A gasp arose in the courtroom, followed by complete silence. Price jerked his head round to look at Goodbody beside him. Anna leant forward in her seat, her chin on her hands. Patrick sat as rigid as a statue. The judge waited, his pencil poised over his notebook.

Mordecai drew a deep breath. 'The child had died,' he said at last. 'What child? What has a child to do with it?'

'Everything,' Tancred replied.

Mordecai stared at him. Then he asked, 'What are you talking about? What child?'

'My daughter's child, the child that had been born to my daughter when she was barely fifteen years old.'

Mordecai stood motionless. He stared at Tancred, willing him to go on, willing him to explain. But Tancred didn't go on and Mordecai knew that Tancred was waiting – for him. Still Mordecai said nothing. And still Tancred remained mute.

It was the judge who broke the silence. 'Yes,' he said quietly to Tancred, 'the child. Please go on. Explain what you mean.'

Tancred turned to the judge. 'The child, a boy, was eight years old when he died. Once he was dead there was no further cause for more payments.' He stopped and turned towards Mordecai and remained silent.

The judge, Mordecai prayed, he must take it on. But the judge said no more. The courtroom was breathlessly still. The pause seemed interminable. Then almost wearily, spelling out the words one by one, Mordecai asked, 'What has the death of this child to do with the payments made to you by Oscar Sleaven?'

'Everything. Oscar Sleaven was the father of the child.'

A noise arose in the courtroom like the wind rustling the leaves of trees as spectator after spectator turned to his or her neighbour. The judge tapped with his pencil.

'Sleaven! Oscar Sleaven?' Mordecai asked. 'You say that Oscar Sleaven was the father of the child that died?'

'Yes,' Tancred replied simply.

'Sleaven was the father? Your daughter, you said, was barely fifteen and Oscar Sleaven was a man of—' Mordecai did not complete the sentence.

Tancred had interrupted. 'Yes, Sleaven was much older. But he was the father of her child.'

'But the money. The money was coming to you,' Mordecai said savagely. 'If what you say is the truth, why was the money from Sleaven coming to you? Why not to her?' Then he made a mistake. 'Was it to keep you quiet?'

'How dare you!' Tancred shouted, colour for the first time flooding into his face. He leant forward over the edge of the witness box, towards where Mordecai stood, thumping the edge with his fist. 'How dare you!' he repeated. The loudness of his shout, the contrast between his former icy composure and now his anger, rang around the courtroom. For almost a minute there was total silence. Then he straightened, squaring his shoulders, the colour fading from his face. He spoke quietly. 'The child's mother, my daughter, had died shortly after she'd given birth. She was not alive to receive the money. These were payments for her child, a boy, to keep him at the home where he was cared for, where he had to be cared for day and night.' He paused. 'Oscar Sleaven provided the money. He could afford it, but at least he did that. With the child's death, the obligation ceased.'

Mordecai stood very still, as though shocked by his own error and Tancred's reaction.

Tancred went on 'From birth the child was damaged. He understood nothing. He was born without a brain. He had to be looked after, night and day. As he was – thanks to the money provided by Sleaven, the money I demanded that Sleaven must pay.' Tancred paused; then turned in the witness box, looked at Mordecai and added, 'He began paying eight years ago, when the child was born. So, you see, I had very good reason from time to time to see or speak to Oscar Sleaven. The meeting in the Tate of which you have made so much was to persuade him to establish a trust in favour of the child.'

He switched his gaze and spoke directly to Price, who was staring up at him, the smile long gone from his face. 'Her mother had abandoned my daughter when she was an infant. That was twenty-five years ago. I did not even know I had a daughter. I did not know she existed. A relative of the mother arranged for the girl to be brought up. I only knew my daughter existed when eight years ago, aged a little over fifteen, she gave birth to her gravely disadvantaged son. As I said, the child was born without a brain. The condition of the child shattered his mother, my daughter. Shortly after the birth—' He paused, bent his head and looked down at his hands, folded before him on the edge of the witness box. 'Shortly after the birth,' he went on, 'when my daughter saw the child she had borne and was told about his condition, she took an overdose of drugs and killed herself. Only then was I informed of her existence and of her fate.' He lifted his head and spoke directly to Mordecai. 'That is the answer to your question as to why the money came to me. It came to me because my daughter was dead.'

Again the noise filled the courtroom, this time louder than before, more like the sound of the ocean breaking on the shore as the listeners turned and whispered to each other. The judge tapped again with his pencil to quieten the noise and said quietly, 'And Oscar Sleaven? You say he was the father of your daughter's child?'

Tancred turned to him. 'He was. My daughter, I learnt later, had been brought up in Australia although she had been born in Hong Kong. Her mother was Hong Kong Chinese.'

The name, Mordecai thought. The name Tancred had thrown out yesterday afternoon. The name he'd spoken so deliberately, so menacingly. Cheung. The name of Price's friend in Paris!

'She was raised in Sydney by a lady called Elspeth Turville, a close friend, as she still is, of a gentleman who came from Hong Kong, a half-brother of my daughter's mother.' Tancred pointed directly at Price who half rose from his seat. 'Yesterday Mr Price was disturbed when he heard the name, for he recognised it. My friend, Harry Cheung.'

'No,' said Price aloud. 'She doesn't know a Harry Cheung.'

Goodbody put his hand on Price's as Price sank back in his seat, shaking his head, then leaning forward with his face between his hands.

'Oh, but she does,' Tancred went on. 'Harry Cheung is her half-brother – and she was the mother of my daughter.'

Tancred had turned to face the jury, who had cast aside the bank statements. They were of no interest to them now. Some of the bundles had even dropped to the floor of the jury box and were left where they had fallen. Every member of the jury was staring at Tancred, riveted. Even the red-faced pugnacious juryman, who sat with his mouth open.

'My daughter was not an easy child, difficult to control, perhaps because she'd been abandoned by her mother as an infant and never knew who her father was. They lived in Sydney and in adolescence she grew increasingly wild. When she was a teenager she took to slipping out of the house, staying out until the early hours of the morning. She got mixed up with an older group, going with them, joining the hostesses in the bars and nightclubs in the King's Cross area of Sydney, experimenting with drugs, meeting men who came there, some who were visiting the city on business. From the clubs they used to go with the men to drink and take drugs in the hotels. That was how she met Oscar Sleaven. When Elspeth Turville discovered that the girl was pregnant she took her to France, Elspeth Turville's native country, sending her to a detoxing centre, urging her to have an abortion. But the girl refused stubbornly. She insisted on bearing the child. When the baby was born and she saw what she had borne and realised the kind of infant he was, the tragedy followed. Only then was I told that I had been her father. I repeat, until then I did not even know she existed.' He paused. 'I was also told the name of the man who had made her pregnant.' He stopped.

Mordecai was standing with both hands, now, on his one stick, his head bowed. Oliver Goodbody, beside the bent figure of Digby Price, stared straight ahead, his features rigid and immobile. There was a sudden scramble from the press box, journalists rushing noisily down the side aisles of the court to get to the telephone boxes or to where they could use their mobile telephones.

'Silence,' the usher shouted as the pressmen pushed their way noisily out of the courtroom and with the exit of the press silence did indeed return to the courtroom. 'So you see' – Tancred turned from Mordecai to the jury – 'I had good reason now and then to meet Oscar Sleaven. The gossip monger, the diarist, Francis Richmond, a silly, malicious man, had a grudge against me because years ago he had visited Bangkok when I was serving there as a diplomat in charge of security. I had to warn him about his activities in the city. He dragged me into his diary in which he recorded false and malicious gossip, as people of his kind often do. But the reason why I met Oscar Sleaven was not for the corrupt one Richmond thought but because of the defective child of whom Sleaven was the father. I had not the means to give the child the care he needed and the child was Oscar Sleaven's responsibility. I made sure that he accepted that responsibility. Then, when Richmond's diary was brought to News Universal, Mr Price' – here Tancred pointed directly at Price – 'Mr Price thought he'd been handed a weapon that would destroy me and he was glad to have it and to use it. He was another I had encountered in my previous life. It goes back to what happened to him in Zambia in Africa many years ago, for which he believed I was responsible. That was his reason. He did not know, however, that twenty-five years ago Helena Cheung, with whom he lives, was the mother of my daughter.'

'That is not true.' Price had risen and was shouting at Tancred. 'It is a lie.'

'Sit down, Mr Price,' the judge said, 'sit down at once or you must leave the court.' Oliver Goodbody pulled Price back into his seat.

Mordecai seized the opportunity of the commotion caused by Price's interruption. 'My Lord,' he called out, almost shouting above the noise in the court, which then subsided. 'My Lord, in view of what the court has just heard, I must consult with my clients. I ask Your Lordship to adjourn to give me time to do so.'

The judge looked at Patrick Foxley, who rose to his feet. 'I have no objection, my Lord,' he said. Mordecai glared at him but Patrick ignored him, standing quite still, his face grave, looking at Tancred.

'I suppose that it is possible, I cannot say more,' Mordecai continued, 'but it is possible that there could be developments in the case. If there were, I would of course immediately inform Your Lordship.'

This time Jack Traynor did not hesitate. 'Very well. I shall adjourn now. I'll be in my room and remain there until I receive word from counsel.' He turned to the jury. 'Please follow the jury bailiff to your room.' Swiftly and without another word he rose and disappeared.

The court exploded in a crash of sound. The jury filed out. 'What's going on?' the spinster jurywoman asked

255

plaintively of another as they went. 'I don't understand what's going on.'

'I'll explain when we're in our room,' said the jury-man in the blazer, taking her by the arm.

In the court everyone was standing and talking. Patrick swept out, alone and without a glance at Tancred or the lawyers on the other side. Tancred stepped down from the witness box and followed, Cranley Burrows taking him by the arm. Mordecai gathered up his sticks and began his inevitably slow exit, hardly looking up from the floor, now and then waving a stick to clear his passage.

'Where to?' Adams asked him.

'The conference room.'

Mordecai settled with a crash into the chair behind the table, flinging his wig to Adams. Goodbody, Spenser and Waite came in, followed by a white-faced Price. Mordecai raised a stick and pointed at Waite. 'Out,' he said. Waite started to object. 'Out,' Mordecai roared. 'Lawyers and clients only. I'm taking charge from now on, as I should have taken more charge earlier in this disaster of a case.'

As Adams led Waite from the room, the others sat, except for Price who leant against the wall at the side of the room.

'Well,' Mordecai began. 'What have you to say? Do you dare now to leave this case to the decision of the jury?'

Chapter Six

The telephone call to Paris came at twenty-five minutes past noon, Paris time, an hour ahead of London and before the court had adjourned. When Helena had replaced the receiver she ran to the library and, sliding back the panel on which was hung the pen-and-ink drawing by Modigliani, she punched in the code and opened the safe. Removing a thick package of dollar banknotes and the velvet box with the slim diamond necklace, also a diamond pendant and two ruby-and-diamond brooches, she closed the safe and slid back the panel. In her dressing room she locked the door and took down a small Louis Vitton dressing case from the top of her wardrobe. At her dressing table she placed the banknotes and the jewellery at the bottom of the case; emptied the few pieces that were in the jewel case on to a silk nightgown and packed it into the dressing case. She added some underclothes, her hairbrushes and cosmetics, and slipped her passport into her handbag. Then she sat at the dressing table and carefully wiped the make-up from her face. This done, she went to the kitchen carrying the dressing case and told the maid, Matilde, that she would not be in for lunch. She was going to the hairdresser, a new salon that a friend had recommended. She was late and was taking her make-up with her. She went through the drawing room and hall, and passed the office at the front of the apartment. The duty secretary looked up, surprised. 'To the hairdresser,' Helena said, 'a new one. I am very late.'

Leaving the apartment, she walked hurriedly down

the rue Casimir Perrier, turned right and when she reached Les Invalides she hailed a taxi, ordering it to take her to the place Vendôme. There she walked through the Ritz and out of the side door. She walked west for a little while before getting into another taxi. 'The airport. Charles de Gaulle,' she said, 'and hurry.'

It was noon, English time, when the court adjourned and a white-faced Price accompanied by Spenser left the conference room in the Law Courts to telephone Paris. Once the door had closed behind them, Goodbody said, 'But how do we know it's true? We have not been served with any witness statements from the Turville woman, or from anyone called Harry Cheung, or—'

'Do you think the judge would refuse leave to serve witness statements late if I were to continue the cross-examination and challenge Tancred's story?'

'No,' Goodbody replied, 'but it would give us time.'

'Time for what?' Mordecai said roughly. 'The question we have to decide is whether I am to continue the cross-examination and call him a liar when we have not a vestige of evidence to show that he is.' He paused before going on, 'That's what he wants us to do for if we go on and fail, the damages will be enormous.'

They sat in silence until Price and Spenser came back into the room. 'We have not been able to reach Madame Helena,' Spenser said. Price sat heavily in a chair beside Goodbody. 'Is it true what he's been saying?' he asked.

'You heard him. What's your opinion?'

'But do we have to accept it, without even hearing from the woman who looked after the girl or anything that corroborates the story?' Spenser asked.

'No, but you heard him. What do you think the jury will make of it?' Mordecai asked. No one answered him, so he went on, 'What evidence have we to challenge it?' He looked round the room before he continued, 'Am I to return to court and say that he's a liar, that he's invented the whole story? If I do, just think of the impression that will make on the jury and the damages you'll have to pay when they realise we have no evidence to prove his story false.'

'Then what's your advice, man?' Price asked brokenly.

'Make an offer, negotiate a settlement and do it now. It is the best chance we have of restricting the damages.'

'Tens of thousands of pounds?' Spenser asked tentatively.

Mordecai snorted. 'Hundreds, hundreds of thousands at the very least. Perhaps more.' There was silence, then Mordecai said to Price, 'The press will now be after the woman Tancred says was the mother of his daughter – and they have a name to help them, the name you were so concerned I should not probe.'

Again there was a silence before Goodbody said, 'Could we not ask for an adjournment for several days, if necessary for some weeks, while we investigate the story?'

'Why should the judge allow that? The burden was on us to come to court and prove the truth that these were corrupt payments – and our duty was to do that today. The judge will see, and will tell the jury, that all we were relying on was the meetings between Tancred and Sleaven, and the evidence of the bank statements. And Tancred has explained both.'

'But is it true?' said Price.

'What do you think? Or, more important, what do you think the jury think?' Mordecai looked around the room, at each in turn. None replied. He continued, 'Foxley won't consent to a long adjournment. Why should he? He'll say we should have come prepared to prove our case.' He turned to Price. 'You were sure you'd come up with evidence to prove Tancred was corrupt and you believed that when we found that money had been passing between him and Sleaven that was sufficient. You thought he would not be able to explain it. Now he has.'

'The story of the child—' Price began.

Mordecai interrupted him. 'The story of the child begins with the story of the mother of the child – and her mother.'

Mordecai waited but Price said nothing. 'How long had you known Helena Cheung before you were brought the diary?' Mordecai asked suddenly.

Price stared at him. 'Why?'

'Spenser says she encouraged you to go on.'

Price put his hand to his head. 'It was I who decided.'

'Ask her about the daughter. Now.'

'She is not in the apartment.' Price paused. 'I knew there had been a relationship between her and Tancred many years ago. I found letters. She was very bitter about him. I did not know there was a child.'

'If there was a relationship,' said Walter Morrison quietly, 'there could have been a child.'

Again there was silence. Mordecai turned back to Goodbody. 'What is your opinion of how the jury will react if I return to that court and suggest that Tancred is a brazen-faced liar as well as a corrupt scoundrel – and then produce not a shred of evidence to back that up? What do you think that would do to the amount of damages the jury would award him?'

Goodbody looked down at his long, slender fingers and shook his head.

Mordecai went on, 'Then there is Lacey and the memorandum he is going to say he made on his return from Paris. He'll say' – he spoke now to Price – 'he'll say you made clear your hatred of Tancred and your determination to publish, that it was a good story that would stimulate circulation and so you'd take the risk. If Lacey does say that, the claim for punitive damages is established.' He turned back to Goodbody. 'That and the story of the mother and the daughter and the dead child. Imagine me continuing to blackguard him publicly in court! Think about it. What is your professional opinion on the effect that would have on the award of damages?'

Goodbody said at last, 'The damages could be enormous.'

Mordecai looked at Walter Morrison, who nodded, and once more addressed Price. 'The only chance of any mitigation in the amount of the vast award of damages you're going to have to pay is to negotiate – and it must be done promptly, before that judge orders us to go on. If I go back into court and continue to attack Tancred, the damages will be astronomical.'

There was a prolonged silence.

Eventually Price lumbered to his feet. 'Do what you think best. I'll be at the Savoy.' To Spenser he said, 'I'll call Paris again from there.' At the door he turned. 'Telephone me what they'll accept.'

When Price had gone, Mordecai said, 'It was a trap, a carefully planned trap. Knowing Price's obsession, Tancred manoeuvred so that it was inevitable that we went on. And we fell for it.'

From his suite in the Savoy Digby Price called Paris. Madame was still out, no one knew where.

Mr Justice Traynor sat in his room, waiting for a message from counsel. At 1.15 he was told by his clerk that counsel were conferring. He sent a message that he'd be back in his room at 2 p.m., walked to his Inn and ate a substantial lunch. He knew it was over.

The jury ate theirs in their stuffy room: solid, heavy food from the canteen, quite unsuitable for the warmth of the July day. 'What do you think is going on?' the middle-aged jurywoman asked the young Asian woman, envying her the coolness of her sari. The young woman shrugged, refusing the food, sipping water.

The juryman in the blazer pushed aside his plate, hardly touched. 'The newspaper has made a fool of itself,' he pronounced.

'Made fucking arses of themselves is what you mean,'

the pugnacious juryman said. 'They've got the money. They won't miss it. But I don't fancy giving it to a bloody politician.' He got up from the table. 'I want a fag.'

'Then go over to the window, there's a dear,' said the other middle-aged jurywoman. He glowered at her but did as she asked. The man in the blazer began coughing and pointed at the sign 'No smoking'. The pugnacious juryman glowered at him and the coughing petered out. But the cigarette was not lit. When the waitress came to clear the dishes he asked her, 'How long are they going to keep us shut up here?'

'All afternoon they say,' she said cheerfully. 'The usher says the barristers are still talking.'

'About their bloody fees I shouldn't wonder,' said the juryman by the window, his unlit fag between his lips.

It was almost five o'clock when the judge took his seat on the bench and the jury filed in, the men now all in their shirtsleeves with their coats over their arms. Tancred was no longer in the witness box but sat impassively in his seat beside Cranley Burrows in front of Patrick Foxley. Neither Digby Price nor Spenser was in court. Mordecai sat bent forward with his chin resting on his hands, which were grasped about the head of one of his sticks; in front of him Oliver Goodbody sat very erect and pale, looking straight ahead at neither judge nor jury.

The clerk called out the name of the case and Patrick Foxley rose to his feet. Before the judge had entered the court he had looked behind him and smiled at Anna. But it was not a triumphant smile. 'I am happy to tell Your Lordship,' Patrick began, 'that neither you nor the jury will be troubled further with this case. The defendants have agreed to withdraw each and every allegation made against Mr Richard Tancred. They accept that the relationship between him and the late Mr Oscar Sleaven was neither corrupt nor concerned in any way with any matter arising from any contract between the Ministry and Mr Sleaven's company. They accept that Mr Richard Tancred, when a minister of the Crown, acted at all times with complete integrity and they apologise unreservedly for publishing the diary of Francis Richmond, which carried the libel about him. To mark their regret and the sincerity of their apology and the complete withdrawal of all allegations that might arise from what was published in the *Sunday News*, the defendants have agreed to pay to Mr Tancred a very substantial sum by way of damages and to bear all his legal costs. In these circumstances I ask leave for the record to be withdrawn.'

As Patrick sat, Mordecai lumbered to his feet. 'I endorse what my learned friend has said. The withdrawal of the allegations made in the defence and levelled in this court is total, the apology complete. News Universal regret their publication of the diary and on their behalf I repeat the apology.' He slid back into his seat and, turning, he whispered to Walter, 'And so say all of us.'

As the judge thanked the jury, releasing them from further attendance, Mordecai went on whispering to Walter. 'Foxley behaved rather well in the negotiation. Adams says there's a woman somewhere who's made him more amenable. Why isn't there one who'd do that for me?'

'No one would,' Walter whispered back.

Mordecai turned round and faced the rigid back of Oliver Goodbody in front of him. He has come worst out of this, he thought.

With a final glance at the young Asian woman who had revived for him such poignant memories, the judge made a perfunctory bow to counsel and left the court. In his room, as he unrobed, he said to his clerk, 'The roody prima donnas weren't too bad after all.' He left the Law Courts by the back entrance and travelled by bus back to Hampstead.

'Fucking waste of time,' grumbled the pugnacious juror, as he ambled out of the courtroom, an unlit cigarette already between his lips. 'Lawyers playing fucking games.'

The public, and especially the press, had heard rumours that there was to be a settlement before the judge had taken his place, so the statements by counsel caused no surprise. Now the journalists swarmed around Tancred and Patrick; they knew better than to come within the range of Mordecai's sticks and left him alone. How much? they kept asking. How much did you get? Tancred smiled his enigmatic smile and pushed his way through the throng. On Burrows fell the task of trying to satisfy them, which he knew he could not. 'As counsel said, the amount is very substantial,' he confirmed. Half a million, a million? they asked him. 'It is a term of the settlement that the amount of damages is to remain confidential,' Burrows kept repeating.

'Any of it going to charity?' one reporter asked.

'It is too early for any decision like that. My client is delighted to have been cleared of the wicked smears about his distinguished service as a minister of the Crown. He has been completely vindicated.'

A million was the opinion of the journalists as they reported back to their offices. The costs would be as much again. Make it a two-million bill for News Universal, they calculated. And this was what was published.

Burrows had kept them at bay sufficiently long for Tancred to slip out of the Law Courts by the back entrance to the car that Burrows had waiting for him. In case he were being followed, the car took a long detour, doubling back on its tracks, eventually emerging on to the M4, along which it drove fast to Heathrow.

But the sensation of the end of the law case Richard Tancred versus News Universal was overshadowed that afternoon by other more important national news that was announced shortly before Patrick Foxley made his statement in court. The Prime Minister had resigned –

for, the official announcement said, personal and health reasons. As was generally known, the statement went on, he had been contemplating retirement for some time and now, on the advice of his doctors, he had decided that this was the time to go. There was to be no General Election, however. Ministers were to remain in their places until a new First Minister was appointed. It was expected that the Chancellor of the Exchequer would be invited by the Queen to form a ministry.

When Adams told him the news in the robing room, Mordecai snorted, 'What was it that Hilaire Belloc wrote? "The accursed Power which stands on Privilege/ (And goes with Women, and Champagne, and Bridge)/ Broke,"' he recited as he ripped off his crumpled collar, '"and Democracy resumed her reign: (Which goes with Bridge, and Women and Champagne.)"'

'Indeed, sir,' Adams replied. 'Indeed. Very true, sir.' He's surprisingly cheerful, Adams thought, considering the result of the case.

In the cab taking him home to Albany, Mordecai was thinking of Oliver Goodbody.

Chapter Seven

When, shortly before one o'clock, Digby Price returned to his suite at the Savoy Hotel, Spenser also slipped away. He knew better than anyone else that in the context of the circulation war and the campaign by Ogilvy Grant's *Telegram* to destroy News Universal, defeat in the libel case, the fall-out on News's reputation by its blunder, and the vast sum of damages and costs would be crippling. In his office in Docklands he telephoned his broker. News Universal's stock price was falling fast. Report of the morning's proceedings had reached the markets before they closed. Nevertheless he instructed the broker to unload what remained of the stock in the nominee's name that disguised his personal holding as soon as possible. The previous sales had made a reasonable price; these, inevitably, would be disastrously low. But he knew he had to sell for whatever he could get. Next he emptied his briefcase and went to his office wall safe where he kept what he had long considered might be his 'insurance policy' in the event of total disaster – the manuscript of Francis Richmond's original diary. It was in Richmond's own handwriting, unedited, unexpurgated.

When Spenser had bought the diary from Job Streatley, he had demanded that Streatley hand over to him not only the typescript that Job had made but also the book in which, in his rounded, old-fashioned handwriting, Richmond had made the entries. Four copies had been made of Streatley's typescript and distributed to the editor of the *Sunday News*, Godfrey Lacey, the

Chairman and one he had kept for himself. Price had ordered the reference to the Prime Minister to be cut; Spenser himself had excised the references to Mordecai Ledbury before the extracts were set in type for printing. It was the original leather-bound book with its manuscript entries that Spenser now removed from the safe and packed into his briefcase. It would be, he trusted, his passport for his imminent transfer of loyalties. He then made a lengthy telephone call. When he had finished he told his secretary to call him a taxi.

'Not your car, Mr Spenser?' she enquired.

'No, a taxi.'

Half an hour later he was being driven away from Dockland. In the cab the driver leant back and told him of the Prime Minister's resignation and they listened on the radio to the reports, and the commentary on the retirement of the old and the identity of the new Prime Minister. The cab finally drew up outside a handsome office block in Battersea Bridge Road. At the desk inside the portico a secretary met Spenser and escorted him to a first-floor office.

He was greeted warmly. 'Come in, my dear fellow,' said Ogilvy Grant. 'Welcome to the *Telegram*.'

When, therefore, Mordecai Ledbury reported to Price at the Savoy the result of his negotiation with Patrick Foxley, Digby Price did not have the assistance of his right-hand man of business. No one knew where Mr Spenser was. He had departed from the News Universal building in a cab; he was not at his home, he had left no message as to his whereabouts. He could not be located. Price also still could not get in touch with Helena in Paris. So when it came to the moment of decision he had to make it alone and on being presented by Mordecai with Tancred's final demand he brusquely agreed. Angry and humiliated, accompanied by a silent Wilson, he left the hotel for Luton airport to board his private jet for Paris.

When they arrived at the rue Casimir Perrier at seven o'clock that evening Helena had still not returned. The maid, Matilde, told Price that Madame had left the apartment in the morning to go to the hairdresser – not her regular hairdresser but another to whom she'd been recommended. She had not taken the car. Price bawled at the maid, reducing her to tears. She did not know the name of the hairdresser. Late as it was, he made Wilson telephone every salon in Paris. He himself called their few acquaintances but no one could tell him anything. Still angry and by now anxious, he paced around the apartment. He went to her wardrobe, but as far as he could tell her clothes were all there. It was only when he chanced to notice that the jewel case on the dressing table was empty that he went to the wall safe and found the money and the jewellery had gone. Wilson, in the outer room, heard his howl of anguish and fury.

After the court had emptied, Anna joined Patrick at his chambers and the two of them took a taxi to Kensington Gardens. By then it was six o'clock; the evening was warm and they walked from the carriage road across the grass in the direction of the Speke memorial. Then they wandered down to the Serpentine and sat on a bench by the Peter Pan statue. 'I used to come here as a child,' he said.

When Anna had parted with a jubilant Emerald and Sylvia at the entrance to the Law Courts, both had been eager to know how much Digby Price had been obliged to pay and they tried to make Anna promise she would find out from Patrick. However, on hearing from the attendant the news of the resignation of the Prime Minister and the probable appointment of the Chancellor of the Exchequer as his successor, they had both bustled off. The Chancellor was due for luncheon on the following Sunday at The Waves. It was imperative that Emerald knew whether his new pre-eminence would prevent his visit; or translate the occasion into the first social occasion attended by the new First Minister. Sylvia, on the other hand, telephoned No. 10 to say that if the former Prime Minister had nowhere to stay in London when he left Downing Street, rather than go to an hotel, he was most welcome at Eaton Square.

On the bench in the park, Anna took Patrick's hand. 'Are you glad it's over?' she asked.

'I am,' he replied. 'But it was an anticlimax for me. I didn't play much of a part.'

'But you won.'

'I didn't. Tancred won. And Mordecai slid out of the fiasco pretty skilfully. His reputation won't be damaged.'

'Did you want it to be?'

'No, but I wanted to beat him fair and square and to be seen to have beaten him. But I didn't. Tancred did.'

'Did you know what was going to be Tancred's explanation of the payments by Sleaven?'

'No. That's what made the case so hard for us, his counsel. When we knew that News had got hold of his bank statements and copies were disclosed to us, as they had to be, I told Tancred that he had to settle unless he had a very, very convincing explanation. He said he had, but he wouldn't tell me what it was. He said he'd reveal it in the witness box and that he'd have the witnesses in London to back it up if that was necessary. It was a high-risk strategy and I had no alternative but to acquiesce. But News was too scared to go on after the jury had heard Tancred. And they were right.'

'How much did Price have to pay?'

'It's confidential, part of the terms of the agreement. But I'll tell you. Seven hundred and fifty thousand pounds general and punitive damages, and Price has to pay all our costs – apart from his own, which are enormous. He has had teams of investigators working for months. He even targeted Cranley Burrows, our solicitor. But all the time Tancred seemed to know what they were doing. He had someone who was informing him. Throughout the months of preparation for trial he was masterminding everything. He planned every move from the very first moment when he came to see me. It was as if he'd planned it all even from before the diary was published.'

'How could he have done that?'

'I don't know. But he seemed to have anticipated every move they made. He gave me the impression he wanted to provoke Price to go on.'

'Why did Price go on?'

'Because he thought he'd win, especially when he got the bank statements that proved Tancred was getting money from Sleaven.'

'Who could have sent those statements to Price's lawyers?'

'I don't know. At the time it seemed a devastating blow, and of course the discovery of the bank accounts made Price certain the payments proved that Tancred was corrupt. He couldn't imagine there was any other reason for the mysterious meetings and the money. And Price wanted to believe it. He was determined to destroy Tancred. There was something between them, I guessed that.'

'Tancred said in court it was something that happened in Africa.'

'Yes, but what it was I don't know and I didn't enquire.'

'What about Helena Cheung in Paris. What part did she play?'

'I suspect a substantial one. She certainly encouraged Price to go on. There was a lot I didn't know, that I wasn't allowed to know. All Tancred wanted from me was to front the exercise in court.'

'And you did it very well.'

'It wasn't very difficult and it wasn't the battle with Mordecai that I hoped it would be. Some day perhaps that will come. Anyhow, it's all over now and what didn't make doing that case very easy was that all the time I have had other things, more important things, on my mind.' He took her hand and leant across and kissed her. 'I'm in love with you,' he said. 'You must know that.'

'You haven't known me very long.'

'Long enough.' He was still holding her hand and he raised it to his lips and kissed it. 'I don't believe in not committing oneself as so many do today,' he said.

'What does that mean?'

'Partners! How I loathe that expression.' He put both his hands round hers but still didn't look at her. 'I love you, Anna. I love making love to you. I want to make love to you all the time. I want to live with you. Which means, for me, that I want to marry you. Which means I'm asking you to take on what my clerk tells me that Mr Justice Traynor, the judge at the trial, calls a roody prima donna.'

She laughed. 'Is that what you are? What about me? A not very talented artist who comes from another very faraway country – a country which, mind you, she'd want to return to every now and then.'

'But not for long. I couldn't be separated for long.'

'No, not for long, not at any one time. But I haven't said yes yet.'

'You must,' he said. 'You mustn't say no.'

'I don't think I shall,' she said and this time she kissed him.

Chapter Eight

'At Gladstone's last Cabinet, when he told his colleagues he was to retire, many wept openly. Thereafter he always called it the "blubbering Cabinet". I cannot say the same of this morning. My colleagues remained remarkably dry-eyed.' The Prime Minister, for he was still the Prime Minister – he was not to go to the Palace until just after three o'clock – was in the Cabinet Room, seated in his usual place facing the windows. Alan Prentice was at his elbow. It was just before one o'clock.

'Gladstone's colleagues were Victorians, Prime Minister. They wept a lot.'

'Did you notice the expression on the face of the Foreign Secretary when I announced that I was going and that I was recommending the Sovereign to send for the Chancellor of the Exchequer?'

'I did, Prime Minister.'

'I would describe it as a face of thunder. I have always liked that expression. In my early days as PM I thought it would be helpful if from time to time I were able to assume a face of thunder. But I never was.'

You are far too devious for that, thought Alan. Even in the manner of your going you will not show your true face to the world.

'When I go to the Palace this afternoon,' the Prime Minister went on, 'I shall not, of course, return. Find out if it would inconvenience Lady Sylvia if I were to beg a bed off her for tonight. I shall say farewell to my constituents tomorrow on my way to Somerset.'

When Alan Price had gone the Prime Minister sat in silence. Then he rose and walked round the Cabinet table and looked out at the garden.

Alan Prentice returned. 'Lady Sylvia is not there but the manservant said he was sure she would be delighted. Lady Sylvia is apparently at the trial.'

'Ah, yes the trial.'

'You'll be pleased to learn', Prentice went on, 'that counsel are negotiating. It seems that the former Minister has won a great victory. It is now merely a question of how much Mr Price has to pay.'

'I hope it is a very great deal.'

'Above all, Prime Minister, it means that your administration will not be tainted with the suggestion of corruption. That would have been a sad end to your distinguished term of office.'

'Thank you, my dear fellow. It is kind of you to say so. Yes, I should like to go with some measure of public respect. I cannot expect honour. Politicians are not awarded much honour nowadays, not even the honour among thieves.'

It was, in fact, not until four o'clock – the difference in time was caused by the delayed return from a royal engagement – that he was driven to the Palace around Parliament Square and up Birdcage Walk, following the route taken by many of his predecessors, some as they went feeling relief and release; others bitterness and resentment at the perfidy of either electorate or colleagues. This Prime Minister fell into the relieved category – except when he remembered Digby Price and the diary that still hung like a sword of Damocles above his head. Defeat would make Price very bitter. There was no knowing what the fellow might not now do.

While the audience was being held, Downing Street telephoned the Queen's Private Secretary and confirmed that Lady Sylvia Benedict would be delighted to entertain the former Prime Minister for the night before he journeyed to his home in the country. So he passed an agreeable evening with Sylvia who had managed at the last minute to get the American Ambassador and one of the former Prime Minister's old friends, a Fellow of All Souls who had been at Balliol with him, an historian who dined much in society and wrote racy reviews for the *Spectator*. The former Prime Minister was in excellent form, reflecting upon political life in the country houses of the Edwardian era, speaking of the code whereby the wives left outside their bedroom doors the plate of sandwiches provided in those days to sustain the guests through the long hours of darkness, even after a gargantuan dinner of half a dozen courses. If the plate was empty that was the signal to their lover that the coast was clear and the husband safely in the dressing room. If the plate was full, it was to warn that the husband was *in situ*. And he told of the contretemps when a greedy guest ate the sandwiches and, seeing the empty plate, the lover entered, to find the husband in full enjoyment of his conjugal rights. Sylvia was amused; the American Ambassador, a New Englander with the features of an eagle and a Puritan heart, was not. The old friend had heard it all before. So the former Prime Minister passed this agreeable evening, scorning to watch the news and the coverage of his resignation before ambling off to bed.

But the morning was not so jolly. There was, of course, the political news of his resignation, and the identity and character of his successor, and the story about the settlement of the Tancred case, accompanied by speculation over the dramatic fall in the share price of News Universal and whether the empire of Digby Price would survive. But the item that made the ex-Prime Minister's morning not so jolly was carried in the *Telegram*'s Diary column, a feature widely read in Westminster and Whitehall. It referred to a recently retired minister who, despite his age and his public posture as a champion of family standards, had for many years enjoyed a secret love affair. The diarist wondered if now that the former minister was free from office, he would be tempted to regularise the irregular but agreeable union.

As a result Sylvia's guest remained in his bedroom until one o'clock and then, declining the offer of luncheon, departed in the official car to which, as a former Prime Minister, he was entitled. He did not go to the constituency office but to the home of his agent, Aidan Wills, where he was greeted affectionately by Penny. She led him through the french windows of the sitting room to the two deckchairs on the stone-flagged terrace overlooking the narrow strip of lawn that led the few yards down to the fence, a lawn bordered by lines of red, white and orange-yellow flowers – salvias, white daisies and—. To his annoyance the name of the orange flowers, always prominent in the displays at the Town Hall on the occasion of the mayor's annual reception, escaped him. He disliked them intensely and contemplated with distaste the mixture of hideous colours in the garden. Penny appeared with a jug of lemonade and a large cream cake for her visitor. She cut him a generous slice, poured him a glass and, lowering her ample frame on to a stool she had drawn up beside him, encouraged him to eat and drink. But he only sipped the lemonade and, despite her protestation that she'd made the cake herself, he declined to eat.

After a sip or two he put down his glass and laid his hand on her bright, shining face. 'You understand, my dear, what this means – my retirement from the House of Commons and therefore from the constituency?'

She nodded, took his hand and held it firm against her cheek before taking it to her lips.

'I shall not in future be seeing you the way I have in the past,' he added.

'I know,' she said. 'But sometimes, surely sometimes I can see you?'

'It will not be easy.'

There was a copy of the *Telegram* on the other deckchair. 'Bring me that,' he said. He turned the pages and pointed to the Diary column. 'See?'

'I have seen it.'

'Has Aidan?'

She brushed this aside. 'I expect he has. It doesn't matter. All I want is to be able to see you now and again.'

'I shall try,' he promised.

She took the newspaper from him. 'How could they have got hold of it, after all these years?' she asked.

'News Universal got it from a man whose diary they published. How it got to the *Telegram* I have no idea. They know no details. But once they get a scent, the hounds will follow it.'

'What will you do?'

'Go home. Ignore it. They won't find out more. Unless . . .' He stopped.

She snatched her hand away from his. 'You know I never would,' she said fiercely.

'They have so much money.'

'Don't say that. I haven't in the past and I won't in the future. It's our secret.'

'They might have followed me here.'

'All you are doing is saying goodbye to your constituency.'

'To more than that,' he replied looking into her eyes. 'To much, much more than that.'

They heard the car draw up at the front of the small house. Aidan Wills came through the sitting room. 'The officers are assembled at the constituency office, waiting to say goodbye, Prime Minister,' he announced.

'No longer Prime Minister,' he said as he rose from the chair.

'You'll always be Prime Minister to us,' said Penny.

He took her hand. 'Thank you for the cake and the lemonade. Thank you – for everything.'

Aidan turned away as he kissed her on the cheek.

Two hours later he arrived home, to the handsome red-brick manor house at the end of a lane, with views of the Mendip Hills and the wooded Somerset farmland.

Joan came in from the garden, a pair of secateurs in

her gloved hands, earth from her gardening shoes leaving a trail behind her. 'Tea?' she asked breezily.

'No, thank you. I'm a little tired. I think I shall have a whisky and soda.'

'A bit early, isn't it? Still, I suppose it's a day for celebration.' She went back to the garden.

Glass in hand, he wandered around the silent house. From a window he could just make out her trousered rear prominent among the flowers in the herbaceous border. She was hard at work with her trowel. No audience now, he reflected. No once-upon-a-time mistress. The autobiography was all that lay ahead. The discreet, necessarily untruthful autobiography.

In London, ministers had been asked to remain at their posts. The only appointment the incoming Prime Minister had to make was a new Chancellor of the Exchequer. In the evening it was announced that the Right Honourable Peregrine McClaren had been chosen.

In the Attorney-General's chambers in Buckingham Gate, the Attorney and the young, red-headed Solicitor-General were in the former's room. 'Have you seen the piece in today's Diary column in the *Telegram*?' he asked. 'They say it's about him. I can't believe it.'

'I have been in Court of Appeal so I haven't myself seen it,' replied the Solicitor. 'But Belinda rang from home and read it to me. The sly old dog! Fancy him . . . and all these years. Belinda says the woman must be Sylvia Benedict.'

Spenser was settling into his new office. Satisfactory terms had been agreed with Ogilvy Grant. He had been put in charge of the takeover of News Universal. 'There'll be a battle with the Monopolies Commission,'

Ogilvy had said. 'But if we don't get it, their Sunday and Daily will have to close.'

'I think, Chairman,' said Spenser, 'that we ought to be able to get it through. Leave it to me.'

In the safe, the safe in his new office, rested the manuscript of Francis Richmond's diary.

Chapter Nine

Tancred passed the night of his arrival in Rome at the Hotel Raphael not far from the Piazza Navona. After checking in he went to a café opposite the Bernini Neptune fountain in the piazza and sat sipping a small cup of black coffee and smoking a Havana cigar, a large Cohiba, the best the hotel could supply. Your only indulgence, Harry had said. Harry was right. As he sat in the floodlit piazza under the warm Roman sky, watching the families, with their small children still abroad although the hour was late, he wondered again, as he had when he had first read the diary, why Francis Richmond had recorded Peregrine McClaren saying, 'Tancred was drinking heavily.' Was that McClaren being mischievous? Or Richmond inventing? In either event, it was untrue. He never permitted his head to become clouded.

Back in the hotel he undressed and lay on the bed in the darkness. He was glad it was all over. And he was glad to be on his own. He needed some solitude.

Next morning early he picked up a hired car from Hertz and drove north into Umbria along the autostrada A1, direction Firenze. At Sinalunga he left the autostrada, turning east towards Perugia along the north side of the lake to Passignano sul Trasimeno and parked in the nearly empty car park. He bought a wide-brimmed straw hat and, looking at his watch, went to the kiosk and booked a ticket on the lake boat for Isola Maggiore. There were only a few other passengers and he sat on the deck in the hot sunshine as the boat sailed slowly over the shallow water towards the island.

It had begun with the knock on the door of his Chelsea flat, late one rainy night almost three years ago. He was working on his Cabinet papers. It was the young actor with the diary. How Streatley had found his home address he'd never discovered, but he had, and he had wasted no time. He could have the diary – for money. 'Your relationship with Oscar Sleaven, your talks and meetings,' Streatley said, 'how easily they could be misconstrued.' And if it got into the newspapers, the harm it would do to him – and to the government, which he, Streatley, so warmly supported! It was, of course, blackmail. Streatley had hardly bothered to dress it up. He had read the diary while Streatley sat opposite him, preening, studying himself every now and then in the looking glass across the room, fiddling with his dyed blond hair. When he'd finished reading he had snapped the book shut and handed it back. 'I'll have to consider,' he'd said. 'Return in three days.'

'Not more than three days,' Streatley warned. 'The newspapers would be interested.'

Streatley was right. They would. And Digby Price of News Universal most of all. Price had a score to settle, from the days way back in southern Africa.

He had been the MI6 man in the embassy in Pretoria, South Africa station and had got wind of an arms deal with what was then Salisbury, Rhodesia and the break-away government of Ian Smith. The weapons were to come secretly across the border from Zambia. He had been responsible for putting a stop to it. Price had been arrested near the border, taken to Lusaka, strip-searched, kept in jail for two days. Price, the only white in the cell with ten others, who had amused themselves with him, abusing him brutally, humiliating him, raping him – while the warders looked through the bars of the cell, laughing. Price had bought his release. No charges, no publicity. What had happened to him no one was to know. It was later that Price discovered who had been responsible for the tip-off that had led to his arrest – and degradation. By then Tancred had moved on. But Price would not forget. Price had pursued him throughout his political career but could never get his finger on anything personal. If Price got his hands on the diary, he would. Price would pay much to get his revenge. Price, he knew, would buy Richmond's diary.

That night the plan began to form in his mind. He was through with politics. For a time he'd enjoyed the battle in the House of Commons and later the responsibility of administering a department of State. He'd been amused by the elaborate performance and the cynical manipulation of his colleagues by the canny Prime Minister. But now he'd had enough. Enough of public life, as earlier he'd had enough of the secret world of MI6. What he wanted was ease and comfort; and for that he needed money. He *was* interested in money, now more than ever. Oh, yes, he'd said what Richmond had recorded: about getting money – and about the Prime Minister. As he considered Streatley's threat, the idea had come to him. A chancy, risky idea but if it came off he'd get what he wanted.

Harry happened to be in London on one of his regular trips and they spent the next two nights together, planning. Helena, Harry told him, was in France. She'd come from Palm Strings, Harry said, where she'd fled after a dangerous entanglement in Moscow. Helena, Harry said, might be persuaded to play a part.

Harry was the only one of the family who'd kept in touch with his schoolgirl half-sister when the family had disowned her and banished her after the birth of her child. Harry was the only one she'd contact as she crossed the world from one rich man's bed to another's. She might be willing to help, Harry had said. For old times' sake? he'd asked, smiling. For her first love, Harry had said. To amuse herself, she said later when she had agreed.

Streatley returned on the Thursday. He'd opened the door to him and kept him standing in the hall. 'Do what you like with it,' he said. 'Now get out. You're lucky I haven't sent for the police.'

'You wouldn't dare,' Streatley had said.

'Get out.' And he slammed the door. Publish and be damned, he'd thought. Or rather, let Price publish and, if all went according to his and Harry's plan, he'd not be damned. He'd get money.

Since his days as one of 'the friends', as MI6 were called, he'd kept his contacts. A few days later he got the message. News Universal had a story about him that they were going to publish. This was just before his ministerial trip to Hong Kong and Beijing. On the stop-over in Hong Kong from London, he and Harry talked again. Next day he went on to Beijing and Harry flew to Paris. Harry was back in Hong Kong when he returned from Beijing and they met in the Mandarin Hotel. By then the story had broken and Harry had engineered Helena's meeting with Price. Soon, if it had not happened already, she'd be in his apartment. A sting, she'd told Harry, a sting always amused her.

Tancred walked off the boat, up the wooden quay through the small village to the restaurant under the awning of vine leaves overlooking the lake. She was sitting alone with her back to him. He saw her dark head as he approached, the hand with the scarlet nails tapping the ash of the cigarette into the ashtray. He put his hands on her shoulders, standing behind her.

She put hers over his. 'You are late.'

He took the seat opposite her. 'You were wonderful,' he said.

'It amused me.' She poured him a glass of white wine. 'Sleaven, I cannot say I mourned him.'

No, he thought. Their daughter, too, had died.

'What will you do now?'

'Move on.'

'Are you all right—' he began hesitantly.

She interrupted him. 'Oh, yes, I took my wages when I left. I had earned them.'

'Where will you go?'

'Now? Back to the mainland, on the last boat.'

'And then?'

'Rome. Los Angeles. I have an apartment up the coast.' She laid her hand on his. 'I shall survive. I always have, I always shall.'

When they had eaten the local fish and finished two flasks of white wine, they wandered back through the village, past the few honey-coloured stone houses with the old women sitting on their doorsteps selling lace to the small number of tourists who came from the mainland. They climbed the hill to the chapel and the ruined villa, and stood looking over the lake. Soon she would be on her way south. And he north.

They came back down the hill and talked of the other woman, Harry's woman, Elspeth Turville. She must have her share, he said. She'd borne the brunt of those years in Sydney raising the difficult girl. He used to visit Sydney and see the child, not often but sometimes. That he had been unaware of her existence, as he had told the court, was a lie. He had known all along. The rest of the story he'd told had been true – or partially true. Not the whole truth. He had been, as the man said, 'economical with the truth'.

But it was true that Helena had given up the daughter she'd borne to the young English student. Like mother, like daughter, fourteen years later, both were teenagers when they had conceived. The difference was that when the Cheung family disowned and banished her, she had lived. She had gone away and lived off the rich in Taiwan, in the States and in Europe. Lived, at the end, off Digby Price. But the other teenage mother, their daughter, had not lived. She had died. That was the difference.

In the late afternoon they caught the boat back to the mainland and stood, leaning over the rail, looking down at the reeds and shallow bottom of the lake as the boat made its slow, stately progress back to Passignano. He told her about Burrows's visit to Pontaix when Burrows had warned him that Price's people had failed to unearth any financial link between him and Oscar Sleaven. If they had no evidence, Burrows had said, they might abandon their defence and make an offer. If they did, the damages would not be great, not as great as they would were News Universal to come across evidence of money passing between him and Oscar Sleaven. Then they'd fight. And if News Universal fought and failed, the damages would be enormous.

So, unknown to Burrows or Foxley, he himself had sent Goodbody the bank statements that showed the Sleaven payments. That was the bait. When Digby Price saw them, Tancred knew that he would go on. For Price would then believe that he had the evidence that proved the corruption. Helena had allowed Price to discover the letters showing that she and Tancred had once been lovers, and convinced him of her bitterness over the lover who had deserted her all those years ago. But not about the child. That, Tancred insisted, must be kept for the court.

They had known that Oscar Sleaven would suffer, exposed not as a corrupter of a minister of the Crown but of a child, their child. He'd gone to Sebastian Sleaven to warn him about what was to happen but he had felt no compassion for Oscar Sleaven. Their daughter had been a child of fourteen when Sleaven had abused her. She, too, had killed herself.

He walked her to the hotel where the car was waiting for her. He held the door as she climbed in. 'I have never been able to resist a sting,' she said. '*Ciao.*' The car drove away. She did not wave, she did not look back. She just went.

He collected his car from the car park. The empty little town reminded him of the Riviera in his childhood thirty-five years ago. Few people; only the cars passing through on their way to Perugia. And not many of them. He drove west, then north towards Lisciano Niccone.

Turning off the main road he followed the winding track up into the hills. It was early evening when he went through the open gate and pulled up in front of the villa with purple bougainvillaea climbing up the white walls.

Harry came from the house and they walked to the terrace and sat in the blue cane chairs overlooking the valley lined with olive trees.

'I expected you sooner,' Harry said.

'I've been with Helena.'

'Where is she?'

'Gone. To Rome and then to Palm Springs.'

Both remained silent for a time.

'Have you seen the newspapers?' Harry asked.

'No. I've seen nothing since I left London.'

'News Universal is crashing. If they go under there may be no money for you.'

Tancred stared at Harry, who looked away over the olive trees to the valley and hills beyond. Then he pushed back his chair, threw back his head and laughed. 'None? There may be none for me?'

'Maybe.'

'And Price? At least there'll be none for Price.'

'Price will be all right,' said Harry. 'Those sort of people always are.'

In London, Oliver Goodbody came to Mordecai's chambers at Albany.

'Why not at Penns?' Mordecai asked as he led him to the drawing room.

'I'm having to resign,' Goodbody said. 'I'll have to make a settlement with my creditors. I'll have to leave my clubs.' Mordecai looked at him. Goodbody appeared to have shrunk, the distinguished face grey and the cheeks fallen in. 'I didn't get sufficient fees on account,' Goodbody went on. 'Spenser was difficult but I never imagined there would be any problem in the end. Now News Universal appears to be collapsing and Spenser has gone. He has joined Ogilvy Grant at the *Telegram*. Heaven knows when or if ever I'll get my fees. In any event, it will be too late for me.' He paused, then added, 'By the rules of the profession I am obligated to pay you your fee personally.'

'When you told me you were coming,' said Mordecai, 'I thought it might not be good news. So I sent for a bottle of Scotch.' He went to the dining room and came back, pushing the trolley. With the Dom Perignon was a bottle of J&B whisky. He poured and handed the glass to Goodbody who said, 'I should never have got you involved. I wouldn't have if I had not been so hard pressed.'

Mordecai looked at him over the rim of his tankard of champagne. 'Forget about my fees,' he said. 'You will not be indebted to me.' He drank a deep draught. Oliver Goodbody sat silent. 'I shall miss you at Penns,' Mordecai went on. 'I don't expect I shall go there myself now very often.'

'I got you into this,' Goodbody began, 'and – I'

Mordecai interrupted him. 'It's over. It was a monstrous case for a monstrous man.' He paused. 'So even the victor may never receive a cent?' he asked.

Goodbody shrugged.

'What a lot of trouble that man Francis Richmond caused with his scribbling gossip,' Mordecai went on. 'A businessman exposed and driven to blow his brains out; a newspaper empire brought to its knees; you ruined.' If he had known, Mordecai might have added a Prime Minister driven into retirement. 'The sole winner', he concluded, 'has been the venal young man who sold the diary. Only bad has come from it for everyone else.'

But Mordecai was wrong, for nothing but good had come of it for Patrick Foxley and Anna James.

Envoi

A few days after their meeting in Albany Mordecai received a letter from Oliver Goodbody, written from his office in Lincoln's Inn Fields.

Dear Mordecai,
I thought you might be interested in what I came across when my secretary and I were clearing the filing cabinets in my room before I left these chambers for the last time. It was on a single sheet of writing paper, which must have become detached from the file on Francis Richmond's estate. It appears to have been written just before he died. The handwriting is very shaky but it was decipherable and my secretary has typed up a copy. I thought you should see it.
From your friend,
Oliver

Enclosure

The Clinic
Job has promised me that he will destroy my diary that I left at home.
I do not know why I have kept a journal, except that it was to amuse myself. Now on a sheet of paper, I scribble my final entry – my epitaph. For soon I shall be dead. I have achieved nothing in my life. I have made no stir in the world. The memory of me will fade like the scent of lavender off a handkerchief flourished in an empty room.
Francis Richmond